Her Perfect Blend

by

Zelda Benjamin

Highland Falls, Book Two

Her Perfect Blend

Cover Art by *Tina Lynn Stout*

The Wild Rose Press, Inc.
PO Box 708
Adams Basin, NY 14410-0708
Visit us at www.thewildrosepress.com

Publishing History
First Edition, 2024
Trade Paperback ISBN 978-1-5092-5841-3
Digital ISBN 978-1-5092-5842-0

Highland Falls, Book Two
Published in the United States of America

Dedication

For Ben, for encouragement and last minute take-out.

Chapter 1

Fiona Campbell stood in the centuries-old barn and listened to the rainfall on the leaky tin roof. A limited amount of light filtered through the cracked walls and the dusty windows. The unusual assault of rain concerned her. The havoc the weather brought on her old barn limited the number of barn seekers and leaf-peepers. And like the townspeople, she worried the weather would put a damper on the upcoming Highland Falls Scottish games.

At last night's meeting, Mr. Paisley, the event committee chairman, attempted to calm the board's concerns. *The athletes have Scotland in their blood. A little rain won't stop them.* If only he could reassure this old barn would make it through October.

Locals bragged how her barn was one of the oldest still standing in this part of the Adirondack region of New York State.

She glanced at the weathered walls. The broad beams had withstood centuries of storms and the test of time. *How much more can they take?* She'd find out soon enough—if the contractor ever got here. She glanced at her watch—twenty minutes late.

Jack and his dad always showed up early.

She wouldn't hold being late against them, not today. The weather was miserable. Behind her, the wagon door swung open, bringing a breath of cold, wet air inside the damp barn. She turned on the heels of her barn boots and stood in place. The man who ducked beneath the doorframe was taller and thinner than Jack Drummond or his father, Ed.

"'Tis a *dreich* out there." The man stepped from the shadows and shook the rain off his jacket. Spangles of water cascaded to the dirt floor, leaving a puddle at his feet. He stepped over the water, walked toward her, and gazed toward the roof. "And in here, too."

In a soft Highland lilt, he described, to a *T,* the drab gray day. The man, however, was anything but dull. She gazed from his russet hair to straight-line Viking features. A tall, lean build made him preternaturally photogenic. He looked like he had stepped off a poster advertising the upcoming festival and games. "If it's a room you need, I'm sorry, the B and B is booked solid."

"The inn next door is more charming than my current accommodations." He glanced at the dusty window with a hazy view of the inn. "'Tis not a room I'm here for today, lass."

"Then why are you here? Are you lost?" She did a quick visual check for the usual signs he might be a barn seeker. She didn't see a camera, a map, or a guidebook listing sites of interest. So, she quickly nixed the idea. No one had stopped to photograph the old barn in over a week.

"No, I don't believe I'm lost. I'm here to see…" He pulled a wet, crumbled paper from the well-worn rain jacket's pocket. "Fiona Campbell?"

"Then you're in the right place." She shook off her girlish infatuation and put on her business persona. "How can I help you?" Was he here to sign up for the games? As the head of the registration committee, she'd already processed dozens of online applications. Occasionally, she met a contestant in person. The event was only a week away. Lots of attractive athletes were already in Highland Falls. So why did this man capture her attention?

"The Drummonds sent me, lass. I'm here to access the barn reconstruction you're proposing. Sorry, I'm late. It's not easy seeing the road signs." He returned her once-over with a quick head-to-toe assessment.

"I thought Jack and his dad worked alone." She forced a smile and turned away from his gaze.

"They're a wee bit busy setting up the viewing stands for the festival." He shrugged and turned his palms up. "I offered to take the call."

"Do you know something about barn wood?" She glanced at his callused palms.

"Aye, lass. I know a bit. We Highlanders are a very self-sufficient group. I've done my share of reconstructing old buildings. I've even sold a few here and there." He glanced from the north wall to the south wall, along the foundation, and to the roof. "This structure must have been a beauty in her prime."

Only someone with a background in preserving old buildings would appreciate her crumbling barn. She nodded. "Do you work for a big company, or is it a family business like the Drummonds?"

"Aye, a family business." He shrugged.

His response, short and to the point, sent a message he did not want to elaborate. The Drummonds would never send someone who didn't understand the nature of this kind of restoration. She took a breath and dismissed the topic for now. "Sounds like you're qualified, Mr....?"

"Please call me Gavin." He extended his right hand.

"Welcome, Gavin." She accepted a firm handshake. "We've already established I'm Fiona Campbell."

"Aye, that you are, lass." He ran a hand through wet hair. "When Jack asked me to check out some lady's old barn...I...uh...I never expected she'd be so bonnie."

His appearance was professional and confident— his crooked smile captivating. Despite the chill in the air, an unfamiliar warm sensation ran along her arms. "I hope you didn't expect me to be as old as the barn?" Heat ran up her neck. She tossed her braid over her shoulder. He was engaging, good-looking, and confident about his knowledge of wood.

"No offense meant." His gaze followed the movement of her hair.

"None taken." She turned and led the way toward the center of the barn.

"That's an interesting structure." He pointed toward a shed sitting in the middle of the barn.

"It's my herb shed. The wood suggests it's older than the outer structure. You have to step inside to appreciate the craftsmanship." She cleared her mind of anything other than today's business.

"You're right. Despite its age, this structure is sturdier than the barn." Gavin examined the outside wall.

"Inside, it's roomier than it appears and drier than the rest of the barn." The long narrow shed would be a tight fit for two people. She stepped over a fluted metal threshold.

Gavin ducked beneath hanging bundles of dried herbs. "You've put it to good use." Inside, he snapped off a spiky stem of rosemary and sniffed.

"The shed is ideal for drying herbs." The comforting scent of wood balsam lingered for a few seconds. "A group of local women and I produce herbal teas and herb-infused butter. In spring and summer, we sell the products at roadside stands."

"Why tear down the structure if it supports local business?" His gaze traveled from her face to a plank on his left. "Unlike the outside walls, this wood has several good years left."

"An internal structure doesn't fit my plans for a new barn." She shook her head and sighed. "I don't have a choice. Eventually, I'll build another shed closer to the inn. On days like this, the rain seeps through the surrounding walls. Some days, the air is too damp to dry herbs. So it has to go, too." Losing the shed was sad. She boasted about her teas made from homegrown herbs. "I need to reclaim the sideboards. If the walls collapse, the planks will be useless."

"Sounds sensible." He nodded. "Jack explained your plan to repurpose the barn into a party venue."

"How do you know Jack and his father?" Jack's failure to mention he was sending a friend to assess the wood nagged at her thoughts.

"Jack and I were mates since our days at Edinburgh University." He followed her to the doorframe at the opposite end.

She stepped away and exited the shed at the opposite end. "I didn't know Jack attended uni in Scotland."

Gavin followed. He stopped short of the threshold

and ran a hand along the overhead support. "This beautiful old-growth timber is not easily available in today's market. Old walls have a magical charm. Don't you agree?"

"Absolutely." Mesmerized by the movement of his fingers and eyes of the blue-black color of Loch Ness, she struggled to form words. A silly emoji bandage wrapped around his finger canceled the sensuous stroke of his hand. "Does your construction company use a lot of reclaimed planks?"

"Not at the moment." He glanced at her and wiggled thick bushy brows. "I'm always looking for quality."

"As do I." She caught the double meaning of the quirky twist of his brows and bit her lip to hide a smile. "In case *you are* interested, the wood is not for sale. Every salvageable plank must be repurposed to maintain the barn's authenticity." History and secrets hidden in the walls were part of the building's charm. What would she find when the walls came down?

"Can't blame a lad for trying." He grinned and turned his attention back to the weathered wood. "Do you know what possessed someone to build around the shed?"

"It's impossible to say." She took a deep breath and glanced at the roof. An enormous raindrop fell through. Too late, she lifted a hand and shielded her face. A giant drop hit the back of her hand and slid uncomfortably into the sleeve of her rain jacket.

"It's drier under here." Gavin placed a hand on her elbow and guided her back into the protection of the shed.

She shook the water from her sleeve. Whoever

built the shed didn't plan for two people standing side-by-side, especially a tall man with broad shoulders. Overhead, bundles of oregano, dill, and thyme hung close to his face. The tightly placed bunches of drying herbs provided some protection—but she and Gavin couldn't stay here much longer.

He removed a flashlight from his pocket and directed the light to a nail on a cross board. "This is an irregular kerf mark." He slipped an arm around her waist and pivoted her toward the wood.

Her body tingled from the contact. She was too stunned to speak. "The...planks were cut by a pit saw." Her voice returned.

"Impressive. You're right. Wood is dated by the cut." He flashed the light along the wood and stopped at a cluster of nails. "Nails like these were forged by hand." He outlined the embedded nails with a finger and smiled.

His excitement was contagious. "They're rose head nails. My handyman, Tim, found similar nails behind a wall in my kitchen. Hammer blows formed the distinct flower-shaped pattern." Except for barn seekers, few people cared about the construction of the old shed.

"Aye, lass." He nodded. "You have a fair knowledge of old building materials."

"When I restored the farmhouse, I learned about old structures." She placed a hand along the wood and traced the movement of his fingers. She checked the wood daily. Today, her fingers tingled. Everything around—the wood—the shed—and the nails —had a strong magical allure. She grew up on Scottish tales of inanimate objects sending messages to humans. Was the wood sending a message about this man? She shuddered and shook off the thought.

"Are you okay, lass?" Gavin reached for her arm and smiled. "No matter how pleasant the company, a cold, damp barn is not the ideal place to discuss business."

"I'm fine." She stepped back. He was a charming addition to a drab day but here for business—not her amusement. "I think about the history of the property. Compromising historical characteristics would be wrong. My plan includes repurposing whatever we can—wood, nails, and doors. The barn was part of this property for many years. Preserving structural integrity is important."

"'Tis a great piece of land." He stepped out of the protection of the shed and glanced out the cracked rear window. "How far back does your property go?"

The raindrops didn't bother him. She pulled the jacket hood over her head and followed. "My land ends a hundred feet from the end of the barn. The rest is state land leading onto public trails."

"Do a lot of local properties border government land?" He raised a brow.

"Most of the older properties do." Residents sent up a red flag when a stranger asked about local land. Fiona, too, was suspicious of big developers interested in Highland Falls. She applauded the locals who took them on in court and succeeded in disrupting their plans. No one wanted fancy houses and high-end resorts interfering with the town's serenity. Regardless of his connection to Jack, Gavin fit the stranger category. She blamed the endless rain for her skepticism and shrugged off her concern. On days like today, everything was disenchanting.

"I'm sure it's *braw* when the sun's shining." Gavin smiled.

"When it's not raining, it's a beautiful view." She had no reason to doubt Gavin's connection to the Drummonds. He was doing a friend a favor. She would be presumptuous to believe he had an ulterior motive. But what exactly did his family build?

"Do you have a time limit on your project?" Gavin tapped the wood around the window. "I don't know how long the frame will support the old glass. What's your proposed starting date?"

The question was relevant. She turned away from the window and stepped behind Gavin. "I planned to start in the spring. Heavy snowfalls last winter and a wet summer have taken their toll." As if to prove her point, heavy rainfall battered the window. The cracked panes rattled. "If the barn remains exposed to the elements, the wood will be useless." She held her breath and waited for the glass to shatter around their feet.

"You're probably right." Gavin stepped away from the window. He placed a hand on her elbow and guided her toward the front of the barn. "Do you have a budget in mind?"

At five-feet-five inches, she wasn't a wee lass, but next to him, she felt petite. He had at least six inches on her, but the attraction was more than his height. His broad shoulders and the protective way he guided her toward the front of the barn made her feel dainty. "I'll discuss the flexibility of my budget when Jack submits a proposal." She never forgot the lessons she learned as the Chief Financial Officer of a profitable hedge fund. Showing all your cards first was never a good idea—

especially to a stranger she was instantly attracted to. "The barn needs to be completed by early spring." She glanced at the leaky tin roof. "I'm planning a wedding."

Once the games were over, the Drummonds agreed to put aside future jobs to complete the renovation.

"Are you getting married, lass?" He stopped, raised his brows, and glanced at her fingers.

"Me, oh no. It's not my wedding. My brother, Ian, and his fiancée, Sophia, plan to marry in the spring. I promised them they would be the first to celebrate a big event in my new barn."

"With the right crew"—A slow smile curled his lips—"We can get it done in time."

"We?" She raised a brow. "I don't doubt Jack and his dad can do it. They're the best contractors in any of the surrounding counties."

"They're going to need extra hands for a project this size." He glanced past the herb shed. "Do you only hire locals?"

"People here do whatever we can to support local businesses." She slipped her hands into a pocket. Had Jack forewarned his friend about the town's attitude toward strangers?

"I'm not surprised. Working with locals is part of the small-town appeal." He kicked at a branch of mint lying on the ground. "I grew up in a town like this."

"Really?" She studied his face. He had big-city sophistication written all over him. "What brings you to our small town? Are you just visiting an old friend?"

"It's great seeing Jack, but I'm here for the games. It was a last-minute decision. The Drummonds were kind enough to offer me a bed. Helping them is the least I can do while I'm here." Gavin tapped a beam to his right.

The porous nature of the wood absorbed the sound.

"I guess Jack's place is the less-inviting lodging you referred to." She laughed. The Drummonds lived in a charming farmhouse a few miles out of town. Gavin must be referring to the amenities. Mrs. Drummond was visiting relatives and left her son, husband, and now, Gavin to manage on their own.

"The accommodations are fine, but the food..." He laughed and stroked a hand along his jaw. "I don't know how much more takeaway I can eat."

"Mrs. Drummond's an amazing cook. You'd eat better if she weren't away." She gazed at the cinnamon-colored scruff on his chin. "And you? Do you cook?"

"Me..." He wiggled a brow. "I'm a terrible cook."

"I won't expect you at the cooking competitions." She laughed. Gavin's lean muscular build indicated he was an athlete. "What's your sport?" This year's list of competitors was overwhelming. No one stood out in her mind. However, talking about the festival was less unsettling than answering questions about local property.

"Shot put." He raised an arm above a shoulder.

"The *clachneart,* stone of strength. I'm familiar with the event. My brother, Sam, competed in shot put competitions." Fiona nodded. "Do you compete often?" His callused hands were a sign of physical labor and hours of practice throwing a twenty-two-pound stone. Of course, brute strength was not the only quality needed to compete in heavy athletics. Perseverance, persistence, and precision were essential. Gavin struck her as the type who possessed all those qualities.

"Not very often. I think I have some wee trophies

or something." He shrugged. "I don't know where they are. So, you're familiar with the event."

"Aye, I am." She refrained from laughing at his poker-faced and subtle humor. His shrug was unpretentious, his modesty charming. "Will you be working with the Drummonds after the games?"

"It depends." He found a dry spot, crossed his arms, and leaned against a sturdy plank. "Do you know the Scottish saying, *Ti fell two dugs wi the ae stane?*"

"To fell two birds with one stone." Fiona knew the phrase well. So what reason other than the games would keep him here this time of year?

"You have an impressive knowledge of Gaelic." He raised a brow. "Do I detect a hint of a Scottish accent?"

"Only when I speak to someone from home." They were discussing things way off the topic of barn wood. "My brother, Ian, and I learned Gaelic at Sunday school."

"You must have been a *bairn* when you came here." He studied her face.

"The classes were in Scotland." She was keenly aware of his calculating appraisal. "I came to New York years later to attend university, stayed for graduate school, and went to work." She gathered her composure and stepped backward. He asked too many personal questions. "What about you?"

"I grew up in the Highlands," Gavin said matter-of-factly. "After graduating, Jack tried to convince me to work with him and his dad. The offer was tempting. Working with them would have been a nice change, but…" He shrugged. "I have family responsibilities in Scotland."

A wife, children? Running a B and B taught her about people—they liked to talk about themselves. Gavin was the exception. He told her the basics about his construction experience. His replies were allusive when she asked for details. An air of mystery surrounded him. "So what's the other bird that brought you here?" She tossed her braid over her jacket collar.

"Family matters," he said. "I'm searching for a great-aunt."

"Is she in Highland Falls?" She raised her voice over a sudden loud downpour battering the sides of the barn.

"I'm not sure. I don't know if Aunt Joan is still alive." Gavin ran a palm along his jaw. "From what Granddad, Hamish, was willing to share—he hasn't heard from Joan in fifty years. Her last known residence was in this town." The corner of his lips dropped. "It's hard to understand the *auld* ones and their secrets."

Such heartfelt words from a rugged-looking man surprised her. He shared an insight about his family that made him sad. "I hope you're successful in finding her." She touched the sleeve of his jacket. "I know all about Scottish family secrets. My family has its share." If he stayed in Highland Falls long enough, he'd discover the town was full of well-kept secrets.

Off to the side, a gust blew open the door. The heavy door banged against the outside wall with a force that rattled the old wood. She froze in place.

"I've got it." Gavin placed a hand on her shoulder and steered her away. He rushed to the door, pulled it closed, and latched a rusted wrought iron pole.

The old hinges creaked as they closed.

She shook off a chill, squared her shoulders, and

followed him. They stood at the door with the wind bellowing outside. Behind them, splashes of water escaped through the roof. Wet strands of hair curled around his face in shades of Scottish autumn. Seconds passed. "I really should get back to my chores." She adjusted her hood. "I'd invite you to the house for a warm beverage, but I'm too busy with my morning schedule to sit and chat."

"No worries, lass. I have enough information for Jack and a thermos of hot tea in the truck."

"Are you okay finishing alone? She fiddled with a button on her jacket. Chores were an excuse to end the visit. Talk about family brought back the memory of the night she got the phone call and the horrific circumstances making her guardian of her brother Sam's five-year-old twins. Hollowness echoed in her chest. In the past six months, the only thing that mattered was her ability to create a stable environment for her niece and nephew. She cleared her mind with a deep breath.

"Are you okay?" Gavin reached for her elbow.

She blew out the breath she was holding. "I was going over a mental list of things I must do. You know beds to make, new guests to check in, and scones to bake."

"Hmm, freshly baked scones." He flashed a smile.

His no-worry smile made her feel terrible she hadn't invited him to the house. "If you're still here after the games, I'll bake you some scones." No way could she have him waiting around for scones to bake. What would the twins think when they got home from school and found an intriguing Scot sitting in her kitchen? Her responsibilities and better judgment pulled her away from Gavin.

"Aye, we've both got work to do." He stepped back, letting her elbow slide through his fingers.

"The sooner you report back to Jack, the sooner I'll have an estimate. I'm eager to get things rolling." She crossed her arms close to her body.

"Mind if I take some photos of the wood?" He held his cell phone in his right hand.

"Go ahead. Take all the time you need." She'd ask her assistant, Cora, to refill his thermos.

"It shouldn't take long. I won't disqualify anything with the slightest potential to be reclaimed. I'll do a quick once-over around the inside. If the rain lets up, I'll walk around the barn and mark the salvageable planks with numbers for my report to Jack."

"I'm anxious to see what you find." She picked at a splintered sideboard and tossed the chips into a nearby pail. "Your knowledge of wood is impressive." She bit her lip. "What kind of construction did you say you do back home?"

"Whatever kind pays the bills." He removed a tape measure from his pocket.

Subject closed. "It was nice meeting you." She extended her hand. He was hard to figure out. He willingly shared a family secret but remained tight-lipped regarding the specifics of his past construction jobs. Had he done something illegal, or was he a secret billionaire? If he stayed in Highland Falls for a while, whatever he was hiding would eventually surface.

"The pleasure was mine, Miss Campbell." Gavin wiped his free hand on the leg of his jeans and shook her hand.

He was a man of impeccable manners. Every fiber

in her body warned her to keep it professional. Yet, he didn't need to be so formal. "Fiona." She offered and pulled her hand away. "See you at the games."

"Aye, Fiona." His dark eyes fixed on her. "I look forward to it."

She slipped out the low stock door at the side of the main entry and sloshed back to the main house. At the front door, she glanced over her shoulder.

Gavin disappeared around the corner of the barn.

How different would her morning have been if Jack or his dad had shown up?

According to legend, the distance a guest of a Scottish landlord threw the stone of strength determined the sleeping accommodations he could expect. Time would tell if this man would earn the best bed in the house.

Chapter 2

Gavin climbed into Jack's truck and jotted notes on a clipboard resting on the passenger seat. Despite bad weather, he had assessed most of the planks. He turned on the wipers, put his foot on the gas pedal, and started the engine but didn't drive forward. On his right, the Thistle Inn offered a picture-perfect view against a gray silhouette of foothills. The house was recently restored with white siding, protruding dormers, and modern windows. Only a small window on the lower level still had older glass. The wavy glass dated the house in the 1800s. Was the history of the place different from the history of the barn? He'd love to see the inside. He removed his cell phone from his pocket, lowered the window, and snapped a photo.

As if on cue, the front door opened.

Fiona stepped onto the front porch and opened a bright-red umbrella. She passed under an old oak tree before walking toward the truck.

The rain picked up.

Huge drops fell from fall leaves and bounced off the red umbrella.

The rain didn't bother him. He enjoyed the view too much. The image captured his imagination, reminding him of a rainy day in Scotland at the tail end of summer. "Did you forget something?"

"I thought you could use some hot tea." She

glanced at the thermos on the passenger seat and handed him a hot cup.

"Thanks." He wrapped his fingers around the warm cup and flipped the lid. A puff of mint-scented steam warned him the tea was too hot to sip. A gust of cold, wet wind blew into the truck's cab. A seductive scent of lemon verbena reminiscent of sunshine and delicate wildflowers mixed with the minty steam.

Fiona glanced at the menacing sky from under the umbrella, then back toward Gavin. "If you'd like local help with your search for your aunt. I can introduce you to my brother, Ian." She rested the umbrella on her shoulder and pulled up the zipper of her rain jacket. "He's speaking here at afternoon tea."

"Afternoon tea?" Gavin raised a brow. "Is that Scottish?"

"I do it for the tourists." She smiled. "My brother would be the first to explain how, although the Scots produce some delicious teas, historically, the idea of High Tea was another name for a workman's late afternoon lunch."

"I've never thought about it before, but it makes sense." Back home, his busy schedule never allowed time for such frivolous activity. He glanced at the thermos resting on the passenger seat and back at the paper cup. A takeaway cup was more his style. "Is your brother a Scottish historian?"

"He's a forensic genealogist who is an expert on the Scots who settled in this area. So he's the one you want to speak to if you're searching for a lost relative." She rested her free hand on the open window.

The scent of lemon lingered wherever her hand touched.

"A forensic genealogist?" Gavin shrugged. "Sounds like an interesting profession."

"Ian's combined areas of expertise are hard to explain. But, when you meet him, you'll understand."

A gust of wind turned the umbrella inside out.

She straightened the umbrella, adjusted her hood, and pulled her braid forward. "Do you know any academics?"

Loose strands of auburn hair escaped her braid and fell softly on her face.

"I try to limit my association with academics. They can be too stuffy." He resisted the urge to push the stray ends back into the tight weave. "I've got a cousin who's a professor of anthropology at Glasgow University. Last time I checked, he was digging for lost gold in the Highlands." He deliberately left out Cousin Logan's importance to the family business. When an interesting artifact turned up at a work site, Logan was the one they called. As he said earlier, it was a complicated company.

"So you know what it's like to put up with them." She swung her head to the side. Her braid followed. "My brother can be that way sometimes. He's also very charming and informative."

"I don't have much to go on," Gavin confessed.

"All Ian needs is a name and a location." She raised her brows. "You do know your aunt's name, don't you?"

"Joan. She's a McIver, or at least, she was." He hadn't shared his family name earlier. It wasn't a secret. She could quickly check the participating athletes. She might find a Gavin or two on the list. A name alone wouldn't connect him to Scottish International Real

Estate and Construction—the family's billion-dollar company. Fortunately, McIver was a common Scottish surname.

"Do you know if she was married?" She glanced at *his* ring finger.

"*Granaidh* is not talking." The Gaelic flowed easily now he knew she understood the language adequately. Damn, she was pleasant and easy to talk to. He hated not telling her the full extent of his family's business. How could he without sounding like a pretentious billionaire?

Finally, the wind died down, and the rain stopped.

"My granddad can be just as tight-lipped." Fiona closed her umbrella. "Do you have any idea when Joan settled here?"

"If I had to take an educated guess, I'd say sometime in the nineteen forties or fifties." He was actually having a conversation about Great-Aunt Joan.

"It's unlikely she would have come here alone. Could she have been a servant or something like that?" Fiona asked.

"You into genealogy?" Gavin wanted to laugh at the idea of a McIver being anyone's servant. Without knowledge of his family, Fiona asked a logical question.

"Osmosis by association with my brother. Sometimes that's all he talks about." She rested the umbrella against the car door, stood on tiptoes, and pointed to the clipboard on the passenger seat. "Is that your report for Jack?"

"Want to see what I've written?" He was obligated to offer her a glance at the sketchy notes.

"Sure, why not?" She rested the clipboard on the

door and squinted at the page. "Your handwriting looks as bad as your cooking sounds." She handed him the notepad. "I'll wait until I hear from Jack."

He inhaled slowly. "Do you make lemon-scented creams with your herbs?" The silky sensation of her hand cream remained on the clipboard. He tossed it in the back seat.

"I don't. I buy my creams at a local shop." She rubbed her hands together. "You have a sharp sense of smell."

"Unfortunately, it comes in handy in my line of work. Not all the smells are so pleasant." Gavin coughed. Had he just compared her uplifting fragrance to mildew or rotted wood? "I'd like to talk to your brother. What time should I be here?"

"Stop by at two." She picked up the umbrella and stepped away from the truck. "The main dining room is sold out. I can offer you something less formal. Hope you don't mind having tea in the kitchen."

"I prefer the kitchen table." He smiled. Tea in the kitchen reminded him of simpler times when he didn't have rushed deadlines, estranged relatives, and a significant portfolio. Back then, he didn't need to be evasive or tell white lies to avoid judgment. Instead, like his cousins and siblings, he worked for his grandfather as one of the crew and received a meager salary.

"Me, too. I enjoy a cup of tea at the kitchen table. See you at two." She avoided a puddle and waved him on.

"Wow." He rubbed a hand through his hair. Today's fortunate stroke of fate led him to an unexpected expert. This morning, he was at a loss on how to search for Great-Aunt Joan. Within a short time, after meeting Fiona, the hunt had direction. Fair Fiona surprised him. She was an enterprising young lady and could be formidable competition. Cautious of the wet conditions, he drove slowly toward the road. At the end of the driveway, he shifted into Neutral and glanced in the rearview mirror.

She stopped at the porch steps and flashed a coy smile over her shoulder.

Gavin was no stranger to the charm of Highland Falls and its inhabitants. Jack's description of the town was spot-on. He described the town as a charming secret hidden in the Adirondacks. *Granaidh*'s surprise announcement of an estranged sister gave Gavin the perfect excuse to visit his mate and see the town. The town was the last known location of his aunt and had recently become the latest international, real estate hot spot. Urged on by *Granaidh*, he called Jack and signed up for the games. The upcoming Scottish event allowed him to slip inconspicuously into the community.

As if on cue, his phone beeped with a message from Jack.

—What's going on?—

—Great wood. Do you think she might sell a few boards?—

He typed back.

—Never in a million years.—

Jack's response was quick.

—My impression, too. What did you think of the fair Fiona?—

A heart emoji followed.

Gavin's phone binged again, and several laughing emojis appeared on the screen.

As soon as Gavin's divorce was final, Jack joined the succession of matchmakers.

Fortunately, texting didn't catch any expectations in his friend's voice.

A loveless marriage left Gavin wary of relationships. He wasn't opposed to falling in love—if such a thing existed.

—*Not what I imagined, but interesting.*—

The way she casually tossed her braid over her shoulder was captivating. Her energy and understated good humor brightened the dreary barn. He smiled. Good thing Jack couldn't see him.

—*Interesting. Did you tell her why you're here?*—

Jack's reply hinted at disappointment.

—*For the games and to find my aunt*—

He added a smiley face.

—*And.*—

—*Nothing else to say.*—

—*She doesn't know you're worth a fortune?*—

Jack added a dollar sign.

Gavin typed.

—*NO.*—

—*Why not?*—

—*We talked about wood.*—

Gavin hated texting.

—*No worries, mate. See you at the pub.*—

—*Change of plans. I'm invited to tea.*—

He looked forward to visiting Fiona in her kitchen.

—*Be careful of what streams you cross.*—

—*Talk later.*—

Gavin understood small towns and took his friend's advice to heart. Fiona was just the beginning of the flow of inquiring townspeople. Sooner rather than later,

Fiona and the locals would learn what Jack and his dad already knew. The family company, SIREaC, gathered prime holdings and developed successful rustic resorts. The company's reputation preceded them wherever they went.

Highland Falls appeared to be the exception. The pitfalls of acquiring property in a small town like this were not new. When the time came, he'd deal with any problems. He hadn't driven very far before his phone rang again. The silly ringtone his daughter, Emily, had chosen always made him smile.

He checked the number. Adrian was calling from Scotland. Almost noon here was dinnertime in Scotland.

"Cheers, cuz." Adrian's voice echoed loud and clear.

"Everything okay?" Gavin put the phone on speaker. He was generally not an alarmist, but he struggled with having sole custody of his eight-year-old daughter. Leaving her in the care of a nanny and his cousin while he was miles away bothered him. "How's Emily doing?"

"She's fine. The nanny picked her up from a friend's house. I'm meeting them for dinner. Want to join us?" Adrian laughed.

Adrian was a lifesaver, stepping in to help out with Emily after his divorce. "Maybe not dinner, but I could catch a flight and arrive in time for breakfast."

Gavin laughed and turned onto the main road. "What's the news on the home front?"

"Your ex is at it again. *Och*—that woman. Just mentioning her is like fingernails on a blackboard."

"What's she up to now?" Gavin blew out a long

slow breath.

"The witch still has one of your credit cards."

"How did that happen?" His heartbeat pounded in his ears. Their divorce was final four years ago. News about his ex wasn't exactly what he expected. Instead, he preferred to hear new details *Granaidh* might have shared about Great-Aunt Joan. "Where is she now?"

"Milan. Should the lawyers get involved? Do you want to press criminal charges? Have her arrested?"

His cousin would like nothing better than incarcerating the woman who abandoned her child and husband for a frivolous lifestyle. "Play nice, and don't forget she's Emily's mother." Once he won full custody of his daughter, Gavin let go of the anger. "Pay the bill and stop the card." What she did *was* criminal. However, a Milan shopping spree wouldn't dent his finances. "She might remember to send Emily a gift." His daughter was the only good thing to come out of a marriage to a money-sucking witch. He was young, inexperienced, and believed he had found the perfect woman. He was an *eejit* attracted to superficial beauty and phony charm. He sighed. Too late, he understood his ex-father-in-law had sacrificed a daughter like an ancient clan chief trying to gain territorial favor.

"Consider it done," Adrian said. "How's the search going for Auntie Joan?"

"I came here with nothing more than a name to go on." When he agreed to find his aunt, he accepted a difficult task. "This is a tight-lipped town. I got a break this morning. I met someone willing to introduce me to an expert on the history of the Scots who settled this town."

"Sounds like a good person to know," Adrian said.

"We'll see. The man is a forensic genealogist." He omitted the invitation to tea. He couldn't confess he was more interested in seeing the sister than meeting her brother. Fiona possessed strong self-qualities he admired in a woman—self-confident, self-reliant, and self-employed. If they'd met at a posh party, he would easily believe she belonged there. So what was she doing here in nowhere Highland Falls? She was an unexpected blip in his plans. He wasn't a fool. Experience taught him not to let a pretty face affect essential decisions.

"Sounds promising. I'll expect more information the next time we speak."

"We'll talk soon." Gavin ended the call, promising to call his daughter Emily later to say good night. Bedtime chats were his favorite moments, and he missed her dearly. If he were back home in Scotland, he would have had considerable information by now. Whenever two Highlanders got together, whisky flowed, and they spoke freely about family history, mutual friends, and local real estate. However, the people he met in Highland Falls were different. They talked openly about where their families were from, but when it came to local real estate, they avoided his questions.

Even Fair Fiona was no exception. She spoke about her renovation plans but changed the subject when he asked questions about the surrounding property. What would she think when she discovered what the family company planned for land Joan might own?

Chapter 3

Courtesy of Mother Nature, Fiona witnessed a flawless change from summer to fall overnight. She helped the transformation by decorating with autumn colors. Hardy orange and purple mums hung over the sides of the second-floor window boxes. Even on a drab day like today, the flowers made her smile. She opened the mudroom door adjacent to the kitchen. Inside the small space, she removed her boots and slipped into a pair of soft shoes. The aroma of freshly baked pumpkin scones flowed from the kitchen through the archway.

"Welcome back." Cora removed a soiled apron and tied a clean one around an ample waist.

"I'm sorry I took so long." Fiona glanced around the kitchen. Thanks to Cora, the counters were clean and tidy. No one would suspect they had been baking since dawn. Fiona appreciated having a clean freak for an assistant. A neat kitchen inspired creativity. She glanced at the clock. "Are all the guests out for the day?"

"Three pipers from Dunedin, Florida, are still in the dining room." Cora filled a fresh teapot. "I'll see if they want another cup of tea." She carried the pot into the dining room.

"I'm sorry my meeting took so long." Fiona followed. She hadn't anticipated spending half an hour discussing old wood, local history, and a bit of personal information with an exciting and handsome stranger.

"Good morning, Miss Campbell." A tall, slim man stood and removed a red plaid tam. "How's the weather outside?"

"There's a break in the clouds." She glanced out the window. The tail end of the truck turned onto the main road. "Would you like another cup of tea before you and your boys head out?" She nodded at the pot in Cora's hand and glanced at two younger boys seated at the table wearing similar blue plaid tams.

"I couldn't drink another drop." The slim man gathered brochures scattered across the table.

"It's a freshly brewed Scottish tea." Cora placed the pot on the table and returned to the kitchen.

"What do you think, boys? We'll have another cup if the lady will join us." The man pulled out a chair between the boys.

Why not? She could use a cup of liquid comfort. "Do you have plans for today?" Fiona removed a cup from the table behind her and poured tea for everyone. The warm, malty blend slid down easily and took her mind off Gavin.

"The boys and I are meeting the rest of the band for a quick practice. We'll explore the area after lunch. Any suggestions?"

"If the rain continues, there's a nice museum in town with a wonderful display of pipes and drums. I can call ahead and tell the curator to expect you." She glanced at her watch. Her brother was most likely collaborating with Mr. Paisley on their latest project. Was she wrong to assume he would have time to help Jack's friend find his aunt?

"Good idea." The man wrapped his fingers around

the cup and finished the tea. "See you at tea time."

All alone in the dining room, Fiona stared out the window. She could only see the east barn wall from where she stood. The wood looked worn and vulnerable, even from a distance. She stacked the dirty cups and plates, sighed, and carried the tray to the kitchen. "Hi, Mabel. You're here early." Fiona placed the dirty plates next to the sink and greeted a vibrant, young redhead leaning against a counter.

"Mom said you'd need extra help today. My only class was canceled." Mabel opened her palms and smiled. "So ta-da. I'm all yours until it's time to babysit the twins."

"Are you sure you don't mind?" Fiona stacked cups and plates into the dishwasher.

"Not at all." Mabel removed a hot-pink elastic band from her pocket and twisted it around a mass of curls.

Mabel's long, curly hair reminded Fiona of autumn leaves. "Are you enjoying your tourism and hospitality classes?" She filled the top shelf of the dishwasher with dirty glasses.

"I can't wait to practice what I learned." Mabel carried a cup of tea to the kitchen table.

"We're serving a new scone recipe at tea time. I could use a taste tester." Cora plated a freshly baked scone for her daughter. "Be careful. It's still hot."

"OMG. It smells delicious." Mabel broke the scone in half and added a dab of butter.

"Can you taste the pumpkin? Your mother and I worked on the recipe for weeks." Fiona inhaled. Getting the right balance of buttery scone and pumpkin spice was tricky.

"Perfect." Mabel gave her a thumbs-up.

"How many will we need? Looks like you've already baked a couple of dozen." Fiona glanced at the counter next to the oven. Trays of scones covered every inch.

"A few dozen," Cora said. "Most of today's guests are day-trippers from Albany. Mabel suggested we send them home with scones. It's a nice touch, considering their trek in this weather." She placed her hands on her hips.

"A goody bag is a great idea." Fiona smiled. "Did you learn that in one of your classes?"

"You can't do enough to please a guest." Mabel glanced over the rim of her cup. "Do you mind adding a recipe card to the bag?"

"Not at all. The recipe's not a secret." Fiona bit into a scone and chewed slowly. She savored the buttery flavor and sweet taste of autumn. "They *are* perfect." She didn't know how she would have survived the early days without Cora. Money was tight when the B and B opened. The best dime she ever spent was hiring her as a chambermaid. From day one, she showed initiative, making perfect little towel sculptures for the guests and offering to help with breakfast. And, now, her daughter was just as valuable.

"Let's get the scones plated." Cora laid out white ceramic serving platters. She pushed one to the side. "We'll save this one for Sophia's shortbread cookies when they arrive."

"Is the cream whipped?" Guests expected scones with clotted cream and strawberries. Fiona regretted she couldn't offer Devon cream. Instead, she replaced the cream with the highest- quality, fatty local ingredients she could purchase. "Are the apples sliced?" Since berries were out of season, she and Cora agreed on locally grown apples.

"Not yet." Cora placed a bowl of red and green apples on the table. "Who was the man you met in the barn? He wasn't Jack or his dad." She wiped her hands on her apron and gazed out the window over the sink. "I recognized the truck. So I figured you'd be okay."

Fiona reached for a peeler and handed one to Mabel. "His name is Gavin. He's a friend of Jack's. He's here for the games. He works construction back home in Scotland and offered to take the call since the Drummonds were busy at the fairground." She shrugged. "His knowledge of weathered wood was impressive."

"Sounds like an interesting young man." Cora filled the electric kettle and turned it on. "It's odd he gave up morning practice to check out the barn? Most competitors spend as much time on the field as possible."

"Weather was bad—maybe morning practice was canceled." Fiona hadn't asked why Gavin wasn't practicing.

"I doubt it. The athletes will compete, even if it's raining. They need to get the feel of a less-than-perfect field." Cora shrugged and walked toward the counter. "What teas are we serving today?

"I'd like to add a milk thistle blend to our usual." She joined Cora at the counter and reached for a box of tea leaves with a picture of a purple rosette on a spikey green stem. "Let's do a taste test." She filled a tea ball and placed it in a purple teapot.

The water came to a boil.

Cora lifted the kettle and poured water over the leaves. She set the pot and three cups on the table.

Fiona glanced at the clock. Four minutes had passed. She poured the first cup and sniffed the pleasantly fragrant tea. "There's a strong grapefruit note."

Mabel put down the peeler, stretched, and yawned.

"I'm sorry if we're boring you," Cora said.

"All the talk about tea and scones is not as interesting as this Gavin guy. Dad took me to the festival grounds yesterday afternoon. I bet he was the hot guy talking to Jack."

So maybe he's not into morning practices. Fiona took a sip.

"Having a father responsible for scheduling practice time for so many cute athletes is nice." Mabel winked. "What's his sport?"

"He's participating in the shot put competition." Talking about Gavin *was* more interesting than discussing milk thistle's ability to detox your liver.

"Cool. I'll tell my friends to make sure we're at the event. This hot guy will be more fun to watch than old Mr. Parker." Mabel rolled her eyes.

"Old Jason Parker was a couple of years ahead of me in high school and quite the heartthrob." Cora laughed and slid diced apples into a saucepan. "He turned fifty last month. When he strolls down the street, he still turns plenty of heads."

"Whatever." Mabel shrugged and carried her empty cup to the sink. She glanced at the wall clock. "The twins' school bus won't be here for at least an hour. If I can use your computer, I'll type the scone recipe and make copies. I'll add something about the town and inn."

"Sounds like a nice touch and good promotion. Use the computer in the office." Fiona handed her a card with a copy of the recipe.

"Got it." Mabel pulled a set of headphones from her backpack, slipped them on her head, and climbed the stairs to the upstairs residence.

"She's going to do well in the hospitality industry." Was the young woman's taste in music as good as her taste in men? Fiona joined Cora at the stove. "Do you think she'll stay in Highland Falls after graduation? With the tourists' boom, there's a need for young people who know the town."

"I don't know." Cora added lemon zest to the pot of simmering apples. "Kids her age don't think like the rest of the locals. They love trendy, new businesses. Your brother's satellite classes are top-rated, even if genealogy is not their major. Mabel mentioned a lodge near Lake Placid with a movie theater." She stirred the pot. "Imagine such a resort close to our town? It would change everything."

"I love the quaint charm of this town and wouldn't welcome any major change." Fiona released an exasperated sigh. "I hope it never comes to that."

On the stove, the fruit simmered.

She inhaled the scent of the perfect comfort food. "The smell is delicious." She reached for a spoon and helped Cora divide the stewed fruit into six serving bowls.

Cora placed plastic wrap on top of each bowl and pushed them to the side. "What did you discover about Gavin besides being Jack's friend?" She scraped the remaining apples off the bottom of the pot into two dessert dishes, dribbled the sticky juice over the tops, and carried them to the kitchen table.

"Why are you asking?" Fiona raised her brows. "Did you hear something?"

"Just town gossip..."Cora shrugged. "You know how everyone gets out of sorts when a stranger is curious about an old house—or old barn."

Fiona dipped a spoon into the saucy mix. "He's searching for a great-aunt. The family lost contact when she relocated here in the late 1950s." Should she tell her friend she suspected Gavin was holding out on something?

Cora would have a chance to form her own opinion soon enough.

"It wasn't uncommon for immigrants who came here during the forties or fifties to never see family again. They were busy building new lives. They often lost touch with family back home." Cora tasted the apples. "My family settled here after World War II. The new ancestry program at the museum encouraged my search for relatives back in Dundee." She sipped her tea. "Have you checked Gavin's application?"

"I don't think I'll find much." Fiona shook her head. "Once I register the athletes, I don't have a reason to review the list. Anyway, I've been too busy with the flood of reservations for rooms and afternoon tea." *But I will tonight.* She doubted she'd find anything of interest on his application. All competitors answered the same questions: name, date of birth, hometown, and occupation. Except for his birthday, she knew the basics. On the other hand, she probably had more information on him than any other registrant. He had a great-aunt, Joan, and a grandfather with a secret—

nothing unusual for a Scot. She discovered he was knowledgeable about old wood. He had a charming smile and a subtle sense of humor—all good qualities in a man. And, he had the most bottomless blue eyes she ever saw—*another good…no, don't go there.* Suddenly, the kitchen was warmer than usual. She stared into her cup. "I'm going to check the rooms for our afternoon arrivals. Which rooms did you assign?"

"The Aberdeen and Skye were the only rooms available. The guests occupying those rooms checked out early." Cora pulled a list from her apron pocket.

"Oh, by the way…" Fiona stopped with her foot on the first step and turned. "You'll have a chance to talk to Gavin. I invited him to tea."

"How…you know we're booked." Cora raised a brow.

"He doesn't mind having tea in the kitchen." She rushed upstairs. Cora didn't have time to ask what was so urgent about Gavin meeting Ian today. "We'll use the tea set Granny sent for Christmas," she shouted from the top step.

Fiona buzzed through her chores at warp speed. When she finished, every corner sparkled, creases disappeared from the handmade quilts, and pillows were puffed to perfection. She gathered the dirty laundry and carried the basket downstairs. She placed one foot on the bottom step and stopped.

Ian sat at the kitchen table. His computer was open to the museum's website.

"You're early." She entered the kitchen and kicked the laundry basket toward the mudroom.

"I visited the dig site on the Logan's property, but with all the rain, there's not much going on." He put the computer to sleep.

"I'm glad you're here early today." She was surprised to see him. Ian was never on time. "I have something to tell you." She walked over to a petite lady's desk in the far corner of the kitchen. The slender legs of the desk wobbled when she opened the drawer. "I met someone who could use your services. Gavin McIver is Jack's friend. He's looking for a great-aunt." She searched through a folder stuffed with athletes' registration forms.

"Doesn't sound complicated." He restarted the computer.

"If you're too busy, you could say no." Fiona shook her head.

"Do you want me to help him or not?" He sipped his tea and glanced at her over the rim of his cup. "What are you looking for?"

"Here it is." She opened a folder and ran a finger down a list of athletes." As she suspected, nothing of interest was on Gavin's registration form. She handed it to Ian.

"Did Mr. McIver mention his aunt's surname—a married name?" Ian opened a file on the Clans of Highland Falls.

"He has nothing more than the name I gave you, Joan McIver." *Or so he says.* She had doubts. Would Ian, an expert on finding lost people, find her?

He typed Clan McIver, Highland Falls, but nothing came up.

"Is he sure she lived in this town?" Ian expanded the search to surrounding counties. "I found a link to the ancient Clan McIver. You might find this interesting." He read verbatim the words on the screen.

"In the seventeenth century, an earl restored the estates of Iver to his son Duncan McIver on the condition he and his heirs should bear the name and arms of Campbell."

"Oh." She placed a hand over her mouth. "Don't you know already everything there is to know about Clan Campbell?"

"New facts are always waiting to be discovered. Clans without a chief often swore oaths to powerful clan chiefs in exchange for protection." Ian turned away from the screen. "Does something bother you about the idea this man might be a distant relative? Did you find yourself a wee bit attracted to the lad?" Ian teased. "No worries if you do—any relatives we might have in common lived centuries ago. Would he be interested in knowing more about the clans' association?"

Ian had an academically infuriating way of going off on historical facts and an uncanny way of knowing exactly what she was thinking. "You can ask him yourself. I invited him for tea." She shoved the list back into the drawer. They spent enough time discussing Gavin McIver. Her afternoon tea guests would arrive soon. "Thanks for bringing the cookies from Sophia's shop." She untied the red-and-white baker's twine. Assaulted by the buttery scent, she chose a shortbread cookie with speckles of tea leaves. A delicate hint of Earl Gray tea put her mind back on track. She glanced at the mud-stained hem of her jeans. "I'll be right back. Keep yourself out of trouble." She grabbed another cookie.

"Don't worry. I'll keep your new friend occupied." Ian chuckled.

She climbed the stairs from the kitchen to her

apartment above the garage. In her room, she changed into clean jeans and assessed herself in the mirror. Her braid could use a redo. Fancy, triple upside-down braids needed more time than she had. She needed something quick and straightforward but more embellished than the one she wore earlier. A simple plait would have to do. She parted her hair in the middle, twisted each section, and tugged on the loops of the braids to make them appear fatter. "Not bad." She turned for a side view, flipped the braids over the top of her head, and secured them with bobby pins. A few strands of hair fell around her face in a softer, messier look. This would have to do. She had already spent too much time changing. She rushed downstairs.

Outside, wheels crunched over the gravel driveway. A transport van had arrived.

In the foyer, she passed Ian as she opened the door to greet guests.

"Don't you look nice?" Cora followed and glanced at the crown of braids.

"I just cleaned up a bit." She tucked a hair behind her ear and ushered guests inside. All the while, she kept an eye out for her one special guest. Maybe he was late—again.

"What a lovely inn." A lady in a puffy winter jacket stepped onto the porch.

"Thank you for braving the weather and coming to tea. Enjoy the fire and warm beverages. Formal tea will be served shortly." In the dining room, she pointed out the different teas on the buffet along the back wall. "The quilted, green leaf cozy cover is green tea. The purple cozy is a thistle tea. The pot with the blue-and-white flag is a peaty Scottish tea. I highly recommend this one on a day like today." She left her guests and returned to the kitchen.

Gavin was seated at the table with Ian. "I hope I'm not too early." He stood when she and Cora walked in.

"Not at all. Glad you made it back." Fiona smiled.

"I couldn't resist your offer of freshly baked scones and tea in this delightful kitchen." Gavin waved a hand in the air." He gazed at her braid and smiled. "You clean up nice."

He cleaned up, too, and even shaved off the scruff along his jaw. A flash of heat warmed her cheeks. *So do you.* His freshly pressed blue-plaid shirt deepened the color of his eyes. "Don't let me interrupt." A commotion in the mudroom drew her attention away.

The twins were home.

The scene before her played out like a scene from a silly movie.

"Uncle Ian." Simon and Sara raced in ahead of Mabel.

Mabel stared at Gavin with her mouth open. She turned toward Fiona and silently formed the words, *hot, shot put guy.*

Gavin's bewildered glance at Sara and Simon amused Fiona. He hadn't struck her as the kind of man who wore his emotions on his face. She should explain the sudden appearance of two children who called her brother *uncle.*

"Mind your manners." Ian took charge. "Say hello to Auntie Fiona's friend, Mr. McIver."

"Auntie Fiona?" Gavin raised his brows.

"These two speed demons are my niece and nephew, Sara and Simon." Fiona smiled and placed an arm around each child.

"Call me Gavin." He shook their hands. "Nice to meet you. How was school today?"

"Do you like frogs, Mr. Gavin?" Simon went into an extended rendition of an incident with a frog named Roger.

"Aye, lad." He winked. "When I was your age, I caught my share of frogs."

"Yuck." Sara scrunched her face.

"Your sister doesn't sound happy about your friend Roger." Gavin smiled.

"He's not my friend anymore. Adam Macgregor squished him."

"Good. The frog was an ugly old thing. And frogs give you warts." Sara grabbed her brother's hand.

Fiona learned to stay a step ahead of Sara and Simon's differences of opinion. "This doesn't sound like nice kitchen talk." She, too, found the subject of Roger distasteful. Anyway, tea was about to be served. Any story with a description of blood and guts was better left untold. "Mr. McIver is busy. Maybe later, he'll have time to hear about your day." Fiona glanced at Gavin.

His narrowed eyes gazed from Fiona to the twins.

The situation often puzzled strangers. She handed Mabel a tray with cookies and milk. "Mind Mabel. I'll be upstairs as soon as tea is done."

"Let's go." Mabel unlatched a rope with a *Private* sign hanging over the stairs.

The little redheads resembled Fiona in so many ways. Unlike most red-haired people, her family had warm skin tones. Even though their mother was fair, the twins inherited their looks from the Campbell side. Strangers often thought they were her biological children.

"Kids." Gavin smiled. "They're always in a hurry."

She nodded and returned the smile. Except for Ian, she rarely discussed the events leading up to their arrival, especially not in front of them. How could she explain to a stranger how she became the twins' guardian and not her family back home? She still questioned why her brother made the decision. Today was no exception. Gavin would have to keep wondering. If he stuck around when the games were over, town gossip might fill in the details—or they might not. Everyone was wary of strangers who overstayed their welcome.

Mabel and the twins had disappeared behind the door at the top of the stairs.

Beep. The tea leaves seeped for four minutes.

"It's tea time." She reached for a tray of shortbread.

Cora grabbed it first.

"I'll carry the teapots." Ian followed Cora with two freshly brewed pots of tea.

What were they doing, leaving her alone with Gavin? She smoothed an imaginary wrinkle from her apron.

"Can I help serve?" Gavin pointed to a forgotten tray of scones.

"You're my guest." Grateful for a distraction, she placed a cup and saucer onto the table. "Pour yourself a cup of tea. I'll be right back." She carried the tray of scones into the dining room. Why should she care what a man she just met thought about the twins or anything in her life? She delivered the scones but didn't stay to chat.

Zelda Benjamin

In the kitchen, Gavin wandered around with a cup in his hand.

"This is a remarkable makeover." He pointed to the crown molding. "Is it original?"

"The town handyman does amazing restoration work." The kitchen was her favorite renovation. The room, although practical, was warm and cozy.

"Is he a long-time resident of Scottish descent?" Gavin faced her.

She nodded. "Many of the residents can trace their roots back to Scotland."

"And you?" He smiled.

"Most definitely a Scot," she said with an exaggerated lilt. Why was he asking again? They determined her heritage earlier.

"No mistaking that, lass." He glanced at the braids twisted across her head and smiled. "But you're not a local."

"No, I'm not." She touched her hair to make sure everything was in place. How much did she want him to know? "I moved from Manhattan three years ago."

"Gave up the high life for a quieter option?"

Like most Scots, Gavin was not at a loss for conversation. "Something along those lines." She shrugged.

"Do you serve afternoon tea every day?" He pointed to a row of teapots ready for the next round.

He had a knack for jumping from one subject to another. At least, it kept the conversation going. "From day one, I only scheduled afternoon tea Monday through Thursday." She didn't regret the decision. Weekend room bookings were heavier than weekdays. Serving tea would cut into her time with the twins.

"You've done well." He leaned against the counter and crossed his arms. "This lifestyle suits you. Did your original plans include converting the barn into a party venue?"

She was strangely flattered by his compliment. He didn't seem the type to carelessly throw praise around. "No." She sighed. "Only recently, the weather has taken a noticeable toll on the wood." Deciding to give up city life and venture into something as complex as a time and money-sucking restoration took time. Repairing the barn or reclaiming the wood could be equally as money sucking. This time, it was a matter of safety.

"What's your vision for the barn?" He glanced out the window.

"Once the shed is gone, I'll have a better idea. The space should be able to accommodate fifty to a hundred people." She raised a brow. "What's your professional opinion?"

"Easily…" He rubbed a palm along his jaw. "Do your plans include a bar and dance floor? Any respectable Scot wouldn't consider a party without whisky and music." He reached for the notepad and pen on the counter. "You might want to consider putting the bar at the far end with a view out a new picture window." He drew a big square. "This is the window." He drew a straight line. "This could be the bar. You'd have to agree on the size and shape. Interior design is not my strong point."

"I haven't thought that far ahead." She laughed and tucked the rough design into her apron pocket. "I'll pass your idea on to my interior designer." A completed party venue seemed so far away. Would Gavin still be here? "What about you? How long are you pursuing the search for your great-aunt?"

"As long as it takes. I don't want to go home empty-handed." He walked over to the table and sat.

His voice was confident and optimistic. She liked those qualities in a man.

"Tell me about the little redheads, your niece and nephew. They sound like they recently arrived." He refilled his teacup. "Would you like a cup?"

"Tea sounds good right about now." She sat across from him. Two little redheads with an adorable Scottish brogue would stir anyone's curiosity. His question was perfectly normal. "Their parents were killed in a car crash six months ago." She blinked back tears.

"I'm so sorry for everyone's loss." The corners of his mouth turned down. He filled her cup and slid it across the table.

"Thank you." She met his glance. Pools of deep blue hazed over with sorrow stared back.

"They're lucky to have you and Ian and such a wonderful place to live." His fingers brushed the back of her hand.

The brief touch was gentle and caring. A shiver ran up her arm. "We all needed time to grieve and adjust in our own way. Having the twins here has helped." She pulled away and wrapped her hands around the warm teacup. His compassion touched her, tempting her to share her doubt and confusion about being made their guardian. *Not today.* She wouldn't open up until he was ready to reveal more.

Chapter 4

Gavin dropped his athletic bag next to a kitchen chair and removed a box of dry cereal and a bowl from the pantry. He glanced at the open window over the sink. The crisp chill and bright sunshine were perfect conditions for today's competitions. It's too bad he didn't have time for a big bowl of hearty porridge. He filled the bowl with little rice kernels. As he added milk, the grains cracked and popped.

"Good morning." Jack entered the kitchen and walked toward the refrigerator. He poured two large glasses of orange juice and handed one to Gavin.

Gavin nodded and sipped his juice. What was Fiona serving her guests for breakfast? Two weeks passed since he was invited to tea at Fiona's inn. Jack and his dad kept him busy with odd jobs around town and at the fairgrounds. The work made him feel better than he had in a long time.

By far, the afternoon he spent in Fiona's kitchen was the highlight of his visit. She asked all the right questions. If only he could give her the answers. For now, he'd let her believe he was just a construction worker with a prominent Scottish family. He rubbed a hand along his jaw. How would she react when she discovered Scottish International Real Estate and Construction was his family's business? Soon enough, everything would be out in the open. Today was not the day. Even Great-Aunt Joan was on the back burner. He glanced at his watch. Today's priority was the precision of his shot put.

"Better get going if you want some practice time." Jack lifted the keys to the truck off the hook by the door.

"Feels good to be back in the game." Gavin swallowed the last crunchy spoonful of cereal. He placed the empty cereal bowl and glass in the sink, followed Jack out the door, and climbed into the truck. He never expected to compete again. A work accident to his right arm had left him with a torn bicep. Months of physical therapy, multiple surgeries, and a determination to be better helped him reach this point. "Thanks, mate, for taking the time to be my official coach."

"Contestants aren't allowed to warm up at the venue without a coach or official present. I'm there for whatever you need." Jack clapped him on the back and started the engine. "You've got this, mate."

The drive to the fairgrounds was quick.

"Catch up with you in a few." Jack dropped him off at the main entrance and drove toward the ground crew lot.

Gavin stepped out of the truck and glanced around. The festive atmosphere reminded him of events back home. A tug-of-war competition was already in progress. The scene was electrified with men in kilts and shouts of encouragement from the crowd cheering for their favorite contestant. Earthy smells of haggis and greasy chips floated from the food trucks.

The phone binged. A UK dialing code appeared in front of the number. Mid-morning here was the late afternoon at home in Edinburgh. "Adrian...everything okay?" An unexpected chat with his wacky cousin worried him.

"No worries, *mac-bràthair thàthar*." Adrian giggled.

"I can tell you're practicing your Gaelic. You got it perfect this time—mother's brother's son." He exhaled. Her giddiness was a good sign. If something bad had happened, she would be a hot mess.

"What are you up to?" Adrian asked.

"I'm walking toward the practice field." He rolled his shoulders. "The competition is today."

"Good luck."

"How was dinner at Granddad's?" At the last family dinner, Gavin learned *Granaidh* had a sister he hadn't seen in decades. A month later, Gavin stood in a muddy fairground without a clear plan for finding her.

"Despite being his usual grumpy self, he accepted my new structure and concepts for a project in Inverness." She sighed.

"You're a talented architect: don't let anyone make you feel bad." Praise was not something *Granaidh* handed out often. He expected everyone to do the job they were hired for—adorable Adrian was no exception. "Did he mention his sister again? Any information would be helpful at this point."

"Not directly," Adrian said. "Logan made an appearance at dinner. He was disappointed you weren't there. And surprised we have another great-aunt."

"Weren't we all?" Gavin rubbed his chin. "Are you sure Granddad had nothing else to say?"

He passed under a power line. Loud static interrupted the call. He stuck a finger in his ear.

"Gavin, are you still there?" Adrian shouted. "What are your plans? Are you coming home after the games?"

A parade of clans and piper bands finished performing. A group of children followed them off the field. "I don't think so." He had every intention of seeing this through to the end. "A search like this is going to take a while." The low point of the situation was a prolonged separation from his daughter.

"Can I help in some way?" Adrian asked. "I'm due for a vacation."

"A trip here wouldn't exactly be a vacation." He would be foolish not to accept the offer. Her flighty curiosity and aptitude for gossip would be helpful. "Tell Emily she's taking a long trip to New York. Give Nannie an extended vacation with pay."

"What about school?" Adrian asked.

"I'll enroll her here." He briefly considered how moving here would interrupt his daughter's routine.

"That'll work…I think." Adrian giggled again.

"Will Emily mind leaving her friends and the academy?" Was he too rash in assuming his eight-year-old daughter would be okay with being uprooted?

"Not if she can spend time with her dad," Adrian said. "You do intend to spend time with her, don't you?"

"Of course, I do." He coughed. The question bothered him. However, she was right. He needed to take a more active role in his daughter's life. Providing a good home and sending her to the best schools was not enough.

"Okay. Leave everything to me. We'll take the company jet to Heathrow. I'll book a sleeper for the transatlantic. She'll arrive rested. Once I have the flight information, I'll contact our New York office and arrange for a driver to pick us up when we land."

"Don't forget to tell the airline she's allergic to peanuts." Gavin reminded her, even if the chance of getting something as basic as peanuts in a first-class seat was doubtful.

"How soon do you want us there?"

The edge of excitement in Adrian's voice told him she was about to run home and pack.

"Wait a couple of weeks. Accommodations are booked solid for the games." He needed time to learn something about Joan. "Don't pack much. Bring a few of Emily's favorite outfits and a warm jacket." Aside from a purse her mother sent from Paris, he had no idea what she liked. He left the shopping and dressing of an eight-year-old to Nannie and Adrian. "We'll buy what she needs when you get here."

"Should I rent a house?"

Initially, renting a place sounded like a good idea—then he had a better idea. He should be where things were happening. "There's a nice B and B on Oak Road. Check out the Thistle Inn and book two rooms— one for you and Emily and one for me. The place is owned and operated by Fiona Campbell."

"Oak Road sounds charming."

"The entire town is charming when the sun comes out." He glanced at the bright sky.

"Sounds like Scotland. We better pack mud boots."

"One more thing…" He had almost forgotten the most crucial detail. "Don't book the reservations in the company name. Use your credit card. I'll reimburse you."

"O…kay," Adrian said. "Consider it done."

Gavin understood she would never question his motives. "Thanks. I'll explain why when you get here."

"Tell me again, what part of New York are we talking about?" she asked.

"Highland Falls, it's a town upstate in the Adirondack Mountains." Distant music continued as the pipers marched off the field. Gavin spoke louder. "I'll text the details."

"I've never been so far north of Manhattan. Send me a picture." Adrian rang off.

Gavin made his way toward the competition field. He didn't mind spectators observing him while he practiced. The practice was more about having time to prepare for the competition than about rehearsing. He was as ready as ever to take on the challenge. He greeted athletes waiting for practice shots.

"You're next." Jack arrived and signed him in.

Gavin circled the spectators, searching for a certain redhead. Holding a shot again fired him up. The excitement of the event was contagious. Participating in the competition was more about a personal challenge than an attempt to beat his fellow competitors. However, his encounter with a sassy redhead innkeeper had him feeling excited again after a long time. She stirred emotions he no longer believed were possible. And now, the games sparked an interest, too. Coming to Highland Falls was a good decision.

"Looking for our fair, Fiona? She might be in one of those tents." Jack pointed toward the sidelines. "Last-minute registration for some events is still open." He nudged Gavin with an elbow. "She's more likely entertaining the twins at a swordplay booth or listening to the Scottish Fiddling Lassies."

"Those would be Emily's choices, if she were here." It's too late now to regret she wasn't coming to the games. When Emily arrives, she's his number one priority. He'd make up for the time.

"Clear the fields." Offside, a burly man shouted and pointed toward a table. "The head field judge will mark and weigh your shots before the competition."

Gavin joined the line by the scales. He was surprised to see Ian behind the table. He glanced at the title on his badge—*Head Field Judge*. "I figured you were more likely to be the competition than a judge."

"Not this year. My schedule is too busy to fit in any practice time." Ian marked the ball with a *V* and handed it back to Gavin.

"Shot put your sport?" Gavin glanced at the mark and placed the ball on a scale.

"No, the shot was my late brother's sport. I prefer throwing the hammer." Ian extended a hand. "Good luck."

Gavin shook his hand and joined the other competitors on the sideline. He listened to Ian explain event logistics. Nothing had changed since the last time he competed.

"Before your throw, each shot will be checked for the mark I placed on it. You will be allowed a five-minute warm-up outside the competition area between the three practice flights. Once the competition begins, no practices are allowed."

Gavin walked off the muddy field.

Last week's rain left the area in less-than-prime condition.

He grabbed a towel, swiped across the sole of his

shoe, and studied the other athletes. The flight of their shots would rest on calculated hand placement, body position, and release. They all were more than capable of making their longest shot.

With safety in mind, the officials did an excellent job of preparing the throwing circle. Dry towels were placed along the path leading up to the ring.

"Not bad, but the shot should have been closer to his palm," a man standing a few inches away commented on the first competitor.

"How's the hand today?" Gavin greeted Jason Parker, the local champ. What he didn't have in height, he made up with a build like a brick wall. Gavin watched him throw a practice shot with enough power to land in the next county.

Over a few whiskies at a local pub, Jason talked about a recent hand injury. He signed up to set a good example for his oldest son, a junior event competitor. "All athletes work through pain." He clenched and unclenched his right fist.

"Aye, we do." Gavin checked his wrist strap. He was no stranger to work or sports injuries. He understood what it took for Jason to decide to compete. "Good luck."

"You too, mate."

Everyone came with a personal story, but they were all equal on the competing field.

Not used to taking second place in business, Gavin came into the event knowing someone could best him. He had no sponsor or recent win under his belt. If he lost, only his ego would suffer. A loss would only dent his pride. He had no money, honor, or fame at stake. Determined to give it his best shot, he approached the judges to verify his mark.

****

Fiona stood offside with the mark checkers.

"Hey, lass. You a checker?" Gavin raised a brow and handed her the steel ball marked with a *V*.

A devastating smile made her stomach flutter as the stone slipped into her hand. "Yes, I am." She found his name on the list and added a check. "I get to be up close to all these handsome men in kilts." Fiona forced a laugh and flashed a smile no different than she gave the previous athletes. Gavin was by far the best-looking man at the event. She saw her share of men in kilts, but he stood out. He wore his red-and-black plaid better than most.

"Hey. No flirting with the judges." Jason elbowed Gavin in the ribs and handed Fiona his shot. "Nice looking lad, isn't he?" He winked. "Good thing this isn't a beauty contest. You ladies will have a difficult time remaining impartial." He winked at the other female judge—the postmaster, Mrs. Grant.

Heat rose on Fiona's cheeks. "It doesn't matter how good you look in a kilt." She reassured Jason and glanced at his knobby knees. "The judging and the rules of participation are concise. There's no room for favoritism. Under the watchful eye of a field judge, the measurement of each throw will be recorded and verified on each judge's sheet." She signed in the last contestant and joined Mrs. Grant in the judge's circle.

"Like you, I signed up to judge for a close-up view of the athletes." Mrs. Grant turned her attention to the next competitor.

Fiona followed her gaze.

Gavin stood in the circle, ready to throw. From his

foot position to his fingertips, everything was perfect. Despite the chilly weather, he had ripped the sleeves off of a dark-blue T-shirt. Muscles and tendons were still tight from earlier practice throws.

Growing up in Scotland, Fiona was no stranger to the games. She was the same age as the twins when her brother, Sam, taught her to hold a shot. *Sit it on the base of your fingers. Place three fingers behind the shot and your thumb and little finger to the side—like a scoop of ice cream in a cone. Don't let it touch your palm.* The memory was difficult to avoid today. She blinked away tears and focused on Gavin's throw.

"I can tell this one is a winner." Mrs. Grant poked Fiona's ribs.

Gavin was competing next. He chalked the ball and stepped toward the back of the throwing circle. His body flexed with whipcord muscles as he prepared for the release. His palm faced forward. His fingers lay under the shot and close to his neck. He kicked in the direction of his throw and spun counterclockwise two times. With the full force of his body, he pushed forward into the release.

For a brief moment, Fiona imagined what it would be like to have those strong arms wrapped around her. She held her breath as the twenty-pound shot took flight. The delivery was perfect. The release was high. Seeing the shot hit the ground, she released a slow, relaxed sigh. She forced her gaze away from Gavin and joined the judges on the field to measure the distance.

"I told you so." Mrs. Grant smiled. "Let's see how he does in the next two."

His second throw was equally as perfect. He was two for two. A short break and regrouping gave the twelve competitors a moment to assess their previous throws. On his third flight, Fiona was surprised to see Gavin drop his elbow before putting.

"That error will cost him." Mrs. Grant shook her head. "He'll lose points for distance with such an amateur throw."

"Going into the finals will leave him tied for first place with Jason." Fiona couldn't imagine him making such a mistake, especially after witnessing two perfect throws. Did he miss the throw intentionally?

The tallying was complete. Gavin lost first place by a quarter of an inch to their local champ, Jason Parker.

"Everyone loves a winner, even a good-looking, second-place winner." Mrs. Grant pointed to the women waiting to take a selfie with Gavin.

"Strong, sweaty men releasing pheromones are always an attraction for women on the make." Fiona forced a laugh.

The blonde snuggled close and whispered in Gavin's ear.

His raised brows suggested the young lady asked the never-ending inquiry—what's under your kilt? She met his gaze and tried not to laugh at the desperate plea on his face.

"I think he needs your help." Mrs. Grant glared at the selfie-blonde. "Better watch out for that one."

Too bad she couldn't help him. She needed to maintain her judge's decorum until the medals were handed out. She shook her head and mouthed—*You're on your own.*

"Sorry, ladies. I've got another appointment." Gavin rushed toward her. "Mind if I join you?" He glanced over his shoulder and placed his hand on her back.

The gentle pressure of his fingers sent a wave of heat along her spine.

"Good game, McIver," Jason shouted and waved.

"That's a tidy champion your town has in Jason Parker." Gavin removed his hand and waved back. "I don't think I've ever been beaten by so close a margin."

"You certainly put up a good fight and..." She glanced over her shoulder at the selfie-blonde. "I'm sure the ladies would agree you cut a dashing image in your kilt."

"The little lass wasn't so interested in my athletic ability as she was..." He took a swallow from his water bottle.

"You don't need to explain. I know what ladies are curious about." Fiona glanced at his Adam's apple as the water slid down his throat.

"Do you?" He smiled.

His smile teased her senses. "No worries. I already know the answer to her question." She winked. "I grew up with a house full of brothers more than willing to oblige the ladies with a visual."

"Good to know." He released a mock sigh and wiped his forehead. "One less thing I'll have to explain to you later."

"Really, what could you possibly have to tell me?" She smiled. She had many things she wanted to ask— what was under his kilt was not one of them.

"Hey, McIver, wait up." Jason crossed the field in their direction. "The guys and I are going to the pub. Why don't you and Fiona come along for a celebratory whisky?"

"Sorry, I've got a previous engagement." Fiona

declined.

"Don't let us keep you from your date." Jason winked.

"You have a date?" Gavin raised a brow.

"I'm afraid so. Sara and Simon are waiting at Sophia's booth." She nodded toward the food booths. "You're all welcome to join us."

"Cookies...I'll pass." Jason winced. "My thirst can only be quenched by a dram or two of good Scottish whisky." He placed an arm on Gavin's shoulder. "You coming, mate?"

"Another time." Gavin stepped close to Fiona.

She had to admit, she liked having him around. He was a pleasant diversion from her daily routine.

"You're getting the better end of the deal, mate." Jason winked at Fiona. "If I were in your shoes, I'd prefer this sweet lady to a bunch of sweaty Scots." He laughed and walked away.

"Sure, you don't want to join them?" Fiona gestured toward Jason and a group of men in kilts.

Gavin shook his head. "I don't need to be there. Let Jason share the victory with his friends. This could be his last competition. He suffered a metacarpal fracture after an event last month." Gavin raised an open palm and clenched his fingers. "Hand injuries are not very common in this sport. Sometimes, repetitive stress and force placed on the small bones can take their toll."

"Did you know our local champ is also part of our pipe band? He needs both hands to play a melody." Fiona sighed. "Enjoying more than one talent is a gift not everyone is fortunate to have. Unfortunately, for Jason, it's not a matter of combining both. It'll be difficult to choose one passion over another."

"Aye, lass. It is." Gavin shrugged. "Tell me, what's your passion?"

"My passion?" Was she ready to divulge her innermost desires to this stranger? Her passions were strong. She approached each with determination and a fieriness that burned deep. "If I tell you, will you share a secret, too?"

"Fair deal." He smiled.

His smile wasn't exactly convincing. *Damn. What's he hiding?* The suggestion to play this game was hers. She couldn't back out now. *Keep it simple.* "Work's my passion. I love owning my own business." They played this game before. She hardly learned anything about him. Maybe this time, she'd get some answers.

"Not exactly what I was expecting," he said.

"We didn't set any specific rules." She retorted. "Your turn."

"Did you love your previous job as much?" he answered with a question.

"We're always presented with opportunities to do things we enjoy. Like Jason, my choices were not easy." She liked her fast-paced job and salary that came along with being the Chief Financial Officer of a hedge fund—until she didn't. "I'm sure you have passions other than tossing the shot or looking for reclaimed wood."

"I do." He laughed. "I'm passionate about extraordinary, sassy redheads with insatiable curiosities."

"Is that all you got?" She scrunched her lips.

"It is for now." He winked.

The man was not only a skilled athlete. He was artfully elusive, as well.

At Sophia's cookie booth, the twins gave kilt-shaped shortbreads to visitors who produced free coupons.

"Doesn't Auntie Sophia smell like cookies?" Sara tugged on Gavin's kilt and pointed behind the counter.

Seeing the twins so comfortable around Gavin warmed her heart.

****

"Aye, she does." Gavin smiled at the little redhead. She reminded him of his daughter at that age. Most chatty little girls couldn't censor their words. "And so do you, lass."

"Gavin's right. You smell so delicious I could eat you." Fiona pinched Sara's cheeks.

"I won't taste as good as a shortbread cookie, Auntie Fi." Sara giggled and handed Fiona a cookie.

Fiona's endearing gesture and Sara's sweet laughter tore at Gavin's heart. Emily would like the twins.

"How about you and I get something to eat," Gavin suggested. "I spotted a food truck selling Scottish eggs and another selling caramel wafers and teacakes."

"Sure, why not? Sugar over-loads are what fairs like this are all about." Fiona bit into the cookie.

"We can start with dessert, if you'd like." He was surprised she agreed.

"Do you want a cookie, Mr. Gavin? What's your clan?" Sara tugged on his kilt again. "I don't see a cookie like your kilt." She squinted and searched trays with rows of kilts the size of Gavin's palm.

"How about this?" He pointed toward a blue-and-black plaid cookie like Fiona's.

"That's Clan Campbell's plaid. Are you a Campbell, too?" Simon glanced at him with wide-eyed excitement.

Gavin took a knee, bringing him to eye level with the boy. "No, but the McIver Clan plaid has a story related to Clan Campbell." He bit into a perfect shortbread cookie. The buttery sweetness reminded him of a holiday back home.

"Scots have a story for everything." Fiona sighed and placed a hand on her nephew's shoulder. "The story can wait. Sophia needs your help." She pointed to a group of pipers gathered around the table.

"I already know the story," Simon said. "Remember when Uncle Ian told us how the McIver clan joined our clan long ago."

"You want to be a historian like your uncle?" Gavin gave Simon's mop of red curls a toss.

"No. I'm going to play football in Scotland. I'm going to be goalie for the Celtics." Simon kicked a discarded cup over the table.

"Aye, lad. Football is a noble sport." Gavin extended his arm, caught the flying object with little effort, and tossed the cup into the trash.

"Nice catch." Simon clapped.

"I don't remember reading anything about football on your application." Fiona tossed her braid.

"Just a passion I didn't mention." Gavin stood. "The lad's information about our clans is *verra* interesting." He wiggled his brows. "Does that make us kissing cousins?"

The way he rolled his *r*'s was so sexy. "After so many generations, I doubt you have any Campbell blood." She cleared her throat. "My brother's a stickler for odd facts. Once he starts researching, he never knows where it will lead. The union of the clans was a fact he came across when he initiated a brief search for your aunt."

"I'll have to thank him for being so diligent." He bit down on a smile. "I'm afraid we McIvers never pay attention to any clan but our own."

"Do I detect a bit of nepotism?" She leaned against a table.

"We strive for preferential treatment." Gavin placed a hand on the table and closed the space between them. "My close-knit family always favors relatives. It's good for business."

****

His face was only inches away. Scattered streaks of gray mixed with the light ginger scruff on his face. If he kept the look, Fiona wouldn't mind.

Simon started a chant. "Kiss Auntie Fi. Kiss Auntie Fi."

"*Shh.*" Fiona glared at Sara and Simon. This morning, she worried the crowds might overwhelm them. Obviously, they were enjoying the event and her current situation.

Sara joined him.

A piper picked up the twin's chant. "Kiss Auntie Fi." He placed a hand on Gavin's shoulder. "C'mon, mate, show us how it's done."

"Let him kiss you, lady," a man in a MacDonald kilt shouted.

As a last resort, Fiona glanced over her shoulder toward her future sister-in-law.

Sophia tossed her hands in the air and laughed.

"You, too?" Fiona sighed.

"We have only one way out," Gavin whispered in Fiona's ear.

"We could run for the food trucks and get lost in the crowd." Her emotions whirled and skidded. She rested a hand on the table. The cookie trays jiggled.

The ruckus caught the attention of the rest of the pipe band. The leader orchestrated a tune, enhancing cheers from the gathering crowd.

The chants made her head spin. Or was it Gavin's closeness? Festivals were for fun and stepping out of the box. Nevertheless, today's fun was getting too personal. She slipped beneath his arm, seeking refuge behind the cookie table. That she wanted to be kissed was obvious.

Gavin followed.

A strong hand clasped her fingers and pulled her close. Suddenly, she was in Gavin's arms. Her breath caught in her chest. Gavin was right. What else could they do? She turned a heated cheek toward him. She wasn't quick enough. His lips feather-touched the corner of her mouth. The gentle touch teased her senses and sent a shiver of delight to her toes.

"Hey, mate. We all know your aim is better than that," a piper shouted.

"Aye, lass. You want them to take away my trophy." Gavin stepped back and touched his forehead to hers. "Let's do it right this time." With perfect precision, the back of his hand lightly traced a path along her cheek and down her neck.

"Yes…" she whispered. Her skin tingled under his fingers. She stood riveted to the spot and waited. This time, he hit the target with professional precision. His lips tasted sweet and buttery. The quick kiss left her wanting more.

He stepped back and ran a hand through his hair. "I've wanted to do that from the day I met you."

Cheers drowned the thudding of her heart.

"Hey, lad. Give us a chance." A burly hammer thrower stumbled close.

"Sorry, mate. This prize is mine." Gavin positioned himself between Fiona and the man. He reached for Fiona's hand. "Let's get out of here."

"Lead the way." She breathed a sigh of relief. The strong-straight fingers holding her hand would never miscalculate a throw. Why did Gavin work through the pressure of competition and let someone else win the prize? She touched her lips. She needed more than an egg and teacake to calm her swirling emotions. The frivolous kiss had melted her defenses.

Chapter 5

A week after the games ended, Fiona drove down Main Street, surprised at the difference a few days could make. The atmosphere in town was more relaxed. Yellow leaves clung to almost-bare branches. The influx of tourists and athletes dwindled to a few stragglers.

She last saw Gavin the day of the games. She assumed he was still here. Town gossip would be buzzing if he left without finding his aunt. She dismissed the thought and parked a few shops down from Sophia's bakery. In front of the bakery, she stopped to admire the window. She laughed at the whimsical pumpkins and spooky witches.

Inside, the only customers were the mayor's secretary, Judy, and Sheriff Maxwell, preoccupied with his morning paper.

"Good morning, Fiona." Judy clutched a neatly wrapped box of cookies as she walked toward the door.

"She's less chatty than usual." Fiona was glad to see Judy leave.

"Not much to gossip about since the games are over." Sophia shrugged.

"Where's my brother?" Fiona looked past the glass partition separating the café from the work area. "I was sure he'd be here."

"Ian's at the museum setting up for a class."

Sophia held a rag in each hand and wiped the counter in circular motions. "Are you in a hurry?"

"Not today. Only two couples are staying at the inn. It's a big difference from the week of the games when we had a full house." Fiona blew out a slow breath.

"I hear you. Today's quiet in here, too. I don't mind the break. I have time to play around with baking and wedding plans. I'm perfecting a green tea shortbread." Sophia pointed to a tray on the counter.

"I don't know how you keep reinventing your delicious cookies." Fiona reached for a perfectly formed leaf-shaped cookie. The top was covered in bright-green sugar. The underside was gray-green. "I love the leaf shape." She bit off a tooth-shaped petal. "Hmm…the subtle sweetness is the perfect complement to any tea. Can you send a dozen for Thursday tea?"

"Sure. Something special going on?" Sophia wiped a crumb from the counter. "I can decorate with sanding sugar in any color to fit the occasion. How about a bright-pink or a dazzling red cookie?"

"I was thinking more of a Scottish hillside. Could you decorate with gray and blue frosting and purple sprinkles?" Fiona glanced at the trays of cookies in the display case.

"Are the cookies for Sara and Simon? Do they miss home?" Sophia tossed the rags into a bucket.

"The cookies are for tea time." Fiona didn't like seeing Sophia sad. No doubt, the twins' story reminded Sophia of her tragic childhood. She, too, lost her parents when she was young. That's where the similarities ended. Sophia was forced to live with a less-than-kind stepmother. Moving to Highland Falls and meeting Ian gave Sophia a new outlook. Fiona sighed. "No worries. Soon enough, the entire Campbell family will be here for the wedding." She picked up another cookie. "Do you sprinkle sugar on top before or after the cookies are baked?"

"Before baking. The size of the crystal prevents them from melting in the heat." Sophia cleaned her hands. "Are you expecting guests from Scotland?" She glanced at Fiona and smiled. "Maybe the cookies are for Jack's friend who kissed you at the fair. What's his name?"

"You know his name is Gavin." Fiona walked behind the counter. "The kiss was nothing. He was indulging the twins. For all I know, he could have a wife in Scotland." She shoved her hands into her pockets. "Anyway, I haven't seen or heard from him since the games. Have *you* seen him?"

"The other day, he stopped in for coffee."

"Oh." Fiona shrugged, not wanting to sound too interested. Her heart drummed in her chest. "Did he say how his search for his aunt was going?"

"The shop was busy. I didn't have time to chat. Gavin bought the sheriff and Mrs. Grant coffee." Sophia pointed to the high-top table in the corner. "They chatted awhile, and he left. Later, Mrs. Grant mentioned he wasn't having much luck finding his great-aunt."

"Did he say anything else?"

"Nothing of importance. Why all the questions? Unless…he's coming for tea again." Sophia grabbed a clean rag, walked around to the front of the counter, and cleaned the display case glass.

"Gavin's not coming for tea anytime soon. I do

have guests from Scotland arriving next week." Fiona placed her arms on the clean glass and leaned forward. "A cookie reminiscent of home would be a nice welcoming touch."

"You don't usually get many foreign guests this time of year." Sophia raised a brow.

"Especially not from Scotland." Fiona thought the reservation odd. "They usually prefer warm and sunny destinations."

"I wonder why they chose to come here." Sophia shrugged. "Maybe they're Gavin's friends."

"Morning, Fiona." The sheriff tucked his paper under his arm, approached the counter, and emptied the last drop from his cup. "Best coffee in town."

"Morning." Was he listening to the conversation? Local law enforcement was not immune from gossiping. The last thing she wanted was to encourage idle gossip.

"Here's a cup to go?" Sophia filled a takeaway cup.

"Have a good day, ladies." The sheriff tipped his hat and reached for the cup.

"Finally, we have the shop to ourselves. I'm dying to hear how the wedding plans are coming along." Fiona plated a couple of sugar shortbreads.

"Is Earl Grey okay? I just brewed a fresh pot." Sophia placed two mugs on a tray.

"Perfect." A hot cup of tea and buttery cookies in a quiet setting were what Fiona needed. She carried the tray to a table.

Sophia followed with a bright-yellow teapot and filled the mugs.

"Hmm...this is good tea." Confident Cora had

everything under control at the B and B, Fiona leaned into the contour of the café chair and wrapped her hands around the warm mug. "Did you and Ian set a date?"

"If Ian can keep his promise not to teach summer session"—Sophia heaved a deep sigh.—"We're planning a summer wedding."

Sophia's wary smile was evidence of her uneasiness. "What's the problem?" Fiona reached across the table and gave her soon-to-be sister-in-law a reassuring squeeze.

"I hope we don't have to invite the entire town." Sophia glanced out the window. "I don't have any family to invite. A small, intimate event would be nice."

"You're going to have more relatives than you can count." Fiona sighed. "After the loss of my brother, my family is looking forward to celebrating a joyous event like a wedding."

"Sounds like a lot of guests." Sophia half smiled. "Will the barn be ready as a party venue?"

Fiona preferred talking about the upcoming wedding. *Who was she kidding?* She would have stood in the damp barn talking to the sexy Scot for hours if her schedule allowed. "I'm working on it. Gavin wrote a fair assessment of the wood needed to repair the walls. Nothing on the roof can be salvaged." She sighed. "He even offered some suggestions for the inside." She still had the simple drawing.

The bell over the door announced a customer.

"Don't leave. I'll be right back." Sophia excused herself.

Fiona observed the comings and goings of City

Hall from her window seat.

Thick, low clouds edged their way over the dome. The brick paths along the square were frosty from last night's rain and this morning's drop in temperature.

She glanced from the threatening sky to the activity in the courtyard.

The museum curator, Mr. Paisley, Ian, and Gavin stood outside City Hall. Ian never mentioned he was meeting Gavin. After a brief conversation, Ian and Mr. Paisley entered the museum.

Gavin didn't join them. Instead, he crossed the street toward the bakery.

Did he see her?

Don't be silly. Maybe he just wants a cup of coffee.

A moment later, the bell rang again.

"Hi. I was on my way to the pub for breakfast. I saw you sitting here all alone and suddenly had a taste for hot chocolate." He smiled.

"Have a seat." Fiona gestured toward the vacant chairs around the table.

He straddled the café chair directly across.

The back of the chair bumped the table, rattling her cup.

"Did Ian or Mr. Paisley have any news on your aunt?" She took a napkin from the dispenser and wiped a spill."

"Not yet." He rubbed his jaw. "I wonder if Granddad was mistaken about her last known residence."

Fiona nibbled on a cookie and licked the sugary crumbs off her lips.

"You missed one." He reached for a napkin and brushed a spec off her chin. "Can I get you another tea or hot chocolate?"

"I'm good." A spark passed between them. Static from the cold, she convinced herself.

"Be right back." He stood and walked toward the counter.

His long, easy stride covered the short distance in three steps. At the counter, two young girls drew him into a loud discussion over which cookies were best with a morning beverage. He pointed to a tray of cookies in the display case.

The girls giggled and smiled at Gavin.

Sophia placed cookies on a plate for Gavin and bagged a few for the girls.

"My treat, girls." At the register, Gavin signaled for the girls to put away their credit cards. He stopped at the condiment counter for a dash of cocoa powder and returned to the table with a steamy cup of hot chocolate and a plate of cookies.

"You made a good choice. Those cookies are a teatime favorite with my guests." Fiona pointed to the *W* iced on top of the cookies. "Paying for the girls' cookies was very kind."

"No big deal." He shrugged. "They're college students here for a class."

"Must be the hands-on class Ian teaches. He uses Scottish artifacts found at a local dig site. Mr. Paisley set up a classroom with a grant he received from the state university system."

"Ian mentioned the class. I'd like to sit in." He removed his jacket, sank into the seat next to her, and folded his arms on the table. "Would you go with me?"

Sleeves of a blue-gray shirt were cuffed around his forearms. The folds of the fabric fell naturally from the slope of his shoulders to his upper chest. Only a custom-made shirt would fit without a wrinkle.

Her pulse skipped a beat. She looked at his face. "No thanks. I've heard Ian speak about ancestry from *A* to *Z*."

Outside, the girls tapped the window and waved.

He gave them a thumbs-up and glanced at the sky. "Looks like snow, not rain."

"That's been the general consensus this morning." Weather, always a good subject for small talk, was a serious topic in Highland Falls. "October is too early for snow. But it would be a welcome change from all the rain."

"The weather's similar to Scotland." He rested an arm on the table. "Sunny one day and blustery the next."

She shifted in her seat and drew in a breath. Gavin's body heat and crisp outdoor scent invaded her space. "Could be why so many Scots settled here." Ignoring the squall roaring through her body, she wiped a drop of tea off the saucer. With a tilt of her head, she gestured at his arm. "You might consider layering a sweater tomorrow. The temperature is expected to drop overnight."

"If you agree to join me tomorrow, you can ensure I do." A smoldering smile tilted his lips.

"Join you...where?" Butterflies tingled in her stomach. Was he inviting her out?

The door opened. A cold breeze blew across the table.

Gavin gathered the napkins and secured them under his mug. "Mr. Paisley mentioned an antique shop in a barn down country. I could use a navigator. I have no idea which way's down country." He chuckled.

"The locals call anything south of their current location down country." Following directions in Manhattan was easy—numbered streets went east or west, and avenues went north and south. When she first moved here, she avoided asking for directions and relied on an app to get her where she needed to go. "You'll get used to it."

Gavin wrapped a hand around his mug. "Apparently, they're having an *Everything Goes Sale* this weekend. He suggested I take a look at the merchandise."

"My brother would agree it's a great place to search for historical facts." Did he expect her to drop everything and be his guide?

"Apparently, my search is the talk of the town." He rubbed a hand along his jaw. "Tim mentioned his grandmother is interested in meeting me."

Residents of Highland Falls, like most small towns, didn't take well to strangers. "Talking to Granny Ulster could be helpful. She knows everything that's happened here." She didn't want to discourage him. Granny would not take kindly if he avoided answering her questions.

"Aye, lass, one of those. My granny would call her a *clipmalabo.* She's a gossip."

"She's been called worse, but always with affection." Fiona laughed. "I should warn you, Granny doesn't like when strangers dig up the past. She'll want to know all about you and your family before offering any information." She gazed straight at him. "She'll expect an answer to every question. Are you up to it?" Granny Ulster had a sixth sense of people. She would instantly know he was hiding something.

"Yeah..." He rubbed his chin. "Maybe I should put Tim's granny on hold and start with the barn."

She caught his uncertainty. Anyway, the barn *was* a better place to look for clues. "Posters advertising the sale are hanging all over town." She pointed to a cluster of signs over the condiment counter wall. When he sprinkled powdered cocoa on his beverage, he must have missed the notice. "You'll find the structure interesting. The barn's built from stone and has a red tin roof." An unofficial date with Gavin would be a pleasant diversion from her usual schedule. He might open up and tell her more about his family's business. "What are you hoping to find?"

"I have no idea. Your brother thinks I might discover some hidden clues." He bit into a cookie and then sipped from the cup.

"If I were in your situation, I wouldn't ignore his suggestions. He's good at tracking down lost people." She glanced at his lips as they touched the rim of the cup.

"This chocolate is delicious." He wiped his upper lip.

"The blend is sold by a local chocolate company. You can buy it any place in town." She pointed behind him toward a display case full of canisters. "You know what they say about chocolate."

"Chocolate's healthy?" He glanced at the display and smiled.

"I've read it can cure everything from a bad day to romantic problems." She returned the smile.

"Since I walked in here, my day has improved by the minute." He gazed directly at her and chuckled. "No problem in the other department either."

Heat rose across her cheeks. "I'll have to ask Jack if you were the boy who flirted with all the girls in college." She set herself up for his suggestive glance.

"I was a little on the wild side." He winked. "Jack was no angel."

A playful glimmer in his eyes challenged her to continue. "And now?" He was better at this game. Flirting was never her sport.

"Are you asking if I'm involved with anyone?" He leveled his blue eyes.

He wasn't dishonest. He was better at avoiding answering her questions. "Exactly." Her heart took a perilous leap as she waited.

"No, no romantic interest at the moment. I'm divorced. I guess you could say I'm taking a little vacation." He folded his hands on the table and leaned forward. "What about you?"

Divorced was good. "I'm way too busy for romance." She tried to dismiss him with a wave. "Not that I've ruled it out. It's just that…" Oh my God, she was stammering like a fool.

"You didn't leave any broken hearts in Manhattan…or Scotland?" He leaned back.

"I was in, what I believed was, a serious relationship when I lived downstate." She avoided his probing gaze and dusted a crumb into her palm.

"What happened?" he asked.

"We had different visions for the future." She'd ended the relationship the day Pete told her he didn't plan on having kids after they married. She could only imagine how he would have reacted to the twins showing up.

"I'm glad you made the move. If you hadn't…I wouldn't be sitting here enjoying your company." He ran a hand through his hair. "Are you in for a road trip?"

"You don't seem keen on looking through dusty old merchandise." She cleared her throat. "Anyway, I promised to spend the weekend doing something fun with the twins."

"Bring them along," he said without hesitation.

"Are you sure you wouldn't mind? They get bored easily on long car rides." When they first arrived, they needed to be constantly entertained. She drove all over the tri-county area, looking for fun events. Frequent stops for snacks and a bathroom took getting used to.

"Don't worry. I know a thing or two about driving with kids." He winked.

"Well…if you're up to it, this little trip might be the adventure we need. The games have kept me busy and less attentive." She studied his face. He wasn't the least bit bothered by the twins coming along. She placed the cup on the table. "You must have lots of spunky nieces and nephews in your nepotistic family?" Fiona expected he would find her comment amusing.

He wasn't laughing.

Maybe she overstepped her bounds, insulting people she had never met. She took another sip.

"My experience with children isn't limited to nieces and nephews." He cleared his throat. "When my eight-year-old daughter was the twins' age, she couldn't sit still or stop chatting. You'd be surprised how quickly they mature."

"You're a dad?" Fiona sputtered into her cup and placed it on the saucer.

"Is it that surprising?" Gavin cocked his head to the side.

Divorced men have children. "I mean...no." She had so many questions she couldn't find the right words for. She sucked in a breath and took a moment to digest the information. "So you have an eight-year-old daughter? Is she in Scotland with your ex?"

"Emily's in Scotland, but she's not with her mother." He shifted in his seat.

Talking about an ex-whatever was never easy. No one was immune from failed relationships. She never judged people by their past mistakes and was momentarily at a loss for what to say next. "And...your ex...where is she?" An ex-wife differed from a current wife. However, she could still be an issue.

"Emily's mother goes wherever her latest boyfriend takes her." He shrugged. "We've been divorced since Emily was four. I have full custody of Emily and employ a full-time nanny. In the last four years, my daughter's only spent a few days a year with her mother."

His tone was even and calm. He showed no sign of disdain for his ex. *Forget the ex-wife.* "Do you have a picture...of Emily?"

"My work often keeps me away. I'm not immersed in Emily's day-to-day activities, but I know every move she makes." He removed his phone from his jacket pocket and opened a photo app. "I received a video this morning. Yesterday, friends invited her to an after-school tea party."

"What a lovely setting." Fiona glanced at a video of three little girls in school uniforms seated around a table. The name of an elite private school was embroidered over the pocket of each jacket. Custom-made shirts, an expensive private school, and a full-time nanny—who are you, Gavin McIver? What she knew about him she liked, but what she didn't know could be a problem.

"Emily's the one with curly red hair." Gavin paused the video.

Under the mop of curls, deep-blue eyes admired the desserts on the tall cake plate. "She's beautiful." Fiona glanced from the phone to Gavin. "She has your eyes. How can you stand being separated?"

"I'll see her soon." He cleared the photo.

"Are you leaving?" She placed a thumb and forefinger on the spoon and stirred what was left of her tea. The spoon dragged tea leaves along the bottom. A diviner she hired to entertain afternoon tea guests told her leaves along the bottom were a sign for the future. Good or bad was determined by other factors. She wouldn't object to Gavin being in her future.

"Hey. If you keep stirring, you'll wear a hole in the cup." He tapped her chin with a knuckle. "No. She'll be here next Thursday." He leaned back and smiled.

Fiona placed the spoon on the saucer. *Clink.* "Are you *all* staying at the Drummonds?" She wanted to tell him a little girl needed more than three dads. Again, she kept her opinion to herself. Anyway, she had a better idea. "I could check my bookings when I got back to the inn. If something's available, I'll give you a nice discount on a family suite."

"We have reservations at the best B and B in town." He laughed.

"You're the reservation from Scotland?" Her tentative smile broadened. What would it be like to see

Gavin every morning? "But the name on the reservation…it's not McIver."

"My cousin, Adrian Bennett, is a McIver on her mother's side. She made the reservation. I'm counting on Adrian's help in the search for Joan." He shook his head and rubbed his temple. "Searching for someone I know so little about is more difficult than anticipated."

"Does your cousin have an interest in genealogy?" Family loyalty was an admirable quality. Fiona added the trait to his list of qualities—kindness, generosity, and endurance. Even a well-guarded family secret was decent…to a point.

"Adrian's interests are more about what's happening now." He shrugged. "Except for our cousin, the archeologist, no one in the family is interested in genealogy. We know all we need to about the McIver clan."

"Our families sound very much alike. Except for a few secrets the *auld* ones keep, I know all the family stories." She understood his sentiment. "Did your granddad bring up Highland Falls when discussing his estranged sister?"

"Not exactly." Gavin rubbed his chin. "I mentioned a magazine article I read about this town. Granddad reacted when he heard Highland Falls."

"My B and B was recently highlighted in a high-end travel magazine article. Sophia's shop appeared in a cooking magazine." She doubted Gavin was referring to similar periodicals. "What kind of magazine mentioned Highland Falls?"

"A trade magazine that comes to my office."

"A construction magazine?" She didn't doubt such reading material existed. "I saw you come out of City

Hall. Were you searching the archives for anything in particular—property deeds or leases? Do you think Joan owned property nearby?"

"I can't rule out anything. I followed Mr. Paisley's suggestions and searched records south of here. I didn't find anything listed under the name Joan McIver." He sighed and lifted his palms.

A tired sadness passed over his features. Was he sorry he agreed to search for his estranged aunt? "I've assisted Ian with similar searches. Sometimes, clues fit together like a simple puzzle. Other times, leads are frustrating and hard to follow. When Ian was searching the history of the MacLennan clan, the course was bumpy, but the result was good, and he met Sophia."

"I'm not sure I see a connection." He leaned back and folded his hands behind his head.

"You're right. Every search is different, but the formula is the same." She sounded like her brother. "A search needs a starting point—like the article about Highland Falls." She wasn't sharing any personal secrets. Everyone in town knew how Ian and Sophia met. "The Scottish plaid and coat of arms on the wall were the starting point of Ian's research into Sophia's ancestry." She pointed over his head.

"Is the tartan authentic?" He turned toward the wall.

"Ian verified the date of origin to the 1700s. The bakery was founded by Sophia's two-times great-grandmother in 1848." She gestured toward the pink-and-white delivery truck parked at the curb. The details were reprinted on the side.

"Did Sophia grow up here?"

"She was living in Brooklyn when she inherited the

shop. Hard work, skill, and perseverance made her a prominent citizen in Highland Falls." The rest of Sophia's story wasn't Fiona's to tell. Would whatever Gavin was hiding be as readily accepted?

"You're right. It's like putting together a puzzle piece by piece." Gavin glanced around the shop. "Sophia's story has a fairy tale ending. Granddad doesn't care about a happy ending. He gets things done by stirring the pot. Aunt Joan's story might not end as well."

"*Pffft*. Fairy tales." Fiona blew out a breath. "Maybe your granddad is right."

"You don't believe anymore, do you?" He raised a brow. "A good Scottish girl like you."

"Your search is proof. In the real world, things didn't happen with the wave of a wand." She shook her head. "I took you for a more realistic man. Hard work, prudence, and perseverance make someone successful, not unicorns and fairies."

"What would Scotland be without its mystical tales?" His brows slowly came together. "It's not exclusive to kilts and bagpipes."

"There's nothing wrong with kilts and bagpipes." She pictured Gavin in a kilt and smiled.

Outside, a fire truck with red blaring lights sped down Main Street.

She followed the lights until she couldn't see them. Soon enough, everyone in town would know where the ambulance stopped. She turned back toward Gavin. "Did you say something?"

"You must have had a favorite tale when you were young—what was it?" He crossed his arms over his chest.

"The unicorn." She hid a smile and gazed out the window again. What he revealed this morning was far more interesting than confessing her favorite Scottish tale. Time would tell what the arrival of his daughter and cousin would bring.

"The unicorn? I expected you'd be more of a Nessie fan." He laughed.

"Nessie's okay, but I always liked a unicorn story. A strong, wild, and untamed creature appeals to me." She glanced at his reflection in the window. A smile curled his lips. "You know the legend of the unicorn, don't you?"

"The one I remember is about a Scottish king. His masculinity and power enabled him to tame even a wild unicorn." He leaned forward and lowered his voice. "If you have the power, taming such a colorful creature wouldn't be difficult."

Loch-colored eyes held her captive. Sitting across from Gavin and listening to his soft, suggestive whisper spun her senses. Her heart beat fast, and her breath stuck in her throat. She fiddled with the cup handle and pushed against the back of her chair.

The door flew open. Two silver-haired ladies entered and paused at Fiona's table.

"Good morning, Fiona." The shorter lady glanced from Fiona to Gavin and then her watch. "Or should I say good afternoon?"

"Did you see the fire engine racing toward the edge of town?" the other woman asked.

Fiona half smiled and waited for the sisters to answer their own questions.

"The foolish old man who owns the bait shop was cooking his catch behind his store. Who knows what the fool used to start the fire? He burned the fish to a crisp." She pointed out the window. "Surprised you can't see the smoke down this end."

"Good to hear no one was hurt." Fiona glanced at Gavin. He was having a hard time containing a laugh. This little incident saved *them* from being today's gossip headline.

The sisters nodded and joined the line at the counter.

"The lunch crowd's starting early. Sophia's a bit swamped." Fiona rolled back her chair and stood.

"So, are we on for tomorrow?" Gavin picked up the dirty cups and carried them to the counter.

"What time should we be ready?" Fiona slipped behind the counter.

He tossed a dirty napkin into the trash and placed the cups on a tray above the trashcan. "Is eight too early?" Over his shoulder, he glanced toward Fiona.

She couldn't decipher the emotion behind his tilted smile. "Sounds perfect." She met his gaze and soaked in her fill. If she denied the fact she was looking forward to spending the day with him, she'd be lying.

Chapter 6

Gavin drove a new four-wheel drive vehicle to the inn the following day. The heated leather seats earned a thumbs-up on a chilly morning like today. The new SUV was a necessity. He couldn't depend on the Drummonds to supply him with a vehicle once Emily arrived. He turned off the road onto the Thistle Inn driveway. Gravel crunched under the tires.

Fiona and the twins stood on the driveway, waving hands covered in bright-colored mittens.

He left the engine running and stepped out of the vehicle. The twins wore puffy jackets and silly hats with animal ears. Would Emily fit into the scene?

"Good morning." Fiona walked toward Gavin. She glanced at his head and open jacket. "Do you have a hat? The weather lady predicted snow later in the afternoon."

"Inside the car." Despite the morning chill, he couldn't deny the warmth of her smile. Auburn waves escaped the confines of a wool cap and framed her face. Any second thoughts about this road trip vanished. "What's all this?" He reached for a brown paper bag.

"I suspected you wouldn't have time for breakfast. I hope you like cherry scones and green tea." She placed two takeaway cups into the cup holder.

"I like fresh-baked anything." He took a bag of scones from her hand. A spark shot through the wool when his gloved fingers touched her mitten.

"Static electricity." She smiled and shrugged but didn't pull away.

"Yeah, that's all it was." He had a different opinion of what caused the spark. "Let's get on the road." He helped Fiona belt the twins in the back and climbed into the driver's seat.

"Nice rental." Fiona adjusted her seatbelt. "Hmm. It smells like a new car. Must have gone from the showroom to the rental lot."

"It's not a rental." He rubbed a hand over the leather dashboard. "I bought it a couple of days ago. I preferred a black vehicle. White was all they had on the lot. I've infringed on the Drummond's generosity long enough."

"A high-end vehicle like this seems like a big expense for a short time." Her hand caressed the back of his seat. "Is this real leather?"

"The dealer didn't have many choices. I took what was available." Gavin liked driving around in the luxury he could afford. What he didn't like was deceiving Fiona. In due time, he'd explain everything. He had no choice but to play it close to the vest until he found his aunt and the property *Granaidh* was hoping for. Once he found Joan, the family business would be an open book. If Joan still owned the abandoned property, convincing her to join the family and convert the land into a rustic resort could be difficult.

If the plan went according to *Granaidh* expectations, finding his estranged sister would be a win for the family. The old man usually got what he wanted. This plan, however, had two potential pitfalls. Aunt Joan might not want anything to do with her brother. The other downside, Fiona, was Gavin's concern. She was an intelligent businesswoman and would see a resort as competition. He shook his head. This was not the time to think about what might happen.

"You should eat now. The drive's at least an hour." Fiona pointed toward the brown paper bag on his lap.

"Good idea." He opened the bag. The buttery scent of the freshly baked scones permeated the air. "A bit of clotted cream would be nice." He took a bite.

"I can run in and get some." She put a hand on the door handle.

"I was only kidding." He reached out to stop her but stopped short of touching her shoulder. Instead, he adjusted the rearview mirror.

In the back seat, the twins were busy eating their breakfast.

"No scones for them?" He crinkled the top of the bag and placed it in between the seats.

"They prefer peanut butter and jelly sandwiches. Known here as PB and J." Her brow wrinkled. "Is it okay if they eat in your new car?"

"No worries. I can always have it cleaned." The question caught him off guard. He wasn't used to chauffeuring kids around. If Emily needed a ride, he called for a company car.

"Be careful with the jelly, and keep your hands clean." Fiona undid her seatbelt, reached back, and placed a napkin on each child's lap. "Use your napkin. We don't want to get Gavin's new car sticky."

Gavin glanced at the rearview mirror.

Fiona reached back and wiped a renegade blob of jelly off the corner of Simon's sandwich in a sensuous swirl. She licked the jelly off her fingertip.

"How's it taste?" He swallowed and imagined the sticky sweetness sliding down his throat.

"Too sweet, but the combination is a big favorite with American kids. I prefer my toast slathered with a good Scottish jam." She turned toward the front and reached for her tea.

"Sounds like you're not a fan." He laughed.

"It's an acquired taste." She smiled. "What about you? Do you like peanut butter?"

"Not the kind they sell in the States with sugar and oil." He shook his head. "Back home, peanut butter has one ingredient—peanuts. How exactly do you make one of those PB and J things?" He encouraged her to continue. This kind of knowledge might come in handy when his daughter arrived.

"Anyone can do it." She lowered her voice. "You toast two slices of bread, preferably the fluffy white kind."

"Don't worry. The secret is safe with me." He played along. The air became warm inside the car. He cracked the window. Listening to her explain something as simple as a sandwich shouldn't have this kind of effect on him, but it did.

"The next step's easy. You open the jar and spread a thick layer of peanut butter on one slice and an equally thick smear of jelly on the other." She clapped her hands. "And voilà, there you have it. That's how easy it is to make a PB and J sandwich."

Her energetic demonstration was captivating but had too many steps. "Sounds like a lot of work for a simple sandwich." He rubbed a palm along his chin. "I make a pretty good piece of toast."

"Toast is a start." Fiona blew out a long, slow breath. "Do you know the secret to serving toast to a young child?" She teased him with a wink.

"There's another step?" He never gave much thought to Emily's eating habits. Nanny took care of meals and other activities. Everything would change when she arrived.

"Are you listening?" She raised her brows.

He nodded.

"The last step is simple but important," Fiona whispered. "You must cut off the crust."

"I don't think Emily's a PJ and J kind of kid." The sugary smell of grape jelly lingered on Fiona's breath. What he wouldn't give for a quick taste. How did he get from a simple recipe to a complicated blend of emotions? He forced a smile, started the engine, and backed out of the driveway.

"You'll find out soon enough." Fiona tilted her head to the side. "You booked rooms for a week? What do you plan to do after your stay here?"

"Let's see how today goes." As much as the idea appealed to him, he couldn't stay with Fiona forever.

"How do you like living here so far?" She adjusted her seatbelt.

"The town's *bonnie*." Behind him, the twins giggled. "When Emily arrives, it will be even better." He missed the silly sound. "How about you? Do you miss city life?"

"The transition from Manhattan to country life had its challenges." She sighed. "I worked hard setting up the inn. Then, one day, I felt like I always lived here."

On the road, Fiona amused him with dozens of anecdotes about her adjustment to country life—and living with two active five-year-olds. Time flew. The unknown of single parenthood was a situation he shared. However, they couldn't be more opposite regarding how they measured success and dove into challenges. Her tenacity, balanced by patience, helped build a successful small business.

Gavin didn't waste time with half-pint projects. He wasn't interested in small-scale deals. Blockbusters excited him. He glanced in her direction.

Her head rested against the back of the seat. Her eyes were closed, and her breathing slow and rhythmic.

Had she always been so laid back, or did life here adjust her outlook? He admired her simple PB and J approach to situations. The amount of time he spent without results searching for Aunt Joan was killing him. He wanted everything done yesterday. Putting aside his secret, he had more than expected in common with Fiona. Once everything was revealed, would a Scottish heritage and single parenthood be enough to bind them?

****

Two peanut butter and jelly sandwiches later, they arrived at the destination. The stone barn was exactly what Fiona remembered from her last visit. The tin roof was freshly painted fire engine red. A lopsided sign over the door read *Red Roof Antiques*.

Inside, she gave each twin a basket, five dollars, and free range while she followed Gavin around the musty old barn. Boxes and crates of stuff that once meant something to someone waited to find a new home. A table crowded with old tea sets and vintage linens caught her attention. She passed a beautiful thistle tea service and didn't give it a second look. Next to her, Gavin picked up an odd object. She had no idea what it was.

"I don't see how anything here will be helpful." He examined the thingamajig and returned it to the exact spot.

"Look what I found." Sara ran toward them with a basket filled with odd knickknacks.

"You've found some wonderful treasures." Fiona pointed to an eraser, a three-legged Dalmatian figurine, and a miniature cup missing a handle. "Why don't you and Simon look for picture books?"

"You make parenting look easy." Gavin ran a hand through his hair. "I'm afraid my parenting skills still aren't fine-tuned. I know it's wrong, but I overcompensate for the time I spend away from Emily."

"The whole thing is pretty much a learn-as-I-go situation." She followed him to a wobbly table. Box-after-box was filled with long-playing record albums. The legs of the old table struggled to support the weight. She searched the boxes and struggled with the musty smell of old cardboard. An old record album with a picture of a woman caught her attention. From the roll-and-go pin curls to the red-orange lipstick, everything about the woman on the cover screamed the 1950s. The background colors and artist's name were faded, but the smoky blue of the woman's eyes was crisp and clear. Was she a singer, a musician, or a cover model? "Did you see this cover?" She removed the album from the box.

The table shimmied.

Gavin steadied the table and stared at the image. "This is remarkable. She's almost the spitting image of Granddad when he was younger." He swiped a layer of

Zelda Benjamin

dust off the worn cardboard with the palm of his free hand. Dust particles dispersed into a fine cloud and disappeared into the air.

Achoo. From the moment, she walked into the old barn, she had the urge to sneeze. "Do you think she's your aunt?"

"Could be." He offered a clean white linen handkerchief. "The strong genetic connection between her and Granddad is unmistakable."

She glanced at the neatly pressed and folded hankie. The finely woven material was overkill for a dusty barn. "I've got this." She removed a tissue from her backpack.

"Find something you like?" An older man in worn overalls approached. He glanced over his wire-rimmed specs at the album in Gavin's hand. "You a fan of violin music?"

"I am." Gavin nodded. His gaze remained on the woman's face.

"You let me know if you want to buy the record album. I'll give you a good deal. When you get to the register, ask for Walter."

Gavin nodded and put the album to the side. He carried the box to a steadier table and flipped through the remaining stack.

Walter turned his attention to Fiona. "You've got a familiar look about you. Were you here before?"

"It's been years." When she accessorized the B and B, she visited similar antique stores.

"I know what it is." Walter's hazy eyes lit up. "You're related to the professor from the university— the one who does all the ancestor stuff."

"Sounds like my brother Ian." This wasn't the first

time someone asked her if she was related to the genealogy guy. McIvers weren't the only ones with strong genetic traits.

"Yes, yes, that's it, Ian Campbell." The man smiled. "He's a regular here. He always finds some odd object to buy. A few months ago, he was here with the shortbread lady from Highland Falls. They bought an old clock with cookies where the numbers should be."

"Do you remember all your customers?" Fiona glanced at the album cover.

"Most of them. However, I can't remember what I had for breakfast this morning." He laughed. "My family decided to sell the property." He opened his palms. "Take what you want. I've got to empty the place." He gestured over his shoulder in Simon and Sara's direction. "Tell the young ones to fill their baskets to the top. I'll charge five dollars a basketful."

Fiona placed a comforting hand on Walter's arm. "Some of these albums must be worth that alone, if not more." She pointed to another stack with vintage crooner songs from the 1940s and 1950s.

The pile teetered close to the edge of the old table.

"Do you know the lady on the album cover my friend found?" She pointed in Gavin's direction.

"Your *friend*? Sure had me fooled, lass." Walter ran a hand through his hair. "Those two redheaded kids are the perfect blend of you and your...*hem"*—he cleared his throat.—*"Friend*. He won't be for long. I see the way he watches you."

Heat rushed to her cheeks. Back in Scotland, lots of people had red hair. No one assumed all redheads were closely related. Would Gavin's redheaded daughter blend in? The idea was silly. She flushed it away.

Luckily, Gavin was too preoccupied searching through the albums to hear the old man's chatter.

"What can you tell us about the lady on the album cover?" She stepped beside Gavin.

"She was a local. She and her husband lived down the road a bit." Walter rubbed an open hand along his chin.

Down the road could mean miles in any direction. She needed a more direct answer.

"By any chance, was the lady's name Joan?" Gavin reached for the album.

"Joan, yes, Joan was her name." Walter rubbed the back of his neck. "I can't remember her surname for the life of me."

"McIver, maybe," Fiona suggested.

"No, no. I'd remember the name. My late wife's cousin married a McIver. You from Scotland?" Walter raised a brow.

"Edinburgh. I came for the games," Gavin said.

"I can tell by your accent. My wife's family was from Glenurquhart. Ever been there?" Walter had a far-off look in his eyes.

"I'm afraid not." Gavin shook his head.

"No worries." Walter shrugged and laughed. "I often can't recall names of my immediate family." He took the album from Gavin and stared at Joan's picture. "But my memory is good with *auld* facts. I remember she and her husband were popular musicians. The interesting thing was their different music styles. The wife was classically trained. The husband claimed he was self-taught. His music had an interesting background and was popular with audiences."

"She was married?" Gavin glanced sideways at

Fiona.

An expression of uncertain expectation highlighted his features. "If she used a married name, that would explain why no one remembered her when you asked about Joan McIver."

"It'll come to me. It usually does." Still stuck on the last question, Walter concentrated on the faded album cover.

"Take your time." Fiona placed a reassuring hand on Walter's thin arm. What fell short in his ability to remember names and exact dates he made up with essential details of Joan's life. Could Gavin piece them together?

"I remember now." Walter turned away from the table. "They had a conservatory in the 1960s. In the summer, they held concerts. The shows were popular with people from the city. You passed the place on your way here."

"We did? I've driven the road hundreds of times and don't remember passing anything like you're describing." Fiona shook her head. "Can you give us any landmarks?" Afraid of overloading Walter's recollections, she refrained from asking too many questions.

"The building is set back off the road. Come with me. I'll show you a map." Walter led them toward the counter. "If you weren't looking for it, you wouldn't notice it."

At the counter, Walter unfolded an old map.

"Do you remember a street name or a mile maker number?" Gavin removed a cell phone from his pocket.

"I don't think you'll find anything abandoned long ago on a traffic app." Fiona stepped behind the counter next to Walter. "Show me on the map where you think the school was built."

"It's hard to say." Walter ran a finger along the old map. "Like I said, it was down the road a bit. Years ago, a crossroad was no more than a quarter mile away. I think the road washed out in a storm."

"That's the direction we came from." She squeezed Walter's hand. "We'll drive slowly on the way back." She glanced at Gavin. "I have some idea of the area he's talking about."

"Is the school visible from the road?" Gavin glanced at the map.

"I doubt it. The property was abandoned many years ago. A fire burned down the bandstand over a decade ago. The area around the school is overgrown from years of neglect." Walter waved a hand in the air. "Just like this old barn—things were built to last back then. Sometimes Mother Nature has other plans."

Fiona experienced firsthand how the elements took their toll on old structures. "What happened to the people?"

"One day, it was like *Trows* came and took them away." Walter smiled. "Do you know what a *Trow* is, lass?"

As a child, *Trow* tales scared Fiona. For weeks, she checked under her bed every night. "They're short, ugly creatures who sneak into houses at night to keep warm. My granny was an endless source of Scottish folklore." How was Joan's story related to such evil creatures? She suddenly doubted whether any of poor Walter's stories were true.

"*Trows* want more than to keep warm." Walter placed his hands on the counter and leaned forward.

"Do you know what they did?"

"I vaguely remember the legend." She shook her head and glanced at Gavin. Did he know the tale?

"I don't remember that one." He shrugged and waited.

"In a way, the creatures were music aficionados. They took musical people back to their caves to hear them play."

Sara and Simon placed baskets on the counter and listened to Walter.

"Forever?" Sara asked with wide-eyed innocence. "Is that what happened to the lady?" She pointed toward the record album. "Can we go to the house and look for her? Maybe she's hiding from the monsters."

"How can you deny a request like that?" Fiona glanced at Gavin's frown. Why wasn't he as excited as she was about exploring the deserted property?

"If the building's been abandoned for so long, the remaining structure could be dangerous." Gavin glanced at the album cover.

"We won't go in, especially if it's unsafe." Fiona noticed a slight tilt of his head. Was he considering a change of mind? "The conservatory is only a PB and J sandwich away."

"Yes, please, let's go find *Trows*." Sara tugged on the corner of his jacket.

"Okay, why not?" He removed a wallet from his jacket pocket. The back of his hand brushed Fiona's thigh.

Every sensor in her body urged her closer. Common sense dictated otherwise.

"How long ago was the house abandoned?" Gavin asked.

"It was decades ago." The right question fueled Walter's memory. He put the twins' assorted trinkets in separate paper bags and handed Gavin the album. "That'll be fifteen dollars."

"Keep the change." Gavin tossed a twenty on the counter.

Fiona intended to pay for the twins' odd items. Excited by Walter's sudden burst of memory, she didn't object. "Do you remember how many decades ago?"

"The lady and her husband moved away after detectives from Scotland came looking for her." He shook his head.

"Detectives?" She glanced at Gavin. He didn't seem at all surprised by the turn of events.

"If my great-grandfather believed she dishonored the family, he would send an army." Gavin nodded.

"Sensibilities were different back then. Still, he sounds like a harsh man." Fiona gave him a sideways glance. Her family encouraged her to pursue her education in the states. What dishonor could such a sweet-looking lady from the fifties bring her family? She turned her attention to Simon tugging on her jacket.

"I'm hungry." He squirmed.

"Let's see what's left in your goodie bag." She ushered the twins out the door. Walter had supplied more clues than she ever expected. And Gavin offered an unexpected insight to his family. She pulled her cap over her ears and led the twins to the car.

Outside, the wind picked up. The air was cold and moist. Snow was on the way.

Gavin turned his collar up against the wind. At the car, he stopped and glanced at Walter. "What do you remember about the husband?" He opened the boot of the car and carefully placed the album inside.

"The husband...?" Walter grinned. "Oh, yes, the husband...Paul. He was a good sort. What he did back home meant nothing to people here."

"Did he do something Joan's family didn't like?" Fiona heard tales about criminals and less-than-reputable people who came to the US and started over.

"He didn't do anything, lass. It's what he was—a tinker, a Scottish Traveler." Walter shook his head. "You call them gypsies."

"If Joan was happy and married to a good man, why would she alienate herself from your family?" She glanced at Gavin for clarification.

"I've told you my family is complicated." He shook his head and climbed into the vehicle.

Gavin's response confused her. She anticipated seeing him happy when he discovered his aunt resided in Highland Falls. She never thought he was the type affected by social class. After all, he was a manual laborer.

Chapter 7

Overwhelmed by an overload of information, Gavin stepped on the brake and hit the Start button. Against his better judgment, they were off to find the conservatory. He tightened his hand around the gear stick but didn't shift into gear. The mysterious disappearance of Joan finally made perfect sense. He chuckled. She ran away with a man belonging to a group of nomads. Thanks to Walter's recollections. Joan was now a flesh-and-blood image from the album cover—a woman who lived and loved. He noticed Fiona staring and turned away.

"What's bothering you?" She placed a hand over his.

"I'm processing everything the old man said." The muscles in his hand relaxed.

"I wouldn't take everything to heart." She glanced out the window toward the barn. "You have no concrete proof this Joan is your aunt. All we have is a story from a man with a failing memory." She tilted a brow. "Unless *you* believe the lady with the pin curls could be your long-lost relative?"

"It's an overwhelming lead. If you knew my family, everything Walter said would make sense. There's no question the lady on the album cover resembles Granddad." He shifted into Drive and pulled out onto the main road.

"Tell me about them—your family."

"The family has a long, complicated history and stringent rules." He regretted misleading Fiona from the beginning. Suddenly, *he* looked at his life choices from a different perspective. He committed his life to the success of the family business at the cost of true happiness—even going as far as agreeing to an incompatible marriage. What if the family's wrong about what's important? "When Joan fell in love with someone unsuitable, she broke the rules." Gavin couldn't believe he actually acknowledged his family was snobs. Aunt Joan's decision was not about money or business ties. She followed her heart—not the rules.

"Maybe they started as friends and never expected to fall in love. A forbidden love would be a nice romantic twist." Fiona faked a swoon. "How sad it must be choosing between family and the man you love?" She sighed. "Admit it, you find this intriguing." She nudged him with her shoulder.

"I find the recent development interesting." The corner of his lip twitched. He wasn't a hopeless romantic. After kissing Fiona at the fair, he wanted more than friendship. "You've got the ancestry bug in your genes—where do *you* suggest we go from here, professor?"

"If you suspect Joan is the lady on the album and want to follow the lead, then I suggest you ask Ian to verify the information. He'll guide you if he finds proof." She removed a phone from her pocket. "I'll text him what we know and where we're heading."

"That's a solid suggestion." Overwhelmed by the unexpected information, he ignored the basics. "Can Ian do a search without a last name?"

"You'd be surprised what he can find. He has endless resources at the university." Fiona answered quickly. "Do you have any idea how old Joan would be now?"

"Granddad opened up a bit and revealed he and Joan are twins. He celebrated his eighty-second birthday last May." Gavin glanced in the rearview mirror.

Sara and Simon whispered back and forth.

Their bond was strong. What broke such a bond between *Granaidh* and *his* sister?

"Twins?" Fiona glanced back at Simon and Sara, too. "He never searched for Joan on his own?"

"Granddad accepted his father's decision to alienate her from the family." Gavin shook his head. "In those days, elders were never questioned."

"If the album dates from the late 1950s, your aunt was barely twenty when she left Scotland." She exhaled. "I hope for your grandfather's sake she's still alive."

"So do I," he whispered. The idea was daunting and never occurred to him. *Of course, it was possible.* Years passed without a word. *Granaidh* assumed his sister died. A ghostly chill sent a shiver down his back.

****

"The house should be on the west side of the road as you head north—about halfway back to Highland Falls." Fiona watched for any sign of a hidden driveway or landmark suggesting a turnoff. Weather, population growth, and the natural rhythm of nature all factored into changing the area's topography. "We'll have to find the haystack to locate the needle." Walter's memory only supplied them with minimal directions. If he was correct, it could be nearly fifty years since anyone lived in the conservatory.

"In about ten minutes, we'll hit the halfway mark between the barn and home." Gavin glanced at the speedometer.

"I sent Ian the information." She checked her phone. "He hasn't answered. Access to an old local map would be nice." Fiona regretted suggesting they find the place.

"Stop the car. I see the house. I see it." Sara pointed toward a downed tree. The tree hid what looked like a side road.

"Should we investigate?" Gavin raised his brows and pulled off the road.

Fiona was tempted to suggest they go home. Sara would be disappointed if they couldn't find the house. Her niece was determined to save the lady from the moment they left the barn. Ian would suggest they inspect the site. She tapped Gavin's shoulder. "You cross the road and check for a path. We'll wait here." Like most roads connecting small towns in the Adirondacks, the quiet road had minimal traffic this time of the year.

After a quick investigation, he flashed a thumbs-up.

"Be careful and follow Gavin." Fiona unbuckled the twin's seatbelts and led them across the road.

"Did you see one? Did you see a *Trow*?" Sara ran toward Gavin and tugged on his jacket.

"You were right, *a bhobain*. There's some kind of a path beyond this old crooked tree." He pushed aside several dead tree limbs and cleared a narrow path.

Something small and furry scampered across the

little clearing, alarming everyone.

"Eek." Sara hopped to the side.

The tiny creature disappeared into a cranny of old roots.

"It's probably nothing more than a field mouse." Fiona took her hand.

"Step carefully. Slippery rocks are hidden in the overgrowth." Gavin offered a hand and guided the twins and Fiona over a gnarled mess of broken branches and wet leaves.

"I'm not so sure about this." Fiona kicked at the dirt beneath the dense overgrowth with the tip of her boot. A somewhat firmer surface existed under the mess. In the past, a gravel or dirt road probably led to the school. Even cleared, the road would barely be wide enough for one car to pass. They walked along something resembling a dicey path for about half a mile. "I see something." Like most abandoned two-story structures, a ghostly elegance surrounded the house. Fiona was fascinated by abandoned places. She was drawn to her B and B the first time she visited the empty farmhouse.

"Let's go." Sara clapped her hands together.

"I'd like a closer look, too." Fiona took her niece's hand and proceeded toward the creepy house.

"Are all the women in your family so persuasive, lad?" Gavin smiled at Simon.

"I'll ask Ian if the trait is traceable." Fiona glanced over her shoulder and laughed. "If Walter's right, the story creates a curious connection to the house. *Trows* and vanishing ladies aside, houses like this have secrets and tales to tell."

"C'mon, scaredy-cats." Sara stepped forward.

"Can't we just see it from here?" Simon froze.

"You go ahead. I'll hang back and take in the whole picture." Gavin touched Simon's shoulder. "I'm with you, lad. We'll let the girls check outside the old house first."

Fiona was touched by Gavin's suggestion. The first day he met the twins, he showed he had a way with kids. She left Simon in Gavin's care and caught up with Sara on the creaky steps. With one hand in Sara's and the other on the wobbly railing, she placed both feet on each step. At the top of the stairs, she stopped and took in the magnitude of the porch. The creaky floorboards were anything but musical. The tune they played advised caution.

"Is the door locked?" Gavin asked from his position at the bottom of the steps

"It might take more than a little elbow grease to open this door." Fiona glanced at the lock. "We've gone this far—might as well try." She jiggled a rusty iron padlock.

"Let me try." Gavin led Simon onto the front porch.

"I'll peek inside." Fiona rubbed a patch of dirt off a window. Years of dirt caked the elaborate bay windows on either side of the door. Inside, the windows were bare. *What kind of curtains had covered the window?* "Nothing much to see." Large pieces of debris loomed in the shadows.

"Is the lady there?" Sara slipped a hand into Fiona's and pressed her nose against the glass.

"For what it's worth, I see some garbage and a wall phone still attached to the wall." Fiona wiped a smudge off Sara's nose.

"What's a wall phone?" Simon tugged Gavin's hand.

"Wasn't good for much except making and receiving phone calls." Gavin accompanied Simon to the window. He pointed to the old-style phone. He rubbed dirt off with a jacket sleeve. "It's hard to tell if the inside structure is strong." He stepped back and snapped photos of the exterior.

"Can you take a picture with that old phone?" Simon pressed a palm on the window.

"You don't. Wall phones didn't have selfies, texts, or games." Gavin turned this phone around and took a selfie with Simon against the old house. He glanced at the photo and shook his head. "A large-scale renovation might bring the building back to its former glory."

"For what purpose?" Fiona removed Simon's hand from the dirty window and handed him a tissue. Was Gavin serious or talking off the top of his head? Could this desolate reminder of the past find a purpose? She experienced the expense of renovating an old house firsthand but had a lucrative plan for the property. What could he possibly want to do with this rundown house? She gave him a sideways glance.

"Can we go in?" Sara tugged on her jacket.

"Not today." Fiona pointed to the ancient lock. She'd seen enough. Unlike her barn, the outside structure looked sturdy. "I suggest you get a safety survey before you explore inside."

"Your auntie's right. 'Tis not safe to go in." Gavin glanced at Fiona. "Let's check around back?" He followed the porch to the rear of the house.

Unsure what they would find, Fiona stepped cautiously with Sara. Simon's rubber boots thumped behind them. As they approached the corner, the property opened onto an overgrown field where a lawn might have been. Broken debris and rocks covered a fire-damaged, open-air stage at the end of hip-high weeds. The only audible sound was a breeze rushing through bare trees.

"The cement platform is still intact." Gavin climbed onto the stage.

"It's a bandstand." Fiona drew in a breath. If either of them doubted they found the conservatory, the tumbledown stage and burned remnants of a shell were proof musicians performed here. Fire-damaged stonewalls, a crumbling overhang, and a few scattered beer cans were testimony to decades of disuse.

"Exactly, but not any bandstand. This one is a replica of Ross' Bandstand in Princes Street Garden." Gavin rested a gloved hand on a blackened rail and stepped down.

"All that's missing is Edinburgh Castle on a hill." Fiona closed her eyes momentarily and remembered visits to the park with her parents and brothers. A cold breeze brushed the back of her neck. The memories faded. She opened her eyes and faced the current reality. What other clues were hidden in the conservatory?

"'Tis just like the one back home." He snapped photos of the ruined bandstand. "I'd like some more pictures of the house."

"Are you sending all the photos to your granddad?" She forced a smile. "If this turns out to be nothing, he'll be disappointed. Remember, we have only the word of a confused old man."

"I agree. Walter's information can go either way. If

this lead goes south, the fault is mine." Gavin positioned Fiona and the twins in front of the house where the light was better. "If nothing comes of our time here, Granddad will appreciate the photos. He has a passion for old houses." He stepped back and snapped several photos of her and the kids—first together and then individually.

"Don't make silly faces." Fiona tickled Sara and made her smile. From what little Gavin told her, she imagined Granddad McIver was not a fun old man. She walked toward him, reached for the phone, and swiped left.

"No worries. I'll send the silly ones to my daughter." He sighed.

The wind picked up, and something between rain and snow started to fall. "Let's head to the car." Fiona pulled Simon's hat over his ears.

"I think we've seen all we can without going inside." Gavin reached for Simon's hand and followed.

Despite the sudden change in the weather, walking back to the car was less treacherous. At the car, Fiona glanced over her shoulder. A portion of the big house was visible through the trees. *What McIver secrets are you hiding?*

Chapter 8

Gavin sat in the Drummond's recently renovated kitchen, waiting for a fancy built-in coffeemaker to finish brewing. A week had passed since he discovered the decaying conservatory, but the image of the old building was still fresh in his mind. The structure showed potential for something other than a resort. He just couldn't figure out what it was.

Jack walked toward the table with a plate of store-bought biscuits. "Find anything interesting?" He glanced at a map sprawled across the table.

"Mr. Paisley discovered an old property map in the museum archives." Gavin smoothed out the creases. "The property lines go way past the old buildings."

"Did you take any pictures?" Jack bit into a cookie.

Gavin anticipated his friend would ask. He purposely divided the ones of Fiona and the twins into a different album. He opened the photo app and showed Jack edited photos of the conservatory, the bandstand, and the overgrown property.

"That's a pretty significant piece of land." Jack brushed crumbs off the map and traced a finger around the perimeter. "Is it all owned by the same person?"

"The only information a clerk at city hall could give me was the name of a trust paying the property taxes." He glanced at Jack. "Does a trust called Sound of Music sound familiar?"

Jack shook his head. "A revocable trust was most likely set up to avoid probate when the owners die." He filled two coffee mugs and set them on the kitchen table.

"That doesn't help much, considering I don't know if Joan or her husband are alive." Gavin sighed. "Just another dead end." He folded the map, reached for a mug, and inhaled the fresh brewed aroma. "When did you learn to make such a good cup of coffee?" He took a sip and glanced at a text message. "It's Ian. I hope he found something useful."

—*I sent the information and album cover to a colleague. She's head of the university music department. Wants to meet you.*—

Gavin read the name and laughed. Only Ian would know a professor of music with the last name Cappella.

"Something funny?"

Gavin showed him the messages.

"Cappella? What's her first name, Melody?" Jack laughed and sipped his coffee.

Within minutes, Gavin received another text. This one came from the professor.

—*Am happy to meet at your convenience. Is this afternoon too soon? I have information about your aunt and uncle.*—

He checked the clock on the wall oven. If he left now, he'd be in Albany in two hours. He'd have plenty of time to get to the airport, pick up his daughter and cousin, and arrive at the B and B in time for tea.

—*Is ten o'clock okay?*—

—*See you soon.*—

"I'll find out soon enough. I'm meeting the professor before I pick up Emily and Adrian." Gavin was relieved he had a vehicle to drive to Albany. Today, Jack and his dad's busy schedule required both company trucks.

"Take this for the road." Jack poured coffee into a travel mug.

The drive from the western foothills to Albany took less than two-and-a-half hours. The scenic byways reminded him of home. He now understood how Joan and her husband chose Highland Falls—but not why. Too soon, rural roads and their secrets faded. He glanced at the navigation system and merged onto the main highway. The drive to the university took only a few minutes. He parked the SUV in the visitor car park in front of a bubbling fountain. The campus was an impressive modernist architectural marvel with tall gigantic columns, bubble domes, and stone walkways. Adrian, an ardent fan of all types of architecture, would enjoy seeing Edward Stone's creation. He passed through a courtyard covered by a colossal glass dome. Signs pointed to the building where Professor Carol Cappella had her office. Outside the office, he stopped and texted Jack a picture of the door sign.

—"She's not a Melody. She's a Carol."—

He added a Christmas wreath and entered the small office.

"Mr. McIver is here." A pleasant young lady with purple hair ushered him through the next door.

Carol Cappella wasn't like any professor he had in college. She was a tiny woman with a surprisingly deep, full, reverberating voice. He instantly liked her. Everything about her was animated—from her eyes to her hand gestures. "I appreciate you taking the time to help." Gavin was on a tight schedule. Adrian and Emily would land in less than two hours.

"My pleasure. Professor Campbell's information about your aunt and the record album is exciting. "She signaled for him to take a seat. "I showed my students the album cover photo. They were quite intrigued."

"I have it here." He placed a brown paper bag on her desk.

"How exciting. My students showed interest in the combined style your aunt and her husband performed." She glanced at him over the wire rim of her glasses. "You are aware of their differences?"

"The man who owned the antique barn mentioned their success as musicians was due to their different musical styles." He rubbed an open palm across his chin. "I can see I came to the right place."

"I apologize. I'm getting ahead of myself." Cappella dismissed her comment with a wave of her hand. "Their musical style is not what you're interested in hearing about today."

"I welcome any information." Gavin would have to thank Ian for this introduction. The woman was a walking encyclopedia of music.

"What do you know about the Tinker, Scottish Traveler lifestyle? Your aunt's husband performed their music style." She pointed to Paul's name. "Tinker is no longer an acceptable term, but I use the word with respect for the Tinker history. I hear New Age groups are still traveling around the UK."

"They are. I met a New Age version of a Scottish Traveler on a trip to Stonehenge," Gavin envied their carefree lifestyle. "They hold on to the hippie culture of the sixties and travel between music festivals and fairs." Gavin sighed. "I spoke to a young man in the group who left a promising career in the space industry to follow his passion for travel and music."

"Having the freedom to do what you love is wonderful. I'm blessed to be in my position." She smiled and typed a few words on her keyboard.

"Not everyone is so fortunate."

"What do you do for a living?" Cappella glanced over the screen.

"I work for my family's construction company." He should stick to the reason he was here. "Did you find something?"

"The tinkers or travelers of old had a unique style of music. The melodies and tunes were popular with local Scottish immigrants who settled in the area surrounding Highland Falls." She turned her computer screen in his direction. "I found several articles on the subject."

He glanced at the screen. Like Ian, she didn't waste any time. "I remember my granny telling stories about Tinkers coming 'round. Granny bought their trinkets and listened to songs created from town gossip."

"What a lovely memory." Cappella clapped her hands.

"Can you send me the links?" Fiona and Adrian might like to see the articles. However, Adrian's outlook would be the complete opposite of Fiona's. Fi would appreciate the family memories. Adrian would be off on a thousand tangents, looking for a connection to a new SIREaC project.

His phone *pinged.* Cappella already sent the links.

"Where did I put the list?" Cappella murmured and sorted through the stack of papers on her desk.

Her impeccable style and well-coiffed hair made

up for what she lacked in office neatness.

"Ah, here it is. One of my students diligently searched for a connection between our university and the conservatory. She compiled a list of State University of New York students who attended a summer program at Stewart's Scottish Conservatory in the 1960s." She handed him a printout.

"Stewart's? Was Stewart Joan's last name?" He searched on his own after visiting the barn. With limited access to the necessary sites, he had no success. Still, he preferred to do the footwork instead of utilizing a think tank in SIREaC's Manhattan office. At this point, with limited facts to go on, tying up valuable resources without solid information would be futile. Discovering Joan's married name was a significant find.

"Yes, that's their surname." Cappella raised a brow. "You didn't know?"

"I tried unsuccessfully to piece together Joan's life before she left Scotland." He never expected such an explosion of information. He rubbed the back of his neck and glanced at the list. The names were separated into two vertical columns. One column listed Joan's students and the other Paul's.

"All this is hard to process. Take the papers with you." Cappella smiled.

"Have you tried to contact any of the students?" The question was a long shot, but he had to ask.

"Not yet." She shook her head. "The information about Joan's whereabouts came from an enrolled student currently at the university."

"Is this student a reliable source?" He glanced over his shoulder through the open door and at the purple-haired girl at the desk.

"She's a very reliable young lady." She followed his gaze. "She has a personal connection to your aunt."

Cappella's unstructured approach to providing details drove him mad. Maybe finding fault with her unorthodox methods was an excuse for what bothered him. He sighed heavily at what the burden of this new information could do to his relationship with Fiona. She often glanced at him like she was trying to figure him out. Once all the dots were connected and the truth about Aunt Joan was common knowledge in Highland Falls, SIREaC's interest in the considerable property would be exposed.

"I presented your story at my lecture on local music history." Cappella studied his face and raised a brow. "I'm sorry. I should have asked permission first."

"Not at all. I appreciate everything you've done so far." He nodded, signaling for her to continue. He didn't want her to think he was displeased.

"Is it urgent to find your aunt—a medical situation or a last wish of a dying relative?"

Although her question was valid, Cappella was off-topic again. "Fortunately, the situation isn't a matter of life or death. Granddad wants to reunite with his sister." He embellished the truth a bit.

"Do you have any idea why the family was estranged?" Cappella asked.

"I have my suspicions." As much as he wanted to avoid such questions, the professor had a right to an answer. "My family would never bless a marriage to a man they considered below her status."

"The tale is as old as time." Cappella sighed. "I suggested an extra credit research project. Interested students will learn all they can about the conservatory and the types of music they taught."

"Sounds like you're off to a good start. Tell me about the student with a personal connection." He redirected her back to her previous comment.

"More than a good start," Cappella said. "The student I mentioned might know where to find your aunt." She smiled. "She saw Joan Stewart a year ago and believes she's still alive."

Joan Stewart sounded surreal. "The possibility crossed my mind." Clever Fiona had done the math and suggested the likelihood his aunt was still alive.

"I expected a connection to the conservatory might come from a local student. She grew up in the neighborhood and remembered a story passed on by a grandparent." Cappella shuffled papers on the desk. "Scots are wonderful storytellers. You already know that." She smiled. "My students are always full of surprises. This time was no exception."

Gavin glanced at his watch.

"A freshman music major from Brooklyn recognized the name. She lived down the street from a music school owned by the Stewarts."

"Is the school still open?" he asked with trepidation. Would she answer the question or go off on a tangent again?

"She texted me an address." Cappella searched an endless list of texts. "Here it is. I'll forward the information."

"Got it." Gavin checked his phone. The message included a street name and address that was foreign. The name of the school, *Coél Na H'alba,* and the translation, music of Scotland, gave him a chill.

Across the desk, Cappella smiled. "Ian mentioned you found the album when you were antiquing with his sister. Pretty girl...isn't she?" She wiggled her brows.

Professor Cappella's creative approach produced results, but her intuitive nature wasn't limited to music. "She's a lovely lass and clever, too." Gavin nodded. What man wouldn't find the sassy redhead attractive? "I wouldn't have pursued my search in this direction without her assistance." He glanced at a photo wall and spotted a girl about Emily's age playing the violin. "Do you teach the Suzuki Method?"

"Many of our violin students started with the Suzuki Method." She walked toward the wall and pointed to a photo in a gold frame. "This young girl is my granddaughter. Are you familiar with the method?"

"My daughter has been taking lessons since she was four years old. She's eight now." He wanted Emily's life to remain routine after his divorce. "She's enrolled in gymnastics, soccer, and violin. Of the three, she likes the violin best."

"She might be interested in our children's performances." Cappella pointed to a photo of children in a chamber orchestra. "Tryouts are next month. Make sure she has time to practice every day?"

"She takes lessons and practices at school. Music's an important part of the curriculum." Now, all the extras her school offered would be his responsibility. "Do you have any local recommendations for someone who teaches the method?" He rubbed a hand through his hair.

"Unfortunately, I don't know anyone in your area." She shook her head. "Imagine if the conservatory could be brought to life again." She glanced sideways. "You seem like a resourceful young man. Maybe you could find investors willing to rebuild the school." She clapped her hands. "I could create an off-campus site like Professor Campbell did for his forensic study students."

"Can any of your faculty teach the Suzuki Method?" A restored conservatory flashed through his mind.

"What a wonderful idea." She giggled and waved a hand. "Listen to me. I'm jumping ahead. Nothing can happen until you find your aunt and establish she still owns the land."

"Yes, that's definitely a complication." Gavin discovered the one specific contingency *Granaidh's* plans relied on. Joan owned a conservatory and property. Would she willingly share with the family? He liked the idea of restoring the music school. He glanced at a small antique clock on Cappella's desk. A handle shaped like a violin bow approached the eleven. "My daughter and cousin arrived this morning from Scotland. Their connecting flight from JFK to Albany will land in an hour." He regretted having to rush off.

"Recruiting your own team?" She straightened a stack of papers.

"Something like that." When he had more information, he'd let Adrian coordinate SIREaC's sophisticated group of property experts in the Manhattan office. By distancing himself from this aspect, he wouldn't have to lie to Fiona. In the past, he dealt with locals resistant to new development. This was different. He couldn't risk alienating Fiona. Would their story end up being another tale of star-crossed lovers?

Gavin stood behind a fence along the runway designated for smaller jets. He adjusted his collar to ward off the wind, glanced at the blue sky and listened to the *whir* of a plane climbing to cruising altitude. He lost sight of the plane behind a cloud and turned his attention to an aircraft that had throttled down and come to a stop.

When the flight's steps were in place, the door opened.

Emily followed an attendant onto the air stairs. She hugged a violin case.

Reunions were always bittersweet.

Could she have grown so tall in the last three months? Only three years older than the twins, she emanated a grown-up air of sophistication. A nanny, a posh private school, and a high-end Edinburgh address separated her from the average kids he'd met in Highland Falls. He was having second thoughts. Did he make the right decision in bringing her here?

"Daddy." Emily handed Adrian her violin and rushed down the steps.

The moment she threw her arms around his waist and hugged him, all doubts disappeared. He glanced at Adrian. She was always stylish and neat as a pin, even after a long flight. "Thanks for doing this. How was the trip?"

"Perfect. We landed at JFK early. We cleared customs and went straight to the company jet. We were up and down in no time." Adrian kissed each cheek and glanced over his shoulder. "I expected to see more foliage."

"The weather's been too wet." Gavin shook hands with the pilot, lifted two large suitcases, and led the way to the parking lot.

"How long is the ride to our hotel?" Emily climbed into the back, fidgeted with the seatbelt, and clicked the latch into the buckle.

"Probably longer than the time to fly here from Kennedy Airport." Gavin tugged the seatbelt. Reassured it was secure, he closed the door.

"Okay." Emily turned her attention to the planes approaching the runway.

"Really, so long?" Adrian raised a brow. "Couldn't you find a private airport closer to Highland Falls?"

"Saranac Lake, north of Highland Falls, has a private airport. The airport was out of the way since I had business this morning in Albany." Gavin climbed into the vehicle and started the engine. He considered the two-runway private airport used primarily by private planes but couldn't chance being seen driving in the opposite direction.

"What's the town like?" Adrian rolled down the passenger window.

"It's a tidy little town—maybe a bit provincial." Too late, he regretted his choice of words. The people he met were anything but provincial—Ian, Mr. Paisley, and especially Fiona.

"What about the tourists?" She adjusted the collar of a puffy jacket.

"They come from the surrounding states and the city." In his spare time, Gavin read everything he could about the town. None of the information uncovered a clue about Aunt Joan. If and when the time came to deal with state laws and regulations, any information would help.

"We're going to change all that, aren't we?"

Adrian gave him a concerned glance. "Our resort will put this charming little town on every traveler's list."

"Isn't it the charm of little towns you try to preserve in your architectural designs?" Gavin was surprised he came to the defense of Highland Falls.

"I guess it is." Adrian gave him a sideways glance. "Are we any closer to finding Granddad's sister?"

Her curious glance questioned whose side he was on. "Not only have I located our Great-Aunt Joan…" He glanced in the rearview mirror.

Emily watched the passing scenery.

"You mean she's still alive?" Adrian clasped her hands together. "Tell me more."

"I found out today. However, I'm not sure about her husband." Gavin stopped at a red light and glanced at Adrian. "They owned a music conservatory near where we'll be staying." Cappella might have been on to something. Rebuilding the conservatory would give SIREaC a more positive image.

"A husband, a conservatory…Oh, this is good. You told me you didn't have any leads." Adrian shifted in her seat. "What happened?"

"I went antiquing with the sister of a local historian," Gavin stated matter-of-factly. Fiona was much more than someone's kid sister. Her passionate energy always left him wanting more.

"You, antiquing?" Adrian tapped him with her elbow and laughed.

"What's so odd about that? The visit to the antique barn led to an excellent lead in finding Great-Aunt Joan."

"You know where Joan is?" Adrian retorted. "Wow, this girl must be someone special to get you to dig through someone's old stuff. I'll have to thank her."

Verra special. "You'll meet her soon enough. She owns and operates the B and B we're staying at." He wasn't about to share his feelings toward Fiona just yet.

"Of course, the Thistle Inn, the charming B and B you suggested. Would we be competing for guests if SIREaC's project is successful?"

"Don't get ahead of yourself. If Aunt Joan holds a grudge, there's a good chance she won't have anything to do with us."

"Why would she hold a grudge?" Adrian asked. "What aren't you telling me?"

"The story is complicated. We'll talk later." He nodded toward the backseat. "Hey, Em, how you doing back there?"

"What's a B and B?" Emily asked.

"It's like a small hotel where you get a delicious breakfast every morning." Gavin glanced in the rearview mirror.

"Do they have a concierge?" Emily asked. "When I stayed in Paris with *Ma* last year, a concierge brought me hot cocoa with whipped cream, marshmallows, and a cherry every night."

"It's a different kind of hotel." Gavin glanced sideways at Adrian. He could use some assistance.

"You know how extravagant *Ma* is." Adrian rolled her eyes.

Gavin nodded. His ex threw around money like she won the lottery. He kept his opinion to himself and offered Emily something better than a paid attendant. "There's a pretty Scottish lady who runs the place. I know firsthand she makes a tidy cup of cocoa, serves delicious cookies, and bakes awesome scones."

"Hmm. Firsthand. Pretty lady." Adrian soaked in every word. "Can't wait to meet her."

Gavin cringed. Once she met Fiona, Adrian would have endless questions. "You'll meet her soon enough." He headed west on the thruway to Highway 30. The first time he drove along the road, the colors were a spectacular blend of red and orange. This year, excessive rain and wind blew the leaves prematurely off the trees. Next fall, he'd take a day trip with Emily.

Would Fiona and the twins accept an invitation?

Time would tell—next fall was a long way off.

Chapter 9

Fiona added a fresh bunch of tea leaves to a strainer. Today's guests, a group of ladies from Hamilton County, arrived early. Since the group was small, she set up two tables of four and a third table for three—just in case Gavin's family wanted tea. She gently bit her lip and glanced out the window for a sign of Gavin's car.

"I noticed you set an additional small table." Cora entered the kitchen with an empty teapot.

"Tea time is the perfect setting for Gavin's family to relax after a long flight." She tightened her apron strings.

"I've never seen you so anxious about a guest's arrival." Cora placed the pot on the counter, took the ties from Fiona's hands, and pulled them into a tight bow.

Fiona wiggled free and filled a pot with mint tea. "You're right. I'm a little edgy about Gavin staying here. He's not the first friend or acquaintance to make a reservation." Tires crunched over the gravel driveway. She ran to the window. "They're here." She untied her apron and tossed it over a kitchen chair.

Cora followed.

Fiona took a deep breath and opened the front door. Gavin and his party were already on the porch. A dark-haired woman with a similar dominant brow ridge stood at the top of the steps. "How was the drive?" Fiona was eager to hear about Cappella. The conversation would have to wait. A curly mop of red hair peeked around his side. "This must be Emily." Fiona smiled. "How was your flight?"

Emily didn't budge.

Gavin placed an arm around his daughter's shoulders and urged her forward. "Come meet..." He glanced from Fiona to Emily and hesitated. "This is my special friend, *Fiona,*" he whispered her name.

The way he said her name sent a shiver to her toes. "Nice to meet you." Fiona leaned down with an outstretched hand. "You're beautiful." A violin case dwarfed the little girl. "Do you play?" Fiona pointed to a case clutched in a small hand.

"I practice at bedtime if you'd like to listen." Emily stepped around Gavin and nodded.

"I'd like that." Fiona refrained from hugging the poised little girl.

Adrian stepped to the front of the group. Her dark eyes gazed directly at Fiona.

For a long moment, neither of them said a word.

"You must be Gavin's cousin, Adrian?" Fiona tossed her braid over her shoulder. The young woman was not how she imagined his cousin would look. She was willowy. Dressed in well-made travel clothes, she appeared to have stepped off the page of a high-end magazine—not a transatlantic flight.

"And you're Fiona—the innkeeper." Adrian nodded. "This is a charming place." She ran a hand along the doorframe. "You've done an amazing job preserving the outside architecture."

"She always knows how to make an entrance."

Gavin stepped inside. His laugh filled the narrow foyer.

"Come this way. I'll sign you in." Fiona didn't take offense. How could she? She didn't know what Gavin told his cousin about their friendship. "Follow me." She led them into the main room. "This room is for guests to enjoy." She pointed to cozy nooks nestled in the corners. "Coffee and tea are always available on the buffet in the dining room."

"Do I smell Earl Gray brewing?" Adrian turned away from a wall with a collection of Highland Falls' historical prints and sniffed the air.

"We're preparing for afternoon tea. Would you like to freshen up first?" Fiona removed two sets of keys from a desk drawer. "The ones with purple bands open the front door. The other keys are for your adjoining rooms."

"Should we meet you in the kitchen?" Gavin slipped the keys into his pocket.

"You're a guest today." Fiona pointed past the archway separating the main room from the dining area. "I set the table for three by the window. Breakfast is served in the dining room at nine. We accommodate guests going out early to hike or see the sunrise with a takeaway breakfast."

"Good to know." Gavin glanced past the arch.

"Follow me." She directed everyone back to the foyer. "Cora will show you to your rooms."

Cora waited at the foot of the stairs.

Gavin let the ladies pass and waited for Fiona. As she passed, he placed a light hand on her back. "I have so much to tell you about Professor Cappella. She was amazing. Your brother's amazing." He leaned closer. "And you're amazing. I wouldn't have ever discovered so much on my own."

"Are you joining us?" Adrian turned and raised her well-groomed brows.

"I'll get the luggage and be up in a minute." He tossed Adrian the keys.

"We'll talk later. I have guests to attend." Ignoring her pounding pulse, Fiona returned to the kitchen. The front door slammed shut. She breathed a sigh of relief. Meeting Gavin's cousin and daughter was a bit overwhelming. They weren't her ordinary guests. Something about them suggested they rarely, if ever, stayed in a B and B.

"Everyone's settled for now." Cora walked into the kitchen.

"Was there a problem?" Fiona noted a strange expression on Cora's face.

"I don't think so, but I'd bet those two gals never stayed at a B and B." Cora shrugged. "However, they were impressed with the room, the bedding, and the custom logo on the amenities."

"I got the same impression." Fiona laughed. She catered to high-end guests who *chose* to stay at the inn. Adrian and Emily didn't decide to stay here. She was glad she ran a cool iron over the duvet after making the bed.

In the hallway, a creaky floorboard on the first step *groaned*.

"Sounds like our new guests are on their way to tea." Cora opened the door a crack.

"Let's go woo them." Fiona would put her afternoon tea up against any posh teatime. With a tray of shortbread in each hand, she left the kitchen.

Cora followed with two teapots.

"How was your flight?" Fiona served Gavin's table first, placing a small tray of cookies in the center.

"We had a sleeping pod and pajamas." Emily glanced at Adrian.

"Wow." Fiona raised a brow. "Sounds like a great way to travel." Even with a lucrative income, she was too practical to splurge on something as frivolous as a first-class ticket.

"You ladies have to taste these cookies." Gavin reached for the tray.

When he arrived, he was excited. Now, an uneasy edginess replaced the joy. "Would you like to help serve shortbread to my guests?" Fiona stepped behind Emily.

"Can I?" Emily turned and glanced at a sprinkle-covered shortbread.

"Don't eat all the cookies." Gavin smiled.

The polite lilt of Emily's accent at each table delighted the guests.

"You did an excellent job." When the cookie plate was empty, Fiona escorted Emily back to her seat.

"I never expected to be taking tea in such grand style." Adrian glanced around. "Is the layout of the room original?"

"The only change is a powder room on this level." Fiona pointed toward the hallway. "Are you in construction like Gavin?"

"All McIvers are born and bred in the business." Adrian glanced sideways at Gavin. "Aren't we?"

"I guess you could say that." Gavin conjured a short laugh. "Adrian's an architect. We'll have plenty of time to talk work and renovations." He reached for a teacup. "Fiona blends most of the herbs she uses in her tea."

In Fiona's short time spent with Gavin, she understood his moods. His short, forced laugh and serious expression were out of place. She couldn't understand why he was so on edge in Adrian's presence. Teatime was a happy time to enjoy with friends and family. She wouldn't let whatever he was hiding ruin Emily's first day. "Afternoon tea is about more than the tea. Shortbread and tea sandwiches get equal billing." She pointed to the cookies on Emily's plate.

"Don't sell yourself *short*." Gavin chuckled.

Fiona refrained from groaning. Silly puns were out of character. "Gavin hasn't had the opportunity to be a guest on this grand scale. Last time he was here, he had tea in the kitchen." She glanced around the table. Emily hadn't touched her tea. "Would you like a cup of hot cocoa instead?"

"With marshmallows and whipped cream, please." Emily unfolded a linen napkin across her lap.

Sara and Simon were polite, well-mannered children but never handled a napkin with such grace.

"Why don't you join them?" Cora placed a fresh pot of tea on the table and pulled out the chair across from Gavin.

"I rarely take tea with guests." Fiona gestured around the room. Only a third of the tables were occupied.

Cora was already serving the table to her right.

"Please join us," Gavin insisted, pulling out a chair.

His smile was genuine. How could Fiona ignore his pleading puppy-dog eyes? She cleared her throat, pretending not to be affected, and sat. Cora had set the table with a mix of Fiona's favorite china pieces. A dark, glazed Brown Betty teapot in the middle of the table was an earthy contrast to her mother's delicate Old Country Rose cups and saucers. The dainty signature pattern of burgundy, pink, and yellow roses stood out next to a plain brown pot.

"Does the pot have a story?" Adrian grasped the handle of the Brown Betty and filled her cup. "It doesn't appear as elegant as your tea service."

"Every teacup and every teapot has a story." Fiona had second thoughts on whether or not she was grateful Gavin had reserved two rooms. She swallowed and clutched the handle of the cream jug. The ceremony of serving tea from this set always calmed her, but not today.

"This pot belonged to Grandma Campbell." Fiona poured cream and politely placed the delicate creamer in front of Adrian. Teatime should be a civilized event, even if the participants have another agenda.

Adrian hung on to every word.

"I've seen similar pots. My English friends believe a simple Brown Betty makes the best cup of tea." Adrian placed the pot back on the warmer and gazed at Fiona.

"The simple design lets the loose tea leaves swirl in the boiling water. The shape allows complete infusion." Fiona reached for the pot and filled her cup. "The Brown Betty gets its distinct color from a dark Rockingham glaze. The glaze also hides tea stains." She could talk forever about her collections, but today, she preferred to turn the conversation in another direction. Two could play the same game. She'd engage Gavin's chatty cousin in conversation that might reveal something about him.

Across the table, Emily used the back of her spoon and drowned marshmallows in hot chocolate.

"Mind what you're doing," Adrian said. "You don't want to stain the linens."

"No worries." Fiona smiled at Emily. "Everything's washable." She turned her attention back to Adrian. "Do you spend much time with Emily?"

"With Nanny's help, we cover the time Gavin's away." Adrian raised a brow. "Gavin's told you about his divorce—hasn't he?"

"She's well aware of my marital status." Gavin coughed.

Why would anyone blatantly ask such a question? Fiona sipped her tea in silence. She gazed at a ray of afternoon sun reflecting off a shimmering gold banding around a saucer. The serene glow reminded her she had the strength to deal with whatever was coming. Entertaining a demanding guest was rare. She blew out a breath and emptied the last drop of tea. This week would be long and more demanding than usual. If Adrian intended to stir the pot, she succeeded.

"Can I pour anyone another cup of tea or a hot chocolate?" Cora approached the table with a teapot.

"No, thank you." Emily yawned.

"I think someone needs to rest." Cora smiled.

"Back home, it's bedtime for you, young lady." Gavin walked around the small table, passing behind Fiona.

A hand brushed across Fiona's shoulder. A quiver cascaded along her arm.

"Thank you for the hot chocolate." Emily scooped the last marshmallow from the bottom of the cup.

"Yes, tea was lovely, too." Adrian glanced at three cookies on the plate. "Do you mind if I take those? The shortbread taste is exceptional."

"I'll let Sophia know how much you enjoyed them." Fiona wrapped the remaining cookies in a napkin and handed them to Adrian. "Her shop is on Main Street. I suggest you stop by if you go to town."

"Can we go?" Emily tugged on Gavin's arm.

"We have the entire weekend to explore the town." Gavin took his daughter's hand. "Now, *a bhobain,* it's time to rest."

The McIver tea party was over. Gavin and his family disappeared at the top of the stairs leading to the guest rooms.

Fiona breathed a sigh of relief and stacked the plates and saucers.

"Gavin's family is not what I expected. The cousin's a little high maintenance." Cora nodded at the staircase and nudged her with her hip. Her arms were full of goodie bags.

"We'll treat her like any other guest." Fiona glanced toward the Hamilton ladies. Most of her guests, especially her tea visitors, were pleasant.

The ladies gathered their belongings and prepared to leave.

Cora handed out goodie bags and walked the ladies to their van.

Fiona gathered the dirty plates and carried them to the kitchen.

"I thought the ladies would never leave." Cora joined her at the counter next to the sink. "I will say you attract the most interesting guests. However, no one as attractive and charming as Gavin ever stayed under this roof." She reached for a wet cloth and rubbed a tea stain off the counter.

Fiona washed a delicate teacup and placed it on a drying mat. "Gavin *is* charming." She laughed. *And even more mysterious now, his family has arrived.*

"The cousin, on the other hand, is something else." Cora rolled her eyes. "She's a little too in-your-face for someone you just met. You probably didn't notice, but I did."

"Oh, *I* noticed. Adrian's all drama but harmless." Fiona folded a dishtowel.

"She's the type who sticks her nose into everyone's business." Cora tossed the cloth in the sink. "Why did she ask so many questions about the inn?"

Cora was never negative about someone she just met. Unlike Cora, Fiona wasn't bothered by Adrian's questions. She welcomed them as a chance to ask questions about their family. "She said more than Gavin ever did."

"What about Gavin?" Cora raised a brow. "If he's helping the Drummonds, why's he asking questions at the property office about land adjacent to the old conservatory?"

"Maybe he hoped he'd find someone living nearby who remembers his aunt." Fiona shrugged and feigned indifference, but Cora was right. Was he more interested in the land than finding his aunt, or were the two intertwined? She glanced at Cora. "I thought you liked Gavin."

"I do." Cora nodded. "If someone shows an interest in local real estate, I'm cautious. He might be charming and a friend of Jack's, but he's still a stranger interested in a piece of property. People are curious. What if he's a developer?" She raised her brows. "In his case, he might not have to buy land to build a fancy resort."

The idea crossed Fiona's mind. She didn't know everything she would like to know. What she did know about Gavin made her smile. He was powerful and sexy on the athletic field. And when he kissed her—she wanted to melt into his arms.

"Are you okay?" Cora glanced sideways at Fiona.

"I guess I'm overthinking Gavin's situation." She shrugged.

"Don't get too involved," Cora warned. "He's handsome and charming. I see how you look at him." She pointed a finger. "When you discover what he's hiding, you might not feel the same."

"Am I that obvious?" Her cheeks warmed whenever she thought about Gavin. He projected an energy she was undeniably attracted to.

"As obvious as *he* is when he watches *you*."

"I hadn't noticed." When Cora knew what she was thinking, she always had an eerie feeling. "In the meantime, Gavin and his family will be treated like any other guest." She avoided Cora's narrowed gaze. "All of today's guests checked in. Why don't you take the afternoon off?"

"You trying to get rid of me?" Cora half smiled. "I could do a little eavesdropping."

"Cora." Fiona's hand flew to her chest.

"I'm only kidding. I would never invade a guest's privacy." Cora entered the mudroom and pulled her coat from a hook. "You have time before the twins come home. Don't look for things to do." She removed the car keys from a pocket. "See you tomorrow."

There's always something to do. Fiona wiped her

hands on her apron and looked around the quiet kitchen. *I could do a quick search on Gavin and his cousin.* A quick search might give her an insight to the business run by his dominating granddad. She shook her head. *No. She didn't have* time to waste. Forming an opinion from random computer searches never revealed the genuine person. She wouldn't find what she already knew in a search—he was a good man and a concerned father. She walked past the laptop on the desk. She tossed the towels into the mudroom washer, set the controls, and listened for the hum of the first cycle.

The mudroom door slammed, drowning out the washer's *whir*.

"Back so soon?" She turned, expecting to see Cora.

Chapter10

Gavin stood framed in the doorway, wearing only a T-shirt and jeans.

"Is something wrong? Why are you outside—dressed for summer?" Fiona gazed at his bare arms.

"I forgot something in the car." He held up a phone charger and stepped into the kitchen.

"Where's Emily?"

"In bed. Emily's head hit the pillow, and her eyes closed." He looked around. "Where's Cora?"

"I sent her home early." The room *was* hushed without Cora or the twins—no whistling kettle or the clamor of pots and pans. Occasionally, a guest lingered while getting a beverage or snack. "Where's your cousin?"

"Upstairs. She's changing into something more suitable before exploring the grounds." He waved a hand in the air.

The cuffs of his shirt hugged his forearms. The room was warmer since he entered.

Fiona reached across the sink and pushed on the window. It didn't budge.

Gavin cleared his throat and pointed to the latch.

"Cora must have locked the window." She shrugged. "Did you warn Adrian not to go inside the barn?"

"Ack. In case you didn't notice"—He shook his

head.—"No one tells Adrian what to do." He lifted the latch and opened the window.

"She definitely has a strong personality." Most days, Fiona had little contact with guests after breakfast. Hopefully, Adrian would come and go without much fanfare. "I…uh…thought she was lovely. I can tell she's very fond of you and Emily."

"You don't have to be polite." Gavin threw back his head and laughed. "When I don't see her for a while, even I have to adjust."

His laugh was contagious. "Every family has a difficult cousin." Talking and laughing with Gavin was easy. Hopefully, their friendship wouldn't change with Emily and Adrian here.

"She's really a good soul." He straddled a chair. "She was a lifesaver after I got custody of Em."

"Is Emily okay by herself?" She was more concerned for his daughter than his cousin.

"I'll watch her on the live video app." Gavin held up a phone. "Her phone is positioned on the bedside table."

"Isn't she too old for a baby app?" Fiona could only imagine how embarrassed a mature eight-year-old would be if she discovered Daddy allowed a stranger to see her sleeping. "Does she know you're watching her sleep?"

"Parents today have all kinds of apps to track their kids." He placed the phone on the table.

"You've got a point. Unfortunately, in today's world, apps like this are necessary." She released an exasperated sigh. "Raising someone else's children is an ongoing learn-as-you-go experience."

"Raising a biological kid is not any easier." He

stood, blew a slow breath, and walked toward the refrigerator. "Can I take a water?"

"You're a guest—help yourself." She pointed toward the refrigerator. Earlier, she forgot to explain the amenities. Meeting his family was a bit overwhelming. "Please tell Adrian the kitchen is open twenty-four hours. The twins and I take our meals in here. We're used to guests coming and going."

"What time should we be down for breakfast?" He unscrewed the cap and put the bottle to his lips.

His Adam's apple bobbed with each swallow. Her heart jolted. "Breakfast is served in the dining room at nine." She leaned back against the counter. "Sara and Simon eat a simple breakfast in here." She nodded at the kitchen table in the middle of the room. "Their breakfast is usually cold cereal or porridge and toast. Guests in the dining have more choices."

"Eating in the kitchen is more my style." He took another sip and rubbed the back of a hand across his mouth. "If you prefer, we eat with the other guests."

"Oh, no. You're more than welcome to eat in the kitchen." When he asked what time breakfast was served, she misunderstood why he was asking. After all, he wasn't just any guest. How many of her guests had kissed her—even for fun? "Sara and Simon will enjoy eating breakfast with you and Emily." Setting two or three places was easy enough. Explaining to Cora would be more difficult. "The twins are downstairs around seven thirty on school days. The school bus stops at the bottom of the road at eight fifteen."

"Don't fuss on my account. I'm not a big breakfast eater—toast and coffee are fine." He smiled. "I can serve myself. I even pour a mean bowl of cereal."

"Tossing a few extra slices of bread in the toaster is no bother." Having Gavin and the kids seated around the table like a family would be nice. She dismissed the image. They wouldn't be here forever. His reservation was only one week. "Do you plan on staying in Highland Falls long enough for Emily to attend school?"

"I'll register her on Monday. She'll have a few days to relax and see some of the town." He finished the water and tossed the empty bottle into a recycle bin.

When he spoke about his daughter, his expression was softer but still serious. "Weekends are less hectic. I don't do afternoon tea on Friday, Saturday, or Sunday. Sara and Simon sleep in and eat breakfast in front of the upstairs TV." She pointed toward the stairs leading to the apartment over the garage. "Do you think Emily would like to join them?" Did registering Emily in school mean he planned to stay awhile? After he found his aunt, what could keep him in Highland Falls? She had a few thoughts. Drawing a conclusion without knowing more about him wouldn't be fair.

"Tomorrow's Friday. Let's see how breakfast goes in the morning." He glanced at the phone on the table. "She might sleep late."

Behind Fiona, a wet, frosty gust blew in the window. "It's getting chilly." She rubbed her arms and turned to close the window.

Gavin reached from behind, right into her space, and shut the window.

Warm breath caressed her neck. For a second, she froze. Regaining her composure, she faced him.

His hand rested on the wall cabinet to her left.

A warm flush heated her cheeks. She turned. "How was your visit with Cappella? Was she helpful?"

"*Verra* resourceful." He pushed a stray hair off her face with a thumb.

"Did she have any leads?" She was hypnotized by the rapid rise and fall of his chest.

"Aye, she did." He sighed. "But...I have more to tell you about my aunt and the conservatory."

Was he about to tell her the family secret he kept so closely guarded? The sexy charm of his accent invited her to lean a cheek into his palm. What was she thinking? She exhaled, placed her palms on his chest, and nudged him away.

The door to the kitchen opened.

Gavin dropped his arm and stepped back.

"Am I interrupting?" Adrian walked into the kitchen.

"Gavin was about to tell me about his visit to Professor Cappella." Fiona glanced at Adrian and folded her arms across her chest.

"I'd like to hear what she had to say." Adrian walked toward the counter. "Is the coffee warm?" She glanced from Gavin to Fiona, didn't wait for an answer, and poured coffee into a mug.

Gavin joined Adrian at the counter with the coffeepot and whispered in Gaelic. A hint of anger resonated in his voice.

Adrian made a face and shook her head.

Not my business. Fiona prepared a tray with sugar and cream and observed them from the corner of her eye.

"Would you like a cup?" Gavin raised a mug in Fiona's direction.

"Just a half, please." Fiona had more than her share of caffeine at teatime.

"Got it." He filled one mug to the top, another halfway, and carried them to the table. He placed the phone in the center.

"Em's out like a light." Adrian turned the phone in her direction and glanced at the screen. "When will you tell me about your visit with the Professor...whatever her name is?"

"Carol Cappella." He stirred his coffee. "She was honest, intelligent, and generous with her information."

"*Carol Cappella* is a music professor?" Adrian giggled. "Is that really her name?"

Fiona crossed her arms and leaned back. The first time she met Cappella, she had the same reaction. Was Gavin taking it purposely slow to annoy his cousin?

"After speaking to Fiona's brother, Cappella enlisted students to help with the search." He smiled at Fiona. "One of her students verified Joan is alive and living in Brooklyn."

The cheerfulness and relief in his voice excited Fiona. Maybe she was wrong, thinking the land was more important than his aunt. "That's wonderful news." Joan was real—not just a picture on an album cover. Would this new information bring *everything* to light?

"You should call Granddad right away." Adrian reached for the phone and handed it to Gavin.

"Let's wait until we contact Joan." He glanced at the screen and slipped it into his pocket.

"Cappella can be like that. I met the professor at a faculty party with my brother and Sophia." Fiona finished her coffee and glanced at the clock. "I wish I had time to sit and chat. The twins' school bus will be at the bottom of the road in a few minutes." Adrian's dropped jaw was no surprise. When Gavin met Sara and Simon, he had a similar reaction. She'd let him explain.

****

The mudroom door slammed.

"If you could see the look on your face." Gavin chuckled.

"Twins?" Adrian raised her brows.

"She's guardian for her niece and nephew. They're adorable kids." The details were Fiona's story to tell.

"Okay…whatever. Her personal life is not my business. From what I've seen, she's an intelligent woman running a successful establishment." Adrian tapped her fingers on the table. "Do you honestly believe she has no idea who you are?"

"What does that have to do with anything?" The weight of Adrian's observation closed in on him. "She knows plenty about me."

"Everything except why you're hanging around." She tilted her head to the side, crossed her arms, and stared at Gavin. "Fiona has no idea about the family company, does she?"

"It's not what you think. Fiona's not the only one." His throat was dry. He reached for the coffee cup and emptied the contents. "The entire town doesn't receive strangers with open arms. At the moment, they're exceptionally accepting of me. I want to keep it that way."

"Why? When they discover why Granddad wants to find his sister, are you worried they'll like you less?" With an open palm, she gestured toward the window. "*Does* Joan own the conservatory you mentioned?"

"It's complicated." Gavin glanced out the window.

The top of Fiona's red hair disappeared around the bend.

"What if Aunt Joan has ill feelings toward the family?" Adrian sighed. "And when your fair Fiona discovers what the family's worth, how will she react?"

"I'm sure Fiona likes me enough to overlook my indiscretion." Gavin lied. Both of Adrian's concerns crossed his mind.

"Really. She doesn't seem like the type to be easily fooled by your handsome face and Scottish charm." Adrian walked toward the sink and placed her mug on the counter.

"Aren't you going to wash it?" He handed her a sponge.

"Wash it? Do I look like I work here?" She glanced at the sponge and placed the mug in the empty dishwasher. "Anyway, what's going on between you and Fiona?"

"She's a bonny lass. We've become friends." This was another subject he would have to set boundaries. "Fiona's interested in old wood, good whisky, and Highland games." He added a list of neutral interests to appease his cousin. *And I love how she flips her braid when upset, delicately sips her tea, and the Scottish lilt to her voice when we're alone.*

"Aye, right. I never met a woman happy just being *your* friend."

"Believe what you want. Neither of us has time for a romantic relationship." Gavin guided her out of the kitchen toward the stairs. He took the stairs two at a time.

"If she knows you're filthy rich, she could be playing along," Adrian said to his back.

At the top of the stairs, he turned. "Really. Have you added relationship counseling to your busy schedule?"

"Don't be a wise ass." She looked up from the step below.

"*Dinnae spraff* such nonsense. She's never given me a reason to believe such a thing." He tried to recall anything Fi may have said supporting Adrian's comment. *Nothing.* "She's a tidy lass and one of the kindest people I've ever met."

"I agree with her kindness. But as far as being interested in you, someone would have to be blind not to notice. I noticed you gave her a little *keek* when you thought she wasn't looking."

Her gaze challenged him to disagree. So Fiona *was* interested. He smiled, despite what Adrian thought about Fiona. "What's your issue with Fiona?"

"At tea, her questions were subtle. She was looking for answers to questions *you* left unanswered." Adrian stepped beside him. "Something you might have failed to mention about your role in the family business."

"Like what?" A few hours of his cousin's chatter were exhausting. He eyed the door to his room.

"Think what a drop of your money could do for this place?" She waved her hands in the air.

"I don't see anything needing improvement." He looked around and inhaled spicy fall scents. He had firsthand experience in the efficient workings of this delightful B and B—perfect housekeeping and generous smiles.

"Are you referring to the property or its proprietor?" she asked.

"You can't talk about one without the other.

Fiona's very aware of successful ways to engage her guests. You'll discover Fiona's congeniality in every crevice of the house. Her business model is not much different from SIREaC's. Look around." He waved a hand in the air. "She preserves local charm and supports the local businesses."

Adrian designed sustainable, sexy, high-end resorts on a much grander scale.

Fiona ran an elegant B and B in her charming way.

"I don't want you to make the same mistake again." Adrian shook her head.

"I appreciate your concern. But you're wrong about Fiona. How can she be a gold digger if she doesn't know I have gold?" Any relationship since his divorce was a personal affair. He stopped judging new relationships by past mistakes. Family members needed to stop butting in with their opinions.

"Then you need to tell her the truth. You shouldn't hide who you are. Letting her think she's getting involved with an ordinary bloke isn't right."

Adrian always stated her opinion in a lengthy dissertation. Gavin knew better than to interrupt her.

"I can tell you, she won't be happy if she finds out from someone other than you." She tapped his chest with an index finger.

"No worries. I planned to tell Fiona about the company and our interest in the conservatory, but you walked in." He didn't know how, but he'd find a way. "Leave it be." He walked down the hallway to his room.

"I will for now." Adrian followed close behind. "We've got more important things to discuss."

"Aren't you feeling a wee bit jet-lagged?" He let

out an exasperated sigh.

"We slept on the flight," she said. "You mentioned Joan's husband. Did you find out his surname?"

"Stewart, Paul Stewart. Why are you asking?" He stopped his hand above the door handle to his room.

"I'll send his name to our cousin, Logan." She removed a phone from a pocket and opened a text app.

"Logan's on an archeology dig in the Highlands?" He glanced over her shoulder and read the message.

"Yes, but he'll know who to contact about searching parish records," she said.

"Parish records?" Completely clueless about where she was going with this, Gavin couldn't escape until he heard her out. He crossed his arms over his chest and leaned against the wall, defeated.

"I read about ancestry searches on the plane." She confessed. "Do you know how popular it's become to discover Scottish roots?"

"Scots have been doing it for centuries—clan and family history are always important. I recently met a man who asked if I knew any McIvers from Glenurquhart."

"Glenurquhart?" Adrian shook her head. "I don't recall any McIvers from Glenurquhart."

"It's not important. I'm just making a point." Gavin had to get her back on track. Like it or not, he couldn't dismiss her. "Let's step inside and finish this chat."

"Don't you want to take advantage of your alone time and get some rest?" She followed him inside and sat in an over-stuffed chair by the window.

If she ever stopped talking, that's precisely what he would do. Although not as trying as an overseas flight, his day was mentally exhausting. Meeting Cappella and filtering through the information she gave him was tiring. But not as taxing as sitting through tea worried Adrian would reveal too much.

"Now that you've told me, Paul, Joan's husband, was a tinker, a Scottish Traveler, the search is more interesting." Adrian pointed toward the window. "Is this usual fall weather?"

"It's been cool and wet since I got here." He shook his head. "You're not here to talk about the weather."

"Giving you a break in the conversation." Adrian laughed.

"Say what's on your mind." Gavin placed his suitcase on the bed and removed a leather travel bag. On the ride here, he explained the sequence of events leading up to his meeting with Cappella—the antique barn, the photo album, even the *Trow* house. He smiled. How would Em react to the *Trows*?

"Something amusing you?" Adrian raised a brow.

"Just thinking of something that happened the other day." He shrugged. "Anyway, I doubt we'll learn much about the husband. A tinker was likely not in one place long enough to have a traceable history. Tinkers have their own customs about marriage, births, and deaths. Those occurrences won't be documented in parish records."

"I agree their customs won't be recorded." Adrian checked her phone. "However, payment for work might be documented in a register."

"You won't find a marriage certificate." He shook his head. "Cappella's word is enough for me to believe he married Joan."

"We don't know if Paul came here first. Joan could

have followed him, or maybe it was the other way around." She looked up from her phone and gazed at Gavin. "What if Mr. Stewart was escaping criminal charges?"

"So what? Paul and Joan built a life here," he said a bit too harshly. He shouldn't fault Adrian for asking questions. Her curious nature was why he asked her to come. "They were liked and protected by this community. The how or why they came here is unimportant in the endgame."

"Oh, I think why they came here is crucial to their story." Adrian sighed.

"Joan had the funds to travel anywhere. She could have bought Paul's ticket, too." Gavin nodded.

"Times were different." Adrian shook her head. "Her father, our great-grandfather, could've denied her account access."

Adrian wasn't buying his take on the story. "It's possible, but why look for complications that won't affect the outcome? I did what I came here to do. I found Aunt Joan." Gavin rubbed a hand through his hair. "Don't dig for problems."

"Where's your sense of romance and adventure?" She stood and walked into the adjoining room.

Was romance in his future? Gavin held his breath until Adrian shut the door between the rooms. That *was* the billion-dollar question.

Chapter 11

"What's today's weather forecast?" Fiona asked the smart device on the kitchen counter.

"The morning temperature is expected to be cold. Skies will be clear with no chance of precipitation. By the afternoon, a frosty northern wind will lower the temperature," the device replied.

Fiona removed a tray of freshly baked scones from the oven and placed them on the table in front of Gavin. The surface looked cramped with three extra settings and large serving platters.

"We'll never leave if you keep feeding us like this." Gavin buttered a scone and placed it on Simon's plate beside scrambled eggs. He did the same for Emily before taking one for himself.

"Thank you, Mr. Gavin." Simon smiled and stuffed eggs into a hole in the scone.

"Is your cousin sleeping late?" Fiona dished out the remaining eggs.

"Mr. Drummond picked her up for the first flight to the city. They have business to attend to." Gavin picked another scone from the tray.

"Will she contact your aunt?" She tucked a napkin into Simon's uniform collar. "Try and stay clean until you get on the bus."

"It's on the top of her list of things to do." Gavin bit into a scone.

"I have no doubt she'll make it happen," Fiona said. Adrian's whirlwind entrance and endless questions left a lasting impression.

"Can you join us?" Gavin stood and offered his chair.

"Not today." She glanced at the plates of crepe French toast, buttery scones, and fluffy scrambled eggs. Earlier, she ate a small crepe and gulped it down with a cup of tea before everyone came to breakfast. She agreed with Cora. Emily's first day at a new school deserved the same breakfast as all the guests.

Although enjoying a hearty breakfast, the twins would have been happy with a bowl of sweet, creamy porridge and a cup of cocoa.

"No problem. Maybe another day." He reached for the maple syrup.

The slight arch of his brow and tilt at the corner of his lips were so attractive and charming Fiona almost took him up on his offer. She ignored the butterflies whipping around her stomach. "I waited for a late arrival. Right now, they need a strong cup of coffee." She reached for the pot.

John Anderson and his wife weren't her average guests. John, her former employer, had encouraged her to pursue her dream. He recommended the inn to many affluent clients who came back every year.

"No worries. I'll see everyone stays neat and clean." He wiped a smear of butter off Simon's lip with his thumb.

"Good morning." Fiona entered the dining room and joined the Andersons at the beverage buffet.

"Good morning, dear." Nadine greeted Fiona with an air kiss on each cheek. "The coffee smells delicious." She poured a cup for her husband.

Fiona checked the buffet for an adequate supply of cream and sugar. A copy of *World Financial News* lay folded next to the creamer. When she came to Highland Falls, she stopped reading business periodicals. With all her money tied up in the B and B, she was no longer interested in the hottest investment. The bold type of center column caught her attention. *"SIREaC's COO Throws Shot Put."* SIREaC must be an important company to make the front page. A shot put competitor in the same headline couldn't be a coincidence. Fiona tilted her head to the side and read the smaller print.

Although the COO wasn't available for comment, this reporter observed Gavin James McIver is spending an unexplained amount of time in the upstate New York town of Highland Falls. Our sources in Scotland said a search for unclaimed family property could be why Mr. McIver extended his visit after participating in the Highland Games. A frequent competitor back home in Scotland, Gavin, won several competitions. Recently, he placed second at the Highland Falls Scottish games.

Yes, he did. An uncomfortable sensation vibrated in her ears. She swallowed, did a double take, and reread the first paragraph.

Mr. McIver is a big fan of restoring old buildings. He is on record as describing recycled wood as magical.

The dining room was usually her happy place. Not now—the print was spinning. Her world moved in slow motion. She blinked and tightened her grip around the coffeepot handle.

*Magical charm w*ere the words Gavin used. Minus a middle name, the shot put competitor had to be Gavin.

He not only worked for SIREaC—he was their Chief Operating Officer. She clenched her free hand. He understood every aspect of construction—from gathering prime material to getting the best out of each piece. Why shouldn't he? A good COO kept an eye out for ways to improve the company. Was he here to find the best location for a projected resort? If so, his primary reason for staying was likely in the company's interest—not Great-Aunt Joan's.

She skimmed over the town's highlights and the games. *With their success in opening rustic resorts in similar areas, this reporter wonders if the company targeted the Adirondacks for their next project.* His reason for staying was right before her—in undeniable print. "Mr. McIver," she said out loud.

The Andersons joined her and refilled their cups.

"Have you met him?" John reached for the paper. "This *is* a small town. If I remember correctly, you're on the board for the games."

"Yes, I met Mr. McIver on more than one occasion." Fiona forced a smile and uttered his name without hinting at the rage churning her insides.

"Is he as charming, honest, and open as people in the industry say?" John added cream to his cup. "I never heard a bad thing said about the man."

Honest, humph. "Definitely quite charming." A moment ago, his charm almost convinced her to ignore her responsibilities. Such a trait would take him far with business associates. Being honest and open helped, too. As their friendship moved forward, he shared bits about his past. He told her about his ex-wife, daughter, and estranged aunt. Fiona helped him find the lost conservatory. He mentioned family but avoided talking about the family business. *A very lucrative business.*

"His family company is renowned for their innovations in green development. When you worked for me, your specialty wasn't land and real estate. Still, you might have come across the name of the company." John rested a finger on the word *SIREaC*.

"It doesn't ring a bell." She had determined investment fund potential for stocks and derivatives, not real estate.

"No business talk." Nadine wrinkled her brow. "We're on vacation."

"Fiona's been away from the financial world for some time. She might like to catch up on the latest trends." John smiled. "A construction boom benefited the world's largest property design firms. SIREaC, a top-ten firm, increased its net worth by consolidating all the disciplines needed to complete a successful project. They do everything—constructions, real estate deals, and property management."

"What would you estimate a company like SIREaC is worth?" Despite the pounding in her ears, Fiona asked with an air of nonchalance. The blame wasn't only on Gavin. She had dismissed the signs of his wealth—a brand-new, high-end vehicle, first-class tickets for his daughter and cousin, even his generosity toward strangers. She refilled Nadine's coffee cup and waited for John's mental calculation of SIREaC's wealth.

"My estimated guess would be the McIver family owns a company with a net worth in the billions." John folded the paper and pushed it to the side.

"That's a considerable portfolio. If you met Gavin...Mr. McIver"—she cleared her throat and flipped her braid over her shoulder—"You'd never suspect he's worth so much."

"I'd love to meet him." John finished his coffee. "I see potential for a lucrative capital investment—if he's interested."

"I'll see what I can do." Fiona topped off his cup. John's hedge fund invested in anything that would make the firm money—land, real estate, stocks, derivatives, and currencies. As their CFO, she often viewed astronomical profiles. She never flinched. How could she tell John the billionaire was eating breakfast in her kitchen? An introduction would have to wait. Whatever her impression of Emily's father, she wouldn't ruin the child's first day at a new school.

A commotion in the main room drew her attention away from the article. The art professor staying in the Highland Room entered with a bag of art supplies slung over his arm. Insulated tumblers were tucked between the brushes and paint.

"Sorry for the disturbance." He leaned an easel against the wall and joined the Andersons.

"Professor Brown is a landscape painter." Fiona made the introductions. "He's doing a painting of the old barn." She sighed. The professor might be the last person to recreate the barn on canvas.

"I'm rushing to catch the morning sun behind the barn." The professor glanced out the window. "Do you mind if I fill my flask?" He adjusted the strap on his shoulder and reached for the coffeepot on the buffet.

"I'll get a fresh pot. Will you be back at nine for breakfast?" Fiona enjoyed accommodating her guests.

"Not this morning." He handed Fiona an insulated bottle.

"Don't leave yet. I'll bring you fresh coffee and scones." She turned toward the kitchen.

"Fiona, wait. Take the newspaper. I've read it all." John handed her the paper. "You might find another interesting article."

No matter how clever or informative, she doubted another article would have the same impact. "Thank you." She rolled the paper and placed it in the pocket of her apron. Could she enter the kitchen and act like nothing had happened? She inhaled deeply and kicked the door open.

"Everything okay?" Cora turned toward the door. She raised her brows and stared at Fiona.

"Yeah, everything's fine." Fiona walked toward the beverage counter in the far corner. "Professor Brown won't be at breakfast. Wrap up some scones. When the coffee's brewed, I'll fill his flask." She avoided looking at Gavin. She wouldn't let his charming smile or handsome face coerce her into believing the reporter was mistaken.

"What was all the commotion?" Cora raised a brow.

"The professor dropped some art supplies." Fiona turned her attention to the coffeepot. Cora knew her too well. No doubt, she sensed something happened. Behind her, Gavin and the kids laughed at something Simon said. Sitting at a table with three giddy kids, no one would suspect he was worth so much.

On the other hand, what did a billionaire look like? In her past life, she worked with many wealthy people. They ate breakfast, laughed, and drove their kids to school. So what if the car was a chauffeur-driven vehicle?

Gavin glanced over his shoulder and smiled.

She ignored an irrational urge to pour coffee over his head. Confronting him would have to wait. How did someone tell you they were filthy rich? He never bragged. His actions after losing to McCoy at the games were modest and unpresuming. His humble attitude was endearing.

Cora bagged two scones and handed them to Fiona. "What's that?" She pointed to the paper in Fiona's pocket. "When did you start reading financial news?"

"Oh, this. John thought I might like to browse through." She pulled the paper from her pocket and reached overhead to a shelf above the counter.

Gavin approached the counter.

His closeness startled her. The paper slipped from her hand.

"Let me help." He caught the paper midair and took a passing glance at the print. "Keeping up with world finances?"

"When I worked on Wall Street, I found their articles cleverly written." *Ha*. This piece on Gavin McIver was innovative prose at its best. The human-interest twist profiled the skill of a successful businessman and his ability to throw the shot. The writer cleverly combined Gavin's extended stay in a sleepy upstate New York town with a subtle suggestion of a new project.

"Is the coffee fresh?" Gavin pointed toward the half-filled pot.

"I made it earlier. I'm brewing a fresh pot," Fiona said politely with no joy or affection. Hurt boiled through her, jagged and painful.

"If you're done reading the paper, I'd like to read

it. I haven't read anything but local news since I came here." He glanced at a stack of local papers on a tray in the corner. "I'm not saying local news isn't interesting."

"I read everything I needed to." She couldn't think of a valid reason to deny his request.

"Simon's amusing Emily with silly stories about school. She might have a crush on him." Gavin placed a hand on Fiona's back and leaned close. "The lad's got the Scottish gift for storytelling."

Fiona's muscles tensed beneath his hand. "A good Scottish lass knows how to listen to a man's stories— whether she believes them or not." Her reply came out harsh. None of this was the little girl's fault. She swallowed past the lump in her throat. "I'm glad she'll have a friend at school."

"Thanks for suggesting we have breakfast with the twins." He squeezed her elbow.

She managed a curt nod and pulled away.

"What's bothering you, lass? Did the professor mess up the dining room?" Gavin rubbed a hand through his hair. "I'll help clean up."

"Everything's under control." Accommodating offers and tender gestures didn't soften her mood.

Gavin returned to the table.

She stepped to the side and paced along the counter while she waited for the hissing coffeemaker to release its last drops into the carafe. The calming smell of fresh brew did little to settle her scorching anger.

The coffee machine gurgled.

"Let me pour *you* a cup." Cora reached for the pot and filled a mug. "You look like you could use some liquid comfort." She handed the mug to Fiona. "I'll see to our guests. When breakfast's finished, you should walk the kids to the bus. Fresh air will do you good."

"I'd rather spend time with John and Nadine Anderson before they go out for the day. I might not have another chance to catch up." Fiona glanced toward the table.

Sara smiled over the rim of a hot cocoa cup.

Simon stuffed a forkful of crepe into his mouth.

"Can you walk the kids to the bus?" She reached for an apron. "The Andersons and Professor Brown are leaving early. When they leave, I'll set the breakfast tables for the remaining guests."

"You sure?" Cora raised a brow and untied her apron. "The breakfast crepes are in the warming drawer."

Fiona loaded a tray with bags of scones and a fresh carafe of coffee. She passed the kitchen table on her way to the dining room without glancing at anyone.

"Can you spare a minute and join us before we leave? I'm driving Emily on her first day." Gavin stood and pulled out a chair.

"Maybe tomorrow." Fiona avoided Gavin's gaze and smiled at Emily. She stopped at the table. "Have fun in your new school. When you get home, you can tell me about your day." Fiona returned to the dining room, filled the professor's flask, and helped him carry his supplies outside. She waited while he set up an easel a safe distance from the barn. "If you need more coffee, come in and help yourself." She handed him the bag of scones and walked around to the mudroom entrance. *All good in here—no forgotten backpacks or gloves.*

The kitchen was neat and clean except for smudges on the table.

She grabbed a wet sponge from the sink and wrung

out the water.

The newspaper was neatly folded into quarter sections on the table with the article front and center.

She was sure Gavin had read it. What else could be responsible for abstract coffee splashes across the page? She had witnessed his steady hand and a purposely, miscalculated shot put throw—testimony to his fast accuracy. He handled a delicate teacup with the best of her tea ladies. Had the article surprised him, causing him to put down the cup with a vigor that blotted the words? He knew she read it, too. *So what will you do, Mr. McIver? There's no way your usually evasive charm will get you out of this.* She tossed the sponge across the room. The sponge landed dead center in the sink.

"Something's upsetting you." Cora entered with a laundry basket and glanced at the newspaper.

"You read the article?" Fiona tossed her braid over her shoulder

"Of course, I read it." Cora shrugged.

"And…" Fiona shifted impatiently.

"I've got plenty to say." Cora glanced at the clock. "Breakfast is in twenty minutes. You're in no state to mingle with guests. Go for a walk and cool down. I've got everything covered." She handed Fiona a set of headphones. "We'll talk later."

Fiona pulled her braid through a hole in a beanie, turned on her headphones, and headed toward the main road. Across the road, a well-placed sign marked a trail leading to the foothills. She looked left and right. The road was clear.

Out of nowhere, a white SUV screeched to a halt.

She immediately recognized the car. Not many

people around here drove such a high-end vehicle. She jumped back. "Darn." A branch caught the hem of her jacket.

"Fiona. We have to talk." Gavin's hands clutched the steering wheel.

"Not now." Earlier, when she looked into those piercing blue eyes, she was happy. The pleasure was long gone.

Now, his gaze narrowed.

A face-to-face confrontation before she gathered her thoughts would not go well. What explanation would he offer? Would he tell the truth about why he was here and what he was looking for? She worked her jacket free of the branch and rushed across the road.

Gavin backed up. "Where you off to, lass?" he shouted.

"I'm taking a hike." Surprised at how calm and composed the words were, she continued walking.

"Mind if I join you?" He stepped from the vehicle and slammed the door.

"It's a public trail," she retorted over her shoulder. *So, I'm not composed.* She glanced at Gavin's expensive shoes, *Italian, of course*, and hoped he might reconsider following her. No such luck. Behind her, leaves crunched under heavy, determined footsteps. She pivoted on her heels and almost collided with him.

Gavin placed both hands on her shoulders. "Are you trying to get away from me?" His brow creased.

"I need some alone time." She blew out a long breath to calm her prickly mood. Long, bare branches extended over the sides of the path. The trail, even when in full bloom, never seemed so narrow. She inhaled the fatty caramelized scent of a pancake restaurant lingering on his breath. She wanted to lean in and let the syrupy flavor on his lips help her forget what she had read this morning. The enormity of the details flashed through her mind. Every sensor in her brain sent out a warning. "What are you doing here? Don't you have some property you need to check out?" If she had the article in her hand, she'd flash it in his face and demand he explain everything the writer insinuated.

"I settled Em in her new class and came back to explain. You were gone." He shook his head. "Cora told me where to find you."

"Did things go well at school?" If she wasn't so angry, she might feel sorry for him. Obviously, he never apologized for who he was.

"Everything was perfect. I'm not here to talk about Emily." He ran a hand over his hair.

"It's better to start with the easier questions." She shot him a look and shrugged his hands off her shoulders.

"And—the other questions?" He placed a hand on her arm.

"Can you walk and talk?" She glanced over her shoulder and pulled away. For a brief moment, she wanted to return to the first time she met him in the leaky barn. Despite the weather, the morning was magical. From that day on, he wove his way into her life. A friendship slowly grew into something more. Was it only one-sided? Maybe he only saw their relationship as a passing friendship.

Today, some unknown reporter shattered everything.

"I'd rather talk face to face than to your back." He stepped closer. A bare branch missed his head by inches. He reached overhead, snapped off the dead wood, and tossed it to the ground.

"There's a bench up ahead. We can sit and talk." She knew business deals were better done face to face. In the end, business was about beating your competitor. She glanced back. The man behind her was the Gavin she loved, not a competitor.

"Let's follow the trail for a while," he suggested.

He was right.

Walking would clear her head. At a bend in the path, she bit back a smile and waited as he came around the curve. He always looked ruggedly well-groomed. Today, he took special care to make a good impression on Emily's new teacher and school officials. She noticed how his dark grey trousers were pressed to perfection and how a blue sweater—*cashmere, of course*—enhanced the depths of his eyes. "Are you ready to sit and talk?" She pointed a gloved hand toward a stone bench along the path.

"Wait." He removed a cinnamon-colored scarf from around his neck and placed it on the bench.

She removed a glove and ran a hand over the scarf. The fabric felt softer than cashmere—cloud-like, expensive, and warm. "I can't sit on this." She handed him the scarf and sat on the cold bench. She patted the bench. "Have a seat. I don't want to be the only one with a cold bottom. It's getting chilly. If you stay out here, wear the scarf and close your jacket." She adjusted her collar against an unexpected gust.

"The scarf's a gift from Adrian. She's a big fan of vicuña accessories." He draped the scarf around his neck. "Vicuña are llama-like animals from the Andes."

"I know what the scarf is made of." She rolled her

eyes and slipped her glove back on. "You're seriously explaining the origins of your obscenely expensive scarf instead of discussing the article that exposed your billion-dollar secret." The scarf, an outrageous extravagance, indicated how far apart their worlds were. He sure had her fooled. Being a single parent and sharing experiences with a man who lived paycheck to paycheck was different from being a billionaire daddy.

"Like I said, the scarf was a gift. I don't indulge in such lavish items." He straddled the bench and faced her.

"Why weren't you upfront about your family's business from the beginning?" She needed the truth—about everything. She met his gaze. "Were you afraid I would fall in love with you for the money?"

"Did you"—He reached for her hand and gazed at her face—"fall in love?"

His fingers caressed the back of her glove.

"You deceived me." Fiona pulled away and slid to the far end of the bench. "I'm trying hard to dislike you." She was never attracted to a man the way she was to Gavin. She couldn't lose focus.

"Is it working?" He wiggled his brows.

"Not very well." She shut her eyes and listened to the sounds of the woods. Her heartbeat slowed. She opened her eyes. "I can't talk about that now...maybe never—not if I don't know who you are."

"I'm guessing a sincere *I'm sorry* is not what you're looking for," he said tentatively.

"I want answers, not hard feelings." She clasped her hands in her lap.

"Everything I told you is true." He drew in a breath and released it. "What I failed to tell you is upsetting you."

"At least we're on the same page." She almost laughed out loud. If she hadn't read the newspaper article, they wouldn't be here discussing this. She'd have to find the reporter and thank him. "That day in the barn, you asked me if I understood the saying, *Ti fell twa dugs wi the ae stane.* You were here for two reasons —to participate in the games and find your aunt." She learned a lot about the kind of man he was on the day of the competition. He was more than brawn. He was humble, confident, and kind. From the beginning, she sensed he was hiding something. And yet, he was open and honest about his relationship with his ex and daughter.

"Do you remember what I said?" He heaved another weary sigh.

She nodded. She remembered everything about that morning. "It makes perfect sense now. Your aunt and *her* property were more than finding a long-lost relative." She believed he was someone entirely different. How could she have been so blind?

"I had planned to come here for the games before I even knew Granddad had a sister." He shrugged. "I read about Highland Falls in an international real estate magazine and wanted to see what the town was all about."

His daft explanation made her muscles quiver. "How convenient your grandfather suddenly mentioned his sister and the chance she might own a piece of land." She stood, swallowed hard, and clenched her fists at her side. "Why *did* Adrian go see Joan today? Are you hoping Joan is kind and forgiving enough to make amends with your grandfather?" Her breath burned in her throat. "Your search for a perfect property could be over. With a little work, the conservatory structure could be the base of a new SIREaC resort."

"You've come up with a pretty good story for someone who doesn't believe in fairy tales. Memories run long in Scottish families. Historically, Scottish feuds are relentless." Gavin rubbed a hand on the back of his neck. "In Joan's case, other complications have come into play."

"Skip the history lesson. I've heard it all before." She met his penetrating glare. "Hypothetically, let's say it all works out with your aunt. What other variables are there? Give me your top three."

****

Was she kidding? His biggest hiccup was right in front of him. He stood and walked a few steps away. Rethinking how to handle the situation, he turned. He noted her clenched hands and dark, unforgiving expression. "Aunt Joan and her property are the least of my problems." He had to convince her he wasn't a competitor. He didn't want to steal Fiona's business—only her heart.

"As much as I enjoyed helping you find your aunt, how you resolve it is your family's problem. However, your plan to build a resort is a big problem for everyone in Highland Falls." She waved her hands in the air.

"There's plenty of business for everyone." Too late, he regretted the comment. What he said was out of character—something an unsympathetic businessman would say.

"How does that work out?" She folded her arms across her chest. "I'll run my cozy little B and B, and you'll run the competition? My success is my ability to maintain a high-end clientele—like the one you'll cater to. You'd have a staff of dozens of workers. At the inn, it's just Cora, *me*"—with an index finger, she thumped her chest—"and an occasional seasonal employee."

"I never lied about my interest in this area for a project. My family only speculated about the possibilities of building a resort on property Aunt Joan might own."

"When I met you, I assumed you were considering building a house out of reclaimed wood. Instead, you planned to build a bloody resort to compete with my B and B and other local accommodations." She stepped away.

Maybe following her wasn't such a good idea. But he needed to clear the air now, not tomorrow or the day after. A flaming flash of red hair swirled in front of his face. He drew in a slow, steady breath and reached for her arm. "SIREaC never puts locals out of business."

"Am I supposed to believe your family got rich by being kind to the competition?" She shook her head and sighed.

Her words cut through him like a dull knife. His early ancestors had no scruples about the way they did business. Today, every McIver earned their position by literally digging their way up. Would she believe him if he told her Cappella's suggestion to find investors to rebuild a conservatory was an excellent idea?

"You didn't think I'd find out you're not the average construction guy living paycheck to paycheck." She pulled away and hugged her arms close to her body.

"I told you my family owned the business the first day we met." He disliked seeing her upset.

"You just failed to mention it wasn't a run-of-the-mill family business." An angry retort hardened her features.

"Now my family's interests are out in the open. None of this should affect how *we* move forward." He was wrong to be evasive and avoid her questions. *Why the hell didn't I tell her?*

"But it will matter. I am my B and B. You swallow businesses like mine with your afternoon tea. We're worlds apart. You're SIREaC, a company with a net worth in the billions. You're the only person I know who wears such an expensive scarf." She pointed toward his neck with a gloved palm. "I put everything I earned into building my business."

She sounded more frustrated than angry. He stepped back. "How do you know what I'm worth?"

"It's not because *you* told me." She smothered a sob. "I borrowed the paper from one of my guests. John Anderson is the head of a very profitable hedge fund. He knows things like that."

"What if I told you I dislike seeing my name in print?" He desperately wanted her to believe he wanted to be a paycheck-to-paycheck guy. Most of the time, he kept his activities low-key. Occasionally, something like his participation in the games caught the interest of an energetic reporter. Usually, such articles never got much notice. Of all people, Fiona read the article. He'd have to be completely transparent to make things right and rebuild her trust.

"That doesn't change who or what you are," she whispered.

"Who is it you think I am?" He ran a hand through his hair. Coming here and meeting Fiona and the twins was life-changing. To save their relationship, he'd willingly confront family expectations and deal with the consequences.

"The COO of a major international development company with your eye on *my* town. I bet your family owns half of Scotland—if not the world." She walked back and forth in front of the bench.

"Not quite half of Scotland and nowhere near that much of the world." He corrected her with a laugh. "Can I ask a question?"

"Go for it." She stopped pacing and quirked an eyebrow.

He hid a smile. Her attitude went from hot to cold in a split second. "What would you have thought if I walked into your barn and introduced myself as Gavin McIver, Jack's billionaire friend?" He remembered his first impression of fiery Fiona with her knowledge of old wood and her understanding of Granny's Scottish sayings. He fell in love with the unpredictable redhead on the spot.

"Don't bring Jack into this." She slipped her gloved hands into her pockets "I would have thought you were a raving lunatic."

"But you didn't, did you?"

The wind picked up.

He adjusted the scarf. Damn. He'd never wear the scarf again.

"Aye," she whispered.

He barely heard her above the creaking branches. "I'm still the same man you met that day. A bloke who likes to work with his hands and build things." He showed her his callused palms.

"Yeah, right." She shrugged.

Her face spoke volumes. She had every right to feel the way she did. This was an excellent time to follow Granny's advice. *Tha sàmhchair òir*—silence is golden and sweet. He respected Fiona's silence. He didn't want to lose her and would try his best to make things better.

Fiona looked past him over the trees. "The money doesn't mean anything. I worked for people with portfolios that could buy out your company. What bothers me is how you deceived everyone after the games."

He replayed how events unfolded and felt a twinge of guilt. "I liked being accepted as an equal. I never intended to deceive anyone with an underhanded plan." *Especially Fiona.* He didn't even know she existed until he walked into the barn.

"We better be getting back." She shaded her eyes from the sun. "Today's a teacher planning day and early dismissal. The kids will be home soon."

Was it an excuse to leave? Mabel and Cora could handle early dismissal. "Can I give you a lift?" The way she said *the kids* touched him.

"No thanks. I need to walk." She crossed the street toward a hidden path in the shrubbery.

"I'll walk with you." Could they move forward from here? If he found a way to tear down the wall Fiona put up, the next obstacle might not be so easy to resolve. Residents of Highland Falls didn't take kindly to strangers, especially developers. He desperately wanted to tell her about Cappella's suggestion for the conservatory. But everything was up in the air until Adrian contacted Aunt Joan.

"What about your car?" Fiona glanced over her

shoulder.

"I'll pick it up later." He watched the gentle sway of her hips and smiled. Where would she stand at a town meeting determining the fate of Joan's property? He wanted her at his side, not across the aisle challenging him.

Chapter 12

"Good morning." Fiona followed the twins down the stairs to the kitchen. At the bottom step, she glanced around the kitchen.

Gavin and Emily were already seated.

She tossed her braid and forced a smile. Yesterday's revelation would not dictate her mood today. A pungent smell of burnt toast greeted her as she walked toward the counter. She glanced at the smoking toaster.

Sara and Simon raced toward the table.

"Sorry about the toast." Gavin fanned the air with a napkin. "When I made Emily's toast, I set the heat too high. Cora rescued me. She turned out perfect slices in the toaster oven." He pointed to a plate stacked high with more bread than they needed. "Here, mate." He handed Simon a perfectly browned and buttered piece.

Simon bit into the bread and smiled.

"No worries." Cora opened the window. "All we need is some fresh air." She nudged a serving cart out of her way. The wheels didn't budge. "Something's stuck."

"Let me take a look." Gavin reached out, gripped the handle, and pushed hard.

The cart rolled forward with a loud squeal.

Simon dropped the toast and covered his ears. From the day he arrived, he was sensitive to offensive sounds.

"Simon doesn't like the noise." Sara put her hands over her brother's ears.

Fiona avoided Gavin's glance. "No worries. I won't use the silly old cart today." Any disturbance, big or small, could offset Simon's day. "Did you pack headphones in your backpack?" She quickly learned how to deal with Simon's sensory processing issues.

A pediatrician offered tips to avoid similar episodes. He suggested warning Simon whenever a toilet flushed or a hand dryer was used in a public bathroom.

"I'll get his headphones." Sara ran to the mudroom.

Gavin joined Fiona at Simon's side. "You've got this, mate." He took the headphones and placed them over Simon's ears. "A bit of oil on the wheels should fix the problem."

A fresh, showered scent of spicy soap invaded Fiona's space. Gavin wasn't the type to ignore a distressed lady or child needing comfort. No matter her feelings toward him now—soft spots in a hard man were difficult to ignore. He had sent her world spiraling into resentment. She was torn between anger and wanting to forgive his error in judgment. A heavy burden of a grudge weighed on her sensibility. She tried to give him a wide berth, but being in the kitchen for breakfast was unavoidable.

"I can have it fixed for you to serve breakfast in the dining room." He smiled.

"No need. Tim will be here soon. He's adding shelves in the mudroom. He'll check the cart, too," she said tartly.

"I'm sure he'll fix it fine." Gavin glanced at the

clock. "Let's get moving." He wiped toast crumbs off Simon's face and ushered him out the door.

Her sharp dismissal was unwarranted. The twins followed his directions without question. She was surprised at how easily he took the role.

"Maybe you should set up for breakfast—now." Cora handed Fiona a tray with fruit tarts. "I suggest four tables of two and one table for three."

"I already set up the buffet for early risers." Fiona reached for the tray. She regretted being so unpleasant.

"See everyone later." Cora smiled as the little group rushed out the door. She turned and glanced at Fiona. Her lips pressed tight.

"I admit my behavior was inexcusable." Fiona left the room.

"*Hmph.*" Cora sighed.

The door shut behind Fiona. She'd be better off staying out of everyone's way today. She couldn't force a casual conversation with Gavin or watch Cora look at her with pity. She didn't have time to dwell on the matter. Several guests were already seated, drinking coffee and tea. She greeted them with her usual conversation starter. "What are your plans for today?" She half listened to their responses as she walked between the tables and offered a choice of pastry and a note explaining the psychology behind each tart choice.

The stairs to the guestrooms creaked.

Was Gavin back? She couldn't hide in the dining room and returned to the kitchen.

A fresh brew replaced the burnt smell.

"I started a pot of coffee and turned on the kettle." Cora hung a clean towel on the rack.

"Did everyone get off okay?" Fiona glanced

around the kitchen. No backpacks or lunch bags were left behind. She licked a raspberry smear off her index finger, turned on the faucet, and washed her hands.

"Without a problem." Gavin stood in the doorway between the mudroom and kitchen.

"Back so soon?" She grabbed a towel and dried her hands.

"It's a short walk." Gavin shrugged.

"I'll go strip the beds." Cora tossed a dirty towel into a basket in the corner.

"I've got…" Fiona tried to object.

But Cora was out the door.

The kitchen was quiet except for the hum of the water heater. She shut off the faucet. The buzz subsided. A steady *plink, plink* took its place.

Gavin walked toward the sink. He reached for the faucet handle

Callused fingers gently brushed Fiona's hand. A familiar tingle ran the length of her arm. She pulled away and hugged her arms around her waist. Regardless of what happened, Gavin was still a paying customer. "Do you have plans for today?"

"I'm house hunting." He reached for a mug.

"House hunting?" *Of course, he was.* Only last week, she wanted him to extend his stay. Now, being under the same roof was uncomfortable.

"I found a promising rental property in town." He lifted the coffeepot and hesitated. "Would you like to come along?"

"I've got a large group scheduled for afternoon tea." Fiona reached for the teapot and filled an empty cup. The menthol scent of fresh peppermint rose above the cup.

"Business before pleasure." He smiled.

He was trying. She'd give him that much. "I know the house you're referring to."

"You do?" Gavin raised a brow.

"It's perfect for your needs." Feigning no show of interest, she sipped cold tea. She poured the last drop into the sink and plugged in the kettle. The decision to move into a house with his daughter was logical.

"This is a small town. Eventually, I hear what's happening in the area." She leaned back against the counter and waited for the water to boil. "Everyone in Highland Falls knows about the house. The elderly owners winter in Florida. They successfully list on an online marketplace for ski season. This year, they headed south sooner." She unplugged the whistling kettle, filled her cup, and tossed the teabag into the sink. "The house is nice but small. Is Adrian moving in with you?"

"No, Adrian won't be living with us." Gavin carried his empty mug to the sink. "She's moving to Manhattan in a couple of days. The city is more her style."

No argument there. She walked to the table and sat. Over the rim of her cup, she watched Gavin add soap to the mug. Tiny bubbles floated above the sink. Why must he be so damn handsome, charming, and kind? She smiled despite her anger. And she was still interested in Joan's story. "Has Adrian met your aunt?"

"Aye, she did." His voice faded.

Her curiosity was piqued. She had chores but would spare a few minutes. Joan's situation had little to do with whether or not Gavin succeeded in getting permission to build on the conservatory property. If

Aunt Joan refused, then Gavin could still search nearby counties. Would Highland Falls escape developers this time?

"Joan's a McIver, all right. She's as stubborn as they come. The reunion was very emotional." He dried the mug with a clean cloth.

"Did you expect less after all these years?" She blew on the tea. "Did the rest of the meeting go well?"

"The mention of Granddad almost ended their meeting." He folded the dishtowel and leaned against the counter with crossed arms. "Joan won't agree to anything unless he'll meet her face to face."

"I'm not surprised. What did your family think would happen?" Joan might welcome a connection to her great-niece and nephew. However, her brother, their contentious granddad, was another story. "Is she healthy enough to fly to Scotland?" Would going home after all these years help Joan forgive?

"She made it clear: Granddad's the one who would have to come here." Gavin shook his head.

"I see the problem. If your grandfather agrees, the meeting should occur on neutral territory." Fiona knew all the stories of Scottish clans' long history of fighting against family to gain reputation, wealth, or territory. The means to achieve these goals often resulted in years of deceit and betrayal between clans. She wasn't sure who would win the modern-day version of such a dispute—Great-Aunt Joan or Granddad McIver?

"Even if both parties agreed, I'm at a loss for a neutral location." Gavin held up open palms. "We own several real estate properties in Manhattan. I don't think Aunt Joan would consider any of them neutral."

"Does the meeting have to be in the city?" Fiona

warned herself not to get involved in his affairs, but the reunion wasn't business. Did he realize Joan offered an olive branch? All Joan needed was a concession. She studied his face. Would she be as forgiving as Joan?

"Adrian offered to fly her up here on the company jet. Aunt Joan refused." Gavin shook his head. "She's never been on a plane and has no intention of starting now."

"Why am I not surprised there's a company jet." Fiona found the absurdity of his wealth amusing.

"It's a convenience." Gavin shrugged.

"A cell phone is a convenience. A jet is a luxury," Fiona retorted. Aunt Joan's problem had nothing to do with flying and everything to do with her affluent family. After all, she walked away from the McIver wealth decades ago.

"What do you suggest?" He showed his open palms.

"I see a simple solution." Fiona was strangely flattered by his need for her advice. She leaned back in the chair and tilted her head toward him with a sly smile. "I'm sure a company like SIREaC has a fleet of vehicles and chauffeurs at their disposal. Why not offer to drive her to Highland Falls? The drive is not so bad. I've done it in about three-and-a-half hours."

"That might work." His brows gathered in. "I'd like Joan to see the conservatory."

No doubt he was up to the challenge. "Problem solved." Fiona looked away, avoiding the extraordinary blaze of his eyes.

"Not quite. You've never met Granddad." He shook his head.

"Good luck with that. My granny always said no

one holds a grudge like a Scot. You've heard the saying—forgive your enemies." She was unsure she should be broaching the subject of forgiveness so soon.

"But remember their names." He scrubbed a hand over his face.

The gesture showed regret. She wasn't referring to Gavin—or was she? Except for a few billion dollars, he wasn't so different from her. She finished her tea and carried the cup and saucer to the sink. "Granny had neighbors she forgave for killing her prize roses. She never fails to mention those miserable Armstrongs every time she passes a rose bush. Granny has forgiven but never forgot," she whispered.

"Where do you stand, lass? Are you as forgiving as your grandmother?" He stepped aside as she approached.

The spicy scent of his aftershave upset her balance. She watched the delicate cup slide to the edge of the saucer and reached for it with her free hand.

Gavin rescued it midair.

The gentle touch of his fingers jarred her memory and sparked a simple pleasure. She took a breath. "*Phew.*" Rational thoughts rushed in. "The grudge sounds petty now but started from a genuine hurt—a wrongdoing on the part of someone Granny cared for." She wanted him to understand what the damage his oversight, intentional or not, had done.

"So, she forgave them?" He gazed at her face and waited.

"She did." She looked away and turned on the faucet. "Forgiving is said to be good for the soul." Fiona temporarily released her bottled-up feeling. Her words were in no way a pardon. Relationships were built on trust and honesty. Gavin violated both.

"'Tis a very wise and honest saying." Gavin grinned. "It's not your granny's forgiving nature I want to hear about." He rubbed the back of his neck. "Can *you* forgive me?"

She turned her attention to the sink. Running water filled the cup. With a soapy pad, she scrubbed harder than needed. When the tea stain disappeared, she shut the faucet and turned toward Gavin.

"Can I take your silence to mean you're considering my apology?" He handed her a dishtowel.

"You had a billion chances to tell me." She glanced at a tea set on the counter. The cup and saucer were part of a set with a beautiful teapot belonging to her great-grandmother. When she first moved here, the pot slipped from her hand and shattered on the floor. She tried to repair the fractured pot. The pieces never fit right. Her heartbreak wasn't as tangible as a broken teapot.

"What can I do to fix everything?"

He asked without any rationalizations, excuses, or justifications for his behavior. He tried his best to make amends. If she didn't still want him in her life, the heavy strain of disappointment wouldn't exist. She could just walk away but didn't want to. "You're a resourceful person. I'm sure you'll find a way." Not enough time had passed to forgive him completely. Emotion still ruled her thinking. Even with high stakes, she'd offer him the opportunity to redeem himself. In the end, it could lead to a stronger relationship.

"Give me a chance." He smiled. "We'll work on the forgetting part later."

Everything he said screamed, please forgive me.

She answered with a tilted nod. "Did Adrian say Joan has forgiven your grandfather?" She already suspected how he would answer.

"Forgiven?" Gavin shrugged. "Adrian didn't say if Joan was forgiving the family." He scrubbed a hand over his face. "Maybe Adrian didn't go about it in the right way. I should have made the first contact. At times, Adrian can be a wee bit abrasive."

Did the burden of being estranged from her family still weigh on Joan? She had many years to think about her decision to part ways. "When *you* meet Joan, your charming constraint will amend any misunderstanding." His subtle charm was one of the qualities that first attracted Fiona.

"I have more than the average share of stubborn Scottish women to deal with."

His fingers fluttered to her neck where loose ends escaped her braid. Would Gavin kiss her? She cleared her throat, pretending not to be affected. "And we lasses have our share of proud Highlanders to contend with."

"Aye, but your arsenals are mighty powerful." He flashed a crooked smile and left the kitchen.

She sighed and sank into a chair. She'd never met his aunt but would bet she could learn a lot from the old girl. Joan didn't seem the type to succumb to a charming smile or money. *Good on ya, Aunt Joan.* If Fiona had to choose sides—it would be Aunt Joan's.

"Don't leave on my account, mate." Tim passed Gavin as he came in through the mudroom door.

"Catch you later," Gavin said.

"Hi, Fi. I didn't interrupt anything important, did I?" Tim pointed over his shoulder. "Is he upset about something?"

"I guess." Fiona shrugged. "What's that?" She nodded at the bakery box in his hand. A folded newspaper rested on top.

"I ran into Sophia at the hardware store. She asked me to deliver your cookie order and this." He placed the box and a copy of the *World Financial News* on the table. "Mr. Paisley from the museum left it at her shop." Tim swiped a hand through his hair. "Never in a million years would I have ever imagined Gavin was worth so much. He seemed like one of the guys."

"Yes, he did. Just a regular guy trying to make a living—no pretense or highfalutin' attitude." Fiona stood and tossed the paper into the trash. "I've seen the article." No doubt, Tim and half the town have read the article by now. "I've got too much work to waste time talking about Gavin McIver."

"Yeah. No problem. Show me where you want those shelves." He walked back through the mudroom door.

"A small window on the back wall doesn't let in much light for herbs." She picked up a basket of soiled linen and towels and followed. Thankfully, the subject of Gavin McIver was over.

"I'll hang some LED lights to simulate daylight." Tim pointed toward the ceiling. "When we redesigned this space, we found a good support beam up there."

"Sounds great." She emptied the basket into the washer and set the dials. "Can I make you a cup of tea?"

"I'd appreciate a cookie or two," Tim shouted at her back.

"When you finish the shelves, come to the kitchen.

I've got a squeaky cart for you to check." Fiona returned to the thankless chore of washing floors.

An hour later, Tim joined Fi for a cup of mint tea, lavender shortbread, and all the town gossip she cared to hear. "Any news about Walter's barn?" She concentrated on untying the red- and-white string on the bakery box. The buttery scent of just-baked shortbread escaped into the air.

"A barn builder from North Carolina is interested in the stones and wood planks." Tim reached for a cookie. "It seems Gavin and the Drummonds got wind of the deal and made an offer for all the materials. Their offer includes tearing down the barn and removing and storing the wood and bricks."

"I'm sad for Walter." For months, she tried to devise something to save her old barn. Ultimately, demolition was the only solution. "Did the family accept the offer from Gavin and the Drummonds?" She sipped her tea. The taste was unpleasant after Tim's news. She walked to the sink and poured the tea down the drain. A few stones in her new barn would be a nice touch and a tribute to Walter's family. She sighed. Bidding against Gavin was out of her league.

"Nothing definite yet." Tim finished a cookie in two bites and gazed at the box.

"Any idea why Gavin and Jack made a bid together?" She handed him another shortbread.

"Gavin has the money. But Jack knows the locals." Tim chewed and swallowed. "Walter's family wants to preserve the history of the area. They want their Adirondack stone used locally." He raised his brows. "Don't you agree?"

"If possible, I'd prefer only to use restored wood or

piece of paper with creases that wouldn't smooth. Wrinkled eyelids, wrinkled sheets, and wrinkled feelings—that was Fiona since Gavin left. She listened at the door to the bedroom the twins shared. The room was quiet. She showered, dressed, and returned to the kitchen with a better frame of mind.

Cora walked through the door to the kitchen with a clean stack of towels. "You look much better." She placed the towels on the counter, poured two cups of coffee, and handed one to Fiona. "Mabel's excited about the new exhibit, too."

"Ian, his students, and Mr. Paisley worked hard." Fiona inhaled the freshly brewed scent and shrugged off the idea Cora was hiding something. On the outside, everything appeared normal. "It's kind of a hands-on whodunit show. Visitors dig for bones and follow a simple path that helps them identify the time, place, and profession of the person to whom the bones belonged." She glanced over her shoulder at the whiteboard. "He's taking the twins to a soft opening today." She pointed toward the bread. "Is it cool enough to slice?"

"Hmm…Just-baked bread and fresh coffee—can you think of a better way to start your day?" Cora carried a loaf to the table and set it on a plate in the middle.

Fiona removed a tub of cinnamon butter from the refrigerator. She put a dab on a plate, broke off a piece of bread, closed her eyes, and savored the first bite of the buttered bread.

"Good, isn't it?" Cora grinned.

"The best." Fiona inhaled the lingering scent of fresh bread. Even with a full house, this was the first morning since Gavin left that she finally relaxed in the kitchen. She relished the moment. The silence didn't last long.

Simon and Sara rushed down the stairs.

"Where's Uncle Ian?" Sara glanced around the kitchen.

"Slow down." Fiona held up a palm and turned toward Cora. "Do all kids walk at a slow run?" Dealing with the challenging milestones of living with five-year-olds wasn't always fun and rewarding.

"They have two speeds—fast and faster." Cora laughed and sliced more bread.

"I smell Cora's special bread." Simon wiped his nose on a pajama sleeve.

Fiona handed him a tissue, pushed a wild red curl away from his face, and kissed his forehead. She wasn't an alarmist, but when it came to the twins anything out of the ordinary concerned her. *Cool as a cucumber.* She learned quickly every cough, sneeze, or runny nose didn't mean a severe illness.

"Who wants porridge and hot chocolate?" Cora placed bowls and mugs on the table.

"Hot chocolate with marshmallows, please." Sara jiggled and wiggled in her seat. Long, red curls bobbed around her face.

"Coming right up." Fiona gave up on getting them to sit still. Even when seated, their bodies were constantly in motion.

Simon reached for a slice of bread and a jam jar.

"Cereal first." Fiona removed a pot from the stove and filled bowls with creamy porridge. "You can't spend the day with Uncle Ian unless you eat a good breakfast."

"And then bread and jam?" Simon put an overfilled spoonful of cereal in his mouth.

"Don't rush. There's plenty of bread for everyone." Cora pointed to half a dozen unsliced loaves on the counter.

Fiona filled mugs with warm cocoa, sat, and glanced around the table. Across from her, the unoccupied chairs and missing redheads, an unfortunate result of an unexpected event, saddened her. Despite the steam from the mugs and warm ovens, she felt a chill. She shook off the woeful feeling. Today was the day she'd put it all behind her.

"I'm finished." Simon carried an empty bowl to the sink.

"Go upstairs with Sara. Get washed and dressed. Your clothes are laid out on the chair." Fiona tousled Simon's unruly red mop. "Grab a comb and brush."

Ten minutes later, the twins joined Fiona in the mudroom.

From her pocket, Sara removed a small brush and a handful of barrettes.

"Fiona glanced at the brush and laughed. "Let's do two braids today." In no time, she twisted Sara's flaming-red hair into two neat braids, just like her favorite sassy book character. "You're next." She sighed and pulled a comb through Simon's curls. "This will have to do." She slipped a wool cap onto his head and guided him out the door. "Stay away from the driveway!" She watched them run toward a wooden play set before returning to her chores.

"No worries. They're playing on the swings." Every few minutes, Cora looked up from the napkins and glanced out the sink window.

Fiona helped smooth napkins for the next half hour

and slipped pretty silver rings onto each one. Mindless chores helped her deal with the everyday stress of being a parent. The crunch of gravel on the driveway directed her gaze back to the window. "Ian never arrives early."

"Let's see who's outside." Cora patted her arm.

"Auntie Fi, Auntie Fi." Simon and Sara ran up the steps.

"What's all the rush?" With her heart in her throat, she did a quick head-to-toe of Simon, then Sara.

"The queen is here," Sara shouted.

"The queen, what queen?" She looked up in time to see a uniformed chauffeur walk around a black town car. Most guests arrived in rental cars or vans to accommodate larger groups. "Who…" Too dazed to do anything else, she waited. The door opened.

A tall, elegant woman stepped out.

Fiona rushed forward. "Can I help you?" The woman wore a luxurious double-faced coat. In a past life, Fiona owned a similar coat. *What a silly thing to think about.*

"I'm Gavin's Aunt Joan." The elegant lady gazed at Fiona and extended a gloved hand. "Didn't my nephew tell you I was coming for tea?"

Familiar blue eyes twinkled. "Welcome." Fiona accepted the outstretched hand. The leather glove was soft with a cashmere cuff. "I'm sure your nephew mentioned you'd be here for tea. It must have slipped my mind." Fiona crossed her fingers behind her back. A little white lie never hurt anyone. What happened between her and Gavin wasn't his aunt's problem. His apology was heartfelt, but his error in judgment did more damage to the integrity of their relationship than the violation itself. Every day, since his departure, she reconsidered her response. She was too angry to forgive. Didn't he trust her to see him without dollar signs? She forced a smile. "Welcome, I'm Fiona Campbell." A sense of awe mixed with admiration and apprehension surged through her.

"You're as lovely as Gavin said." Joan walked toward the front door with a confident familiarity.

"He must have arranged your reservation with my assistant." Fiona glanced over her shoulder, but Cora was gone. "Please come in." Aunt Joan was too classy to show up without a booking. What else did Cora fail to mention?

"Would you mind if the driver brings my luggage inside?" She pointed toward a man in a black jacket.

He removed a suitcase, a tote bag, and a violin case from the vehicle.

"We overestimated the time it would take to get to Highland Falls. My nephew is still working. When he finishes work, Gavin will meet me here." She glanced at the empty parking spots. "Oh, dear. I'm unfashionably too early for tea—aren't I?"

"No worries." Fiona's stomach fluttered. The sensation had little to do with Aunt Joan's unexpected arrival—and everything to do with the idea of seeing Gavin. Earlier, something as simple as an empty chair at the kitchen table sparked a warm feeling. Any mention of his name sent her emotions soaring from high to low. With the twins in tow, she followed the older woman. At the front door, Fiona stopped and faced the driver. "You're welcome to stay."

"Thank you, ma'am." He tipped his cap. "This is a round trip. I'm driving back to the city."

"You can leave the luggage here." Fiona pointed to

a nook in the hallway.

"It's been a pleasure driving you, Miss Joan." The chauffeur placed the luggage against the wall. He took both of Joan's hands. Long, wrinkled fingers disappeared in his giant palms. "Tell the boss to send Al if you ever need a ride."

Joan and Fiona stood in the doorway and watched the black vehicle drive away.

"I shouldn't be surprised by the expense my nephew went to bring me here." Joan chuckled. "The McIvers haven't changed a bit...always flaunting their wealth."

It wasn't Fiona's place to agree or disagree. "Let's get you comfortable while we wait for my other guests." She suspected Joan's generation, unlike Gavin, had a need to tell the world about their financial status.

Inside the main room, Cora sat behind the desk folding napkins.

Fiona glanced at Cora. She didn't look the least bit surprised when Joan entered. This was not the time to question her. "This is Gavin's Aunt Joan." She raised her brows and tilted her head toward Joan.

"I'm so pleased to meet you, Mrs. Stewart. I see you met Fiona and her darling niece and nephew." Cora glanced sideways at Fiona, stood, and gathered the folded napkins. "I'll be back with tea and fresh-baked bread with jam." She rushed from the room.

"Hmm." Joan inhaled. "Smells like homemade bread. Do you bake fresh bread every day?" She removed her leather gloves and placed them into a purse.

"Cora bakes her infamous buttermilk bread for special occasions." Fiona pointed toward Cora as she disappeared behind the kitchen door.

"What's today's occasion?" Joan glanced around the empty room.

"I would say your arrival is special." Fiona smiled. Joan's unexpected arrival could signal a sign of change—not only for Fiona and Gavin but the entire town.

"Auntie Fi." Simon tugged her arm. "It's our special day. We're off from school."

"You and your sister are special every day." Fiona smiled. Joan's arrival superseded any school holiday.

"This must be the *bairn* from the photos Gavin texted." Joan smiled at the twins hiding behind Fiona. "I had a long phone conversation with him yesterday." She sighed. "He told me about your visit to the conservatory."

"I didn't know the conservatory existed until Walter told us part of the story. We decided to investigate with Sara and Simon." Fiona was at a loss again. What could she say to make Joan feel better about the condition of the conservatory? After all these years, returning to a place with so many memories must be bittersweet.

"The photos of you with your niece and nephew brought back memories. You don't often see three such attractive redheads in one place." Joan shook her head. "However, the state of the conservatory grounds was a shock. My late husband, Paul, and I had a caretaker for many years. We believed we might come back someday. The caretaker passed away a few years after Paul. He had lived on the grounds from the day we bought the property. When he was gone, I didn't feel the expense of maintaining the property was necessary."

"Old buildings need a lot of care." Fiona glanced out the side window toward the barn. "I'm sure you did your best."

"So true." Joan followed her glance. "Do you have plans to restore the old barn? Is the odd little shed still inside?"

"Until the roof started leaking, I grew herbs inside. I plan to renovate the barn soon. Your nephew put together a proposal to recycle the salvaged wood." How much had Gavin told his aunt?

"He mentioned he's working with a friend who owns a local construction company." Joan raised a brow.

"He was helping his friend, Jack, the day we met." Fiona shrugged and feigned indifference.

"Oh." Joan smiled. "Just by talking to Gavin, I gather he's different than the McIvers I grew up with— more his own man. What do you think?"

Beneath Joan's droopy white brows, McIver's blue eyes gazed at Fiona. "I've only met Adrian and Emily. Adrian's definitely unique. Emily's a lovely, well-mannered little girl. I don't know the family well enough to make a comparison." Fiona wanted to believe Gavin was the man she met in the barn—an average guy who liked to work with his hands. She shifted uneasily. "We've cleared the breakfast tables. We're almost set up for tea. I'd be happy to serve you here." She gestured toward a peacock-blue chair tucked in the corner. "Would you prefer Earl Grey or a hearty Scottish blend?"

"A cup of Scottish tea sounds wonderful." She removed her coat and tossed it over the back of the chair.

Behind Fiona, the twins peeked in and out.

She couldn't imagine Joan wanting the constant chatter of two inquisitive five-year-olds. She turned on her heels and waved them away. "Go back outside and wait for Uncle Ian."

"I'd love their company." Aunt Joan looked around the little room. "You'll have to tell me who did all this restoration work. I remember the property before it was converted to an inn."

"Our local handyman, Tim Ulster, is an excellent carpenter." Fiona glanced at the crown molding. "You might know his grandmother, Jenny Ulster."

"Oh...I do. Jenny was a force in her day—the Grand Dame of secrets." Joan chuckled. "Is she still alive? She must be in her nineties."

"Very much so. Sharp as ever and still the keeper of town mysteries." Fiona laughed.

"So many untold stories," Joan snuggled into the deep chair. "Come sit with me." She motioned for the twins to join her.

"Are you sure you're okay with this?" Fiona hesitated. She shuddered at the thought of what their little mouths would reveal. Neither Simon nor Sara had the restraint of Tim's Granny.

"We'll be fine. I'm sure my early arrival interrupted your routine." Joan waved her off and hummed a fast-paced tune. "Do you know the song about the *Boo Coo*?"

"A booo...cow." Simon giggled and snuggled next to Joan.

Sara stood by the side of the chair.

The cheeky lyrics should keep the twins occupied

for a while. Fiona hummed the tune and entered the kitchen.

"I turned on the kettle." Cora looked up from the table and waved a bread knife toward a row of teapots. "Which teapot do you want to use?"

A kettle hissed on the stove.

"Did you know Gavin's aunt was coming for tea?" Fiona shut the burner and reached for a two-cup Brown Betty. She poured boiling water over the infuser and watched the water turn a rich brown. Dark teas steeped best in four to five minutes. Cora had plenty of time to fess up.

"Yes. I did." Cora placed a slice of bread onto a plate.

"And…" Fiona placed her hands on her hips and stared at her friend.

"So much happened in the last two weeks. I didn't want to add this minor hiccup to your plate." She waved the knife in the air.

"This is more than a minor hiccup." Fiona threw her hands in the air. "If Gavin joins his aunt for afternoon tea, where will you seat him?" The mention of his name and the possibility of him coming through the door at any moment sent Fiona's stomach swirling like a mixer on high speed.

"Joan's a single guest at a table with two couples. I set the table for six, just in case. No problem there, right?" Cora raised a brow.

"Sure, not a problem." The conversation was as silly as the *Boo Coo* song. Joan was a lovely lady who came to tea. Gavin would be another guest—nothing more.

"Maybe Joan would like some bread and jam while

the tea steeps. We have some time before afternoon tea. I'll make up the remaining rooms while you entertain our visitor." Cora carried a tray out the door.

"I'll bring the tea when ready," Fiona said to Cora's back. She removed the infuser and wiped a leaf off her finger. The leaf held up nicely, retaining its oils and aroma. Three or four more pots could be steeped from this bunch. Behind her, the mudroom door slammed shut. "Ian?" She glanced at the clock. Ian promised to be here by one thirty—it was already past one. Was it possible he was actually on time today? "You're here early."

"'Tis not your brother, lass."

The strainer slipped from her hands into the sink.

The melodic sound of Gavin's sexy Scottish accent startled her.

Chapter 14

Fiona stepped away from the sink and the mess of tea leaves. The cadence of Gavin's Scottish burr sent a tingle to her toes. She placed a hand on her breast to still her racing heart. For a moment, she was dumbstruck. Gathering her composure, she greeted him with a guarded smile. Her heart beat faster. He looked perfect in all the right places.

Gavin hesitated in the doorway. He glanced at the teapot on the counter. "I hope you're not setting a place for me in the dining room. I prefer taking my tea right here—in the kitchen." His jaw ticked as he assessed her.

He walked toward her in what seemed like excruciating slow motion. "You must be eager to meet your aunt face to face." Fiona wiped her palms on her apron and gripped the teapot handle. "She told me you had an interesting phone conversation." She stepped away from the sink and placed the pot onto the kitchen table. An image of Gavin and three adorable redheads eating breakfast clouded her sensibility. She missed those mornings. Today, the table was the perfect security barrier between them.

"Joan's driver texted he dropped her off and was heading back to the city. I didn't have time to go home and change. Jack and I were making last-minute adjustments on Ian's exhibit." He hooked a thumb into

a worn jeans pocket and stepped closer to the table—
across from her.

"Joan won't mind you're still in work clothes." She
certainly didn't. "She's teaching the twins *boo coo*
songs." She blew out a slow breath. "I wish you told me
to expect her."

"Simon's and Sara's *boon coo's brooken oot.*" In a
heavy Scottish accent, he gave the song a personal
twist.

She couldn't hold back a laugh and applauded.

Gavin bowed from the waist. "Sorry, lass, I
apologize. I thought arranging Joan's visit with Cora
would be less complicated. I know how busy you are. I
suggested the inn so she wouldn't be alone in an
unfamiliar house." He shifted his weight. "I hope her
early arrival is not an inconvenience."

"Not at all. Joan's delightful." How could she stay
angry after his performance? What would happen if she
let go of her displeasure completely? "How long will
Joan be staying in Highland Falls?"

"We haven't discussed her plans." Gavin ran a
hand through his hair.

"What are your plans for the rest of the afternoon?"
She chewed on her lower lip. What she really wanted to
know was, would *he* come back soon?

"I'll take my aunt to my house and let her get
settled." He flipped a chair around and straddled the
seat.

"So, Emily and Joan haven't met?" She wiped a
drip off the teapot with the hem of her apron.

"They'll meet this evening. I made dinner
reservations at a trendy new restaurant at the edge of
town. Most of the time, Em and I dine on take-away

and my infamous toasted cheese." He smiled.

The alluring curve of his lip sent her heart racing again. "Where's Emily now?" She hadn't forgotten toasted cheese was his specialty. He told her many things the day they visited Walter's barn and the conservatory. The only thing he failed to mention was he was filthy rich.

"At a play date." He shook his head. "I'm getting better at letting her out of my sight."

"I'm having a similar problem with Sara and Simon." She never spoke to anyone about having separation anxiety.

"Can you join us for dinner?" He rubbed the back of his neck.

"I don't have time to eat out." She waved a hand around the cluttered kitchen. "Eating out is usually a stop at the twins' favorite fast-food place and lots of ketchup." She didn't miss the fancy dinner dates in her past city life.

"I detest ketchup." He cringed.

"I'm not a fan, either." How could she resist a man who sang the *boo coo* song and disliked ketchup?

"Maybe you and I could sneak away one night and try something new." He reached a hand toward her but stopped short of touching.

An inviting smile made it hard to resist. "Your invitation is tempting." Was she ready to offer an olive branch? "I'd only consider if we split the check."

"I'll let you pay for the whole meal, if it makes you feel better. And...no ketchup." He crossed his heart.

"I have no problem paying for your dinner." An evening out with an adult male was hazardous, especially one as appealing as Gavin. Was she willing to take the risk? "Nothing fancy. I hate the thought of wearing heels."

"Not your thing anymore?" He glanced at her legs and smiled. "When you left the city, did you leave all your fancy clothes behind?"

The question came from a man who undoubtedly had a row of thousand-dollar suits in a closet. She preferred him the way he was—in worn jeans and work boots. "I have no use for professional attire and party dresses." She shrugged. "I don't miss dressing up." Her old clothes, donated to Dress for Success, were part of a lifestyle she'd willingly give up again. Could Gavin say the same?

"Do you *trust* me to come up with something super casual with good food?" He stood and slowly stepped toward her side of the table.

The word *trust* was a challenge. "Finding an informal place shouldn't be difficult in Highland Falls. Even the new trendy cafes cater to the outdoors set." She gripped the edge of the table as he turned the corner.

He glanced from her face down the skirt of her apron, stopping at the tip of her work boots. "Nothing but jeans and hiking boots. I promise." He crossed his heart again.

"Let me know what you come up with, and I'll think about having dinner with you." Just as he came too close, the microwave alarm *binged*. She sidestepped toward the counter and removed a glass pitcher of foamy milk. She concentrated on the contents, tilted the container, and separated the foam before pouring warm milk into a creamer. The silence in the kitchen was as thick as the foam she discarded. She glanced at her watch. *Today, of all days, it would be nice if Ian were on time.* Tea guests would arrive soon. "How long ago did you see Ian?"

"He'll be a little late." Gavin smiled and looked around the kitchen. "Where's my aunt?"

"I was about to serve tea." *Then you walked in and turned my afternoon upside down.* She placed the teapot, the creamer, and a pretty cup and saucer on a tray. "She mentioned you had a long phone conversation. Are you eager to meet her in person?"

"*Verry.*" He stroked his chin. "She's not like the McIvers back home."

Joan said the same about Gavin. The sexy, melodic way he rolled his *r*'s made her tingle. "Joan hasn't been home in decades—people change." She put the last touches—a linen napkin and a small delicate spoon—on a tray.

"Thanks for being so accommodating." He came up behind and placed a hand on her back. "Can I help serve?"

"You were right to send her here." She glanced over her shoulder. "I got the impression she's happy to be in Highland Falls. You must have so many questions."

"The questions can wait. I'll let Joan settle in tonight. She can visit the town and the conservatory tomorrow." A hand slid from her back and caressed the edge of the tray.

Gavin's fingers lightly brushed her fingertips. A fresh outdoor scent surrounded him, making her light-headed. Nerves in her fingers tingled with the desire to touch him. Tightening her fingers over the edges, she pulled the tray close. The tea service jiggled.

"Are you sure you don't need my help?" He stepped in front and curled callused fingers over hers.

"I've got this." Holding her emotions in check, she gripped the tray and stepped aside. "You'll have to excuse me. I'm a little behind schedule." In the past, his touch, presence, and the gleam in his eyes had brought tranquility to her hectic schedule. How would she get those feelings back after her heart was so badly bruised?

Gavin held the door, let her pass, and followed her into the sitting room.

She walked past him, placed the tray on a side table, and poured a cup of tea for Joan.

Sara and Simon rushed toward Gavin.

"Where's Emily?" Simon looked behind him.

"You'll see her later at the museum." Gavin ruffled Simon's hair, stepped into the room, and stared at his aunt. "I can't believe how much you look like Granddad."

"And you are more handsome than the pictures Adrian showed me." Joan stood and reached for Gavin's hands. She squeezed gently.

Yes, Gavin was handsome. What did it feel like to encounter a family member after so many years?

"Did you enjoy the drive?" Gavin guided Joan to a chair, sat, and poured a cup of tea.

"The Adirondack Northway is as beautiful as I remember. Paul and I frequently drove our camper van into the city for concerts or to pick up students." Joan glanced out the front window toward the foothills. "Have you driven the thirty-mile high route?"

"I haven't done much sightseeing." Gavin tugged his fingers through his hair. "Unfortunately, my time is limited. I prefer to fly to the city."

On a private jet, no doubt. "I'll refill the tea." Fiona reached for the teapot.

"It's not necessary, dear. One cup of tea is fine for now. Unless you…" She looked from Fiona to Gavin.

"I'm good." Gavin placed an empty cup on the tray.

"Are you taking the lady to the old house?" Sara stepped between Gavin and Joan.

"The big scary place?" Simon asked.

"Did you know *Trows* lived there?" Sara faced Joan. "We found your picture in the old barn where Walter works. Simon was scared, but I wasn't."

"I was not." Simon made a face at his sister. "You're a frog."

"Simon." Fiona forced an authoritative voice and stepped between the twins. "You need to make better choices with your words."

Sara stuck out her tongue.

Fiona threw her hands in the air and turned toward Gavin.

He winked and mimicked her gesture.

Both of them needed more experience in the parenting department.

"Sara was worried the *Trows* took you to their cave." Gavin winked.

"Oh, no, *a bho bain.*" Joan reached for Sara's hands.

"They wanted you to play your violin," Sara said.

"Who told you about those silly creatures?" Joan smiled. "I haven't heard anyone mention a *Trow* in years."

"Auntie Fi and Gavin." Sara pointed to Fiona, then

Gavin. "Are you going to the house?"

"Sara's infatuated with the *Trows* and begs for a tale every night." Fiona relied on her brother's knowledge of Scottish folklore to create new bedtime stories.

"When I go, I'll need a brave little girl like you to come along." Joan winked at Sara. "For now, the scary old house can wait. I'd love to visit Walter at the antique barn and see the town."

"Sounds like a pleasant way to spend the day." Gavin glanced at Fiona. "We can all drive to the barn, if Auntie Fi asks Cora and Mabel to cover this weekend."

"I don't know." Fiona shook her head. "Weekends are busy." She glanced around the room full of redheads. A stranger walking into the room might mistake the scene for a cozy family reunion. She understood Gavin's willingness to accommodate his aunt. His demeanor forced her to reconsider past thoughts about Joan's property being Gavin's priority.

"Will you come?" Sara asked Joan.

"Oh, I wouldn't miss it for the world." Joan wiggled her brows. "Will you be able to get away, dear?"

"The inn is booked solid. Mabel, Cora's daughter, will be here soon. I'll ask if she can help out." Fiona had made her decision before Gavin suggested Cora cover for her. She hated disappointing the twins. At least, that was her excuse.

"I understand the demands of running a business. We shouldn't keep you from your responsibilities." Joan glanced at Gavin. "Let's walk outside." She shifted in her seat. "I'm a bit stiff from sitting in a car for three hours."

"Can we go, too?" Simon pleaded.

"Can't think of a better tour guide." Gavin ruffled Simon's hair.

Fiona's heart skipped a beat. "I'll get your coats." She gathered cups and plates and carried a tray full to the kitchen. She met everyone at the front door with an armful of jackets, hats, and gloves. When everyone was zipped and tucked, she followed them onto the porch. The air was brisk, and the sky was clear blue. Overhead, a flock of winter geese soared in a V-formation. Winter weather arrived early this year. So did the geese. Despite the cold, the day was perfect for walking. She waited until the group disappeared around the corner of the inn, sighed, and returned to the kitchen.

Cora stood at the sink, rinsing teapots. "The kids seem comfortable with Gavin and his aunt." She pointed out the window.

"They like being with Gavin." Fiona removed a plate of sliced cucumbers, dill spread, and freshly made egg salad from the refrigerator.

"And you...?" Cora glanced over her shoulder.

"I'm working on it." She forced a smile and gave a tense nod. The group looked like a model family out for a walk. Sara and Simon needed happy moments like this. She slathered the spreads on Cora's bread, placed three-tier cake stands on a cart, and stepped back. "What do you think?" She gestured toward the stands.

"I think you should be outside with Gavin." Cora came to her side, placed an arm around Fiona's waist, and squeezed.

"You never give up, do you?" She smiled at Cora. "We're definitely not on the same page. I'm asking if I should place the cucumber sandwiches on the top tier and Sophia's shortbread cookies on the bottom. And you're"—She pointed to the serving stand.—"Well...you know what you're talking about."

Cora laughed. "I'd place the cookies on top and mix the sandwiches on the middle and bottom tiers." She rearranged the cucumber and the egg salad sandwiches. "How did Gavin act toward his aunt?"

"He was affectionate, considering he never met her. I believe he's glad he found her. And, not for any reason connected to the property." Fiona reached for a towel and wiped a dab of egg salad off the tray.

"Did she say how long she's staying?" Cora asked.

Fiona shook her head. "She invited the twins and me to join them tomorrow. She'd like to visit Walter. I told her I'd run it by you first."

"What a wonderful idea. Mabel's free. She asked if you'd need extra help." Cora winked.

Whether or not this was true, Cora made it impossible for Fiona to refuse the invitation. With Joan here, Fiona was almost sure Gavin wasn't going away. Could she find a way to engage in a healing process to restore trust and goodwill? She placed the last sandwich on the bottom tier. Rather pleased with how they turned out, she took her phone from her apron pocket and snapped a photo.

Guests were already seated in the dining room using a simple technique Mabel suggested. Using whimsical teacup-shaped place cards avoided confusion. Guests no longer scrambled for what they imagined was the best seat. Cora had a lot to be proud of. Her daughter understood the art of hospitality. After graduation, she would be successful in any tourism field. If Fiona had mentioned Mabel's skill to Gavin, could he have found her a spot in a SIREaC resort?

A soft buzz of conversation filled the room.

Fiona approached Joan's table.

The other guests, a couple from Albany and two retired professors from Manhattan, were already seated. At the last minute, one of the professors invited his nephew. The dark-haired man occupying the seat intended for Gavin wore a hideous plaid jacket resembling a box of shortbread cookies.

Fiona looked away and suppressed a giggle.

Gavin escorted his aunt to her seat. "Good afternoon." He glanced around the table and gazed at the young man.

A playful twinkle in his eyes suggested he was amused by the man's jacket. "Your tea will be served in the kitchen." She glanced at Gavin.

"My favorite place to drink tea." Gavin wiggled his brows and walked away.

"He's...so easy to please." She swallowed, smiled, and retrieved a Brown Betty from the serving cart.

"You have an amazing setup." The shortbread box man adjusted the wire rim of his glasses. "Do you run this place on your own?"

"I'm afraid my nephew, Frank, is lacking in social graces." The gray-haired professor, wearing similar glasses shifted in his seat. "He surprised me this morning. He's in the area on business. Your assistant was kind enough to accommodate my request."

"What business brings you to Highland Falls?" Fiona tossed her braid with her free hand and filled his cup.

"I'm with the New York State Department of

Tourism. Keywords from an article related to Highland Falls and the Scottish Games recently came to my attention. We're highlighting the town in our spring catalog." He reached for a cucumber sandwich. "I would be happy to share the information. You might find the keywords helpful in customizing your advertising strategy."

Fiona inhaled deeply. He hadn't told her anything she didn't already know. Mabel used the inn for a class project on search engine optimization. The ad she created did well.

"The tourist office appreciates publicity from any source. This article was in a financial paper." The young man smiled. "Have you read the piece?"

"I glanced at it." She forced a tone of indifference. He already took too much of her precious time. "If you don't mind hanging out in the kitchen while I clean up, you can discuss this after tea."

"I can't think of a better way to spend my afternoon. I'd like to walk around your property, if that's okay. I noticed an old barn on my way in. Is the structure original?" he asked.

"The inside of the barn is off-limits for now. You're welcome to explore the rest of the property." How would the state react if the roof caved and crumbled on their employee like a shortbread cookie? The image, although amusing, was not good for business. The last thing she wanted to do was ruffle the feathers of a representative from the state tourist board.

"If you intend to explore before dark, young man, I suggest we let the lady serve tea." Joan stood and took the teapot from Fiona's hand. "I'll take care of the pouring. See to your other guests." Joan offered the professor and Frank a Scottish solid brew. "Don't be surprised if your spoon stands straight up." She laughed and suggested they add milk or cream.

"Cream, please." The professor held up his cup.

Joan covered the bottom of the cup with just the right amount. She looked up and smiled at Fiona.

Thank you. Fiona mouthed the words and moved to the next table where overnight guests sat. A burst of childish giggles from across the room interrupted her greeting.

Gavin and the twins came in to sample the buffet. How long was he standing there? Did he notice the scene at his aunt's table? She'd tell him the news later.

"Is that your family...and such a handsome husband?" A craggy-faced man drew Fiona's attention back to the table. "Where were you hiding them?"

"You can't get the shades of their hair out of a bottle." The lady to his right shook a head of unnatural, brassy red hair.

"No, you can't." Fiona followed their glance. She might be prejudiced, but all Campbell children were beautiful. Granny would say Gavin cut a handsome figure, as well. This wasn't the first time someone thought the twins belonged to her and Gavin. Absent-minded Walter at the antique barn had made the same comment. With hair running the spectrum from Gavin's spicy ginger to the kids' classic shades of red, the assumption was easy to make.

"They're a perfect blend of their parents," the brassy redhead said.

"Oh, no." She shook her head. "We're not family." What would life be like if they were a family? *Don't go there.* She shouldn't be thinking about such nonsense—

not after Gavin missed the mark and avoided discussing what he really did for a living. "What I mean is the children are my family. The man is just a...family friend."

****

Gavin leaned against the buffet and watched Fiona stroll from one linen-draped table to the next. She ran a tight ship. With Cora and Mabel assisting, she worked magic.

A man with a weather-beaten face at the table in the far corner said something.

When something bothered her, she tossed her braid like she did now. What did the man *say* to ruffle her feathers?

"Your phone is beeping." Simon tugged on his arm.

"Thanks, mate." Gavin checked his text. "Uncle Ian is turning up the driveway. Let's get your coats."

Fiona must have gotten the text, too. She headed toward the kitchen but was detained by a guest at the sideboard.

Gavin escorted the twins to Ian's car and adjusted their seatbelts. "Have fun." He waved and rushed back to the house.

Fiona stood at the sink, looking out the window.

A thick red braid hung along a kissable neck, down her back, and ended at the half-tied bow of her apron. He stepped close, debating if he should adjust the bow.

"Thanks for walking the twins out." She glanced toward the door from the dining room.

"Are you expecting someone?" Gavin followed her gaze.

"The young man at Joan's table. He's with the state

tourist board." She bit her lip. "I wasn't sure if he followed me. I don't have the time to answer his questions. I'd still be standing at their table, if your aunt hadn't intervened."

"Do I need to talk to him? I could tell him you're too busy." Gavin cracked the door enough to see if the man was still seated at the table. "Is it the dark-haired chap dressed like a box of shortbread cookies?

"The jacket is a bit much." She giggled. "I don't recognize the plaid." She dried her hands on a towel and peeked over his shoulder. "I'm not sure why he thinks I have the answers. So many townspeople are better equipped to answer his questions. I'll direct him to City Hall."

"Maybe he wants a less official view of how things work." If Gavin were in the man's shoes, he'd prefer talking to her than pointy-nosed Judy at City Hall. Did Mr. Tourist Board have more than business on his mind? Gavin had no right to be jealous—especially after what he had done. "If you're good here…" He glanced at his watch. "I'll start putting Aunt Joan's luggage into the car. I hope you won't mind if she leaves before tea ends. I want her to get settled before dinner."

"No worries. Joan's had a long day." Fiona draped the dishtowel over her shoulder and stepped away. "Bring her back soon."

"You can count on it." Gavin cupped her cheek with a palm and smiled. He'd be back…with or without his growing entourage.

Chapter 15

On the short ride back to town, Aunt Joan expressed her observations at the B and B. "I never met two people so conscious of avoiding each other. And, the *bairn*...they're very fond of you. What's the problem between you and the lass?"

"I'm afraid 'tis all my fault." When he read the article, he realized he had made the biggest mistake of his life. "I started with a misconception of how I earned a living."

"Ach." Joan nodded. "What did Fiona think you did for employment?"

"I told her I worked for my family's construction company." He scratched behind his ear. "She just didn't know the extent of my involvement in the business or the company's worth."

"How was that possible?" She raised her brows. "SIREaC is recognized worldwide."

"I alluded to being an average bloke living paycheck to paycheck." He stopped at a stop sign by the crossroad into town and waited for the car to his left to pass. Joan took his right hand off the wheel and turned the palm.

"With calluses like these, anyone would believe you earned your living with your hands." She stroked his face. "I know what the family demands. Your hand shows how hard you worked to earn your place in the

McIver Empire. You have nothing to be ashamed of. You make an honest living."

"With a big paycheck." Gavin smiled. He admired his aunt. Her heart was in her music and belonged to a man the clan didn't accept. If she had stayed in Scotland, what role would she have in the family business?

"An abundance of wealth comes with its problems." She shook her head. "Couldn't you find a way to tell her the family is filthy rich?"

"It was complicated." He never had reason to flaunt his wealth. Business associates understood the power he brought to the table. "Fiona is more concerned with SIREaC's plan to build an exclusive resort in her town than how much I earn. Big money doesn't impress her. She left a lucrative position with a successful hedge fund to start a B and B." He rechecked the crossroad. *All clear.*

"I gathered she's done well." Joan nodded. "Tell me about this new SIREaC resort. Are you here to find a property?"

"The project is off the table for now." He learned the hard way that being open and honest was the way to go.

"Ach. Hamish sent you to find me, didn't he?" She stared out the window. "And my property."

What could he say? Anyone who knew the family would know *Granaidh* was behind this. Only three of Joan's six siblings were still alive. Did they know the extent of Granaidh's secret? If they did, they played dumb when their brother mentioned their sister.

"Are you aware I wrote to my brother often?" she whispered.

He shook his head. "He'd never mentioned you until I told him about an article I read about Highland Falls—an up-and-coming tourist town in the Adirondacks. His reaction piqued my curiosity. After several questions, he revealed he had a sister he hadn't seen in years."

"All those years, he never said a word to anyone." She sighed. "You're a smart lad. You must suspect there's more to the story."

"Aye, but only speculation about your relationship with Paul. Granddad didn't say much." Gavin now had the opportunity to hear the story from the source.

"Was finding me difficult?" She closed her eyes and leaned her head on the headrest.

"I had help. We researched and discovered your picture on an old record album cover." He glanced sideways. "I couldn't deny the lady on the cover resembled Granddad."

"You and Fiona?" She opened her eyes.

"She introduced me to her brother. He's an expert on the Scots who settled here. With his guidance, Fiona and I connected the dots to your Brooklyn music school." He changed gears and drove up the hill toward his temporary home.

"Sounds like you and Fiona work well together." She smiled.

"We could," he said with regret. Could Fiona forget the trappings of his family wealth and see him the way she did the first day they met—the person he wanted to be? Some nights, he lay awake thinking the attraction was one-sided.

"She's a smart lass." Joan patted his knee. "Try explaining the company's structure. You're one of the many cogs in the big wheel. She'll understand you were doing your job."

"My job?" Gavin laughed hard and short. He never questioned his role. No one in the family ever disputed their role. He enjoyed scouting locations for new projects. This time, it got personal.

"Don't worry. I'm glad you found me. People like us learn not to take things to heart." She dismissed his concern with a wave of her hand. "You'll feel better after you hear *my* proposal. My plans will send my brother into a tizzy." She smiled. "Hamish was always a manipulative clone of our father. I'll bet he hasn't changed, has he?"

"Doesn't sound like it." He held back a low laugh. SIREaC controlled so many lives. Except for Aunt Joan, no one dared to leave the business entirely. A few of his cousins straggled off. However, they never went too far from the hand that fed them. His cousin Adrian ran an architectural company specializing in green designs. Most of her business came from family projects. Uncle John's son was an archeologist contracted at sensitive SIREaC dig sites. They took baby steps and stayed within the nepotism of the company. Joan was different. She had made a clean break. He glanced toward her and smiled. *Good on you, old girl. You had a happy ending.*

"Enough about cranky old Hamish. Why did you wait so long to tell that bonny lass the truth?"

"When the right moment presented itself, I had every intention of telling her." He ran a hand through his hair. "I had several opportunities. Instead, I was evasive and turned the conversation away from SIREaC and the search for a resort property."

"Directness has never been a McIver trait." Joan chuckled. "Does anyone in town know SIREaC is interested in the area?"

"At first, only my mate, Jack, and his dad knew." At the top of the hill, he shifted gears again. "Unfortunately, I didn't get a chance to explain to Fiona. A reporter from *World Financial News* beat me to it. Her response to finding out about the company's wealth proved she was nothing like other women I dated." *Or married.* His ex enjoyed every moment of her marriage to someone within the company's hierarchy. Not Fiona. She held the responsibilities of his position against him—not his money. If he worked for a local company like the Drummonds, he wouldn't struggle to return to her good graces.

"If Fiona doesn't care about the size of your paycheck, what's she upset about?"

Aunt Joan's perception was eerie. "She sees a new resort as a threat to the town and her business."

"I understand their sentiments. I lived here long enough to know the town never took well to developers." Joan nodded. "How long have you been here?"

"A few weeks." He slowed and turned onto Clover Street. The house he rented was in the middle of the block.

"You're still here, which means the townspeople didn't see fit to run you out. They must like you, despite who you represent." She flashed a smile. "This town will never be interested in a resort like SIREaC recently built on Long Island."

"How do you know about the company projects? I believed you broke ties with every McIver years ago."

Gavin pulled into the driveway and shut off the car.

"I did on my terms." Joan gazed at Gavin. "The one thing you learn growing up in a family like ours is how to protect your interests."

"The family did a good job of keeping your existence a secret. They will be shocked to hear you've kept up with the company's success." Gavin chuckled. Joan was one surprise after another.

"Hamish knows." She scrunched her lips. "I have a good idea what he's after. Building on a property already owned by a McIver would make things easy. All he would need was a few building permits and to comply with environmental standards for the area."

"SIREaC has no right to your property, does it?" Gavin unlocked the car doors.

"I'm the only McIver with a claim to the conservatory," she said coldly. "I still own my SIREaC shares."

Gavin was not surprised. He could almost predict where the situation was going. "You managed your wealth and led a life you chose." He laughed. The story was getting better by the minute. Joan's story solidified his decision to do away with plans for a resort. The town was wrong for a SIREaC project—but the conservatory was perfect for Cappella's suggestion.

"I would never relinquish what's rightfully mine. Keeping up with the family company was in my interest." Joan opened the passenger door.

Gavin rushed around the vehicle and helped her out. He wanted to hear more.

A cold breeze blew off the foothills.

"It's in your best interest, young man, to pay close attention to the organization's internal workings. You never know when such information will come in handy." Joan stepped onto the paved driveway and looked him straight in the eye. "Once a McIver, always a McIver is written in the bylaws created by my granddad, Dougal, your great-grandfather. He guaranteed the business would always be passed down equally to his descendants. The slightest disagreement can set family against family. Scots have been doing that for centuries."

"I never had a reason to question how great-grandfather set up the line of inheritance." Gavin's parents were partners in the law firm representing SIREaC and handled all the legal issues. Today, the company that started at the turn of the last century ran smoothly and profited under the scrutiny of Dougal's descendants.

"Just remember, Dougal McIver wasn't about to let all his hard work fall to waste if future generations couldn't agree on whatever was in vogue." She pulled up the collar of her coat. "Feels like the weather will be nasty tonight. I can feel it in my bones."

"Let's go inside. I'll turn on the kettle while you get settled." Gavin removed Joan's suitcase and violin case and followed her toward the tiny house. "The house isn't much by McIver standards, but it suits my current needs."

"It's a lovely old house." She approached the front door and stepped inside. "I remember the first owners, the Simmons."

"They're still the owners. I'm renting for the winter while they're in Florida." Gavin carried her luggage down a short hallway to the first bedroom. "Emily has the room next door." He nodded toward a room with faded floral wallpaper. "I moved most of my stuff to the dormer bedroom." He gathered a few odd items. "I'll join you in the kitchen." Upstairs, he tossed his belongings onto the bed and returned to the kitchen.

Joan was seated at the wobbly kitchen table.

"I remember playing cards in this room." She drew an invisible pattern on the table. "The left legs wobbled back then, too."

Gavin wiggled a table leg with his foot. He'd find time to fix the table and other repairs. "Some of the cabinets' handles need adjusting, too." He glanced at the whitewashed farmhouse cabinets. A proper kettle stood on the counter. "Would you like tea?" He carried the kettle to the sink. One of the things he learned from observing Fiona was to wait for a rolling boil before pouring. He never acquired even the simplest of kitchen skills. A local woman prepared food, assuring him and his siblings ate well. When Emily came to live with him, he hired a nanny who could cook.

"Tea sounds lovely." She glanced around the room. "A kitchen is the best room in a house."

"Sorry, I don't have loose tea." He removed a box of teabags from a cabinet. The choices at the supermarket overwhelmed him. A stock boy suggested a popular U.S. brand. Gavin filled two cups with steaming water and set them on the table.

"Teabags are fine." Joan glanced toward the entrance foyer.

"Do you need something?" He should have given her a quick tour of the house and pointed out the ladies' room.

"I don't see my tote bag. I must have left it at the inn." Joan reached for a spoon and removed the teabag from her cup.

"I'll check the car first." Gavin grabbed his jacket. Outside, the temperature dropped, and the wind picked up. He didn't spend long searching for the missing bag.

Back in the kitchen, Joan opened a package of digestive biscuits and placed them on the table.

"I didn't find the bag in the SUV. Is there anything you need tonight, or can you wait until tomorrow?" He reached for a biscuit.

"When I travel, I usually put my bedtime medications in my purse." She looked in her handbag. "I don't know why I didn't this time."

"No problem. If there's no rush, I'll return to the B and B after dinner. I'll drive you and Em home first." Only recently, Gavin and Emily established a nighttime routine. Back home, she was used to nannies and wouldn't mind Joan tucking her in.

"Does Emily travel with you a lot?"

"She lived in Edinburgh with a nanny and Adrian until recently." He was surprised she didn't ask about Emily's mother. If she kept up with the local news as she did with the happenings at SIREaC, she would have most likely read the details of his divorce. The sudden eligibility of the grandson of one of the wealthiest men in the country made all the trashy tabloids.

"Adrian is a charming *clipmalabor*—just like her grandmother." Joan half smiled. "From the day she said her first word, my sister Clara could talk your ear off."

Joan's face showed neither bitterness nor joy at the mention of her sister. He pulled out a chair across the table from his aunt. "I remember driving from Aberdeen to Edinburgh with Adrian and her grannie. I was lucky I got in two words the entire trip." He smiled.

"When Adrian entered my Brooklyn music studio, seeing her was quite a shock. She's Clara sixty years ago." Joan walked to the trash, tossed her teabag, and returned to the table. "Tell me what happened with Fiona—did you ever apologize for your lack of candor?"

Just like that, Joan dismissed any discussion of the family. "I've given it my best shot. Apologizing is easier than forgiving." His fast-paced life often left him inattentive to others' feelings.

"Maybe you're trying too hard. When the right time comes, just be you. Fiona doesn't need something colossal or unforgettable to show your sincerity." Joan reached for a biscuit and dunked it in her tea.

Joan's interest in Fiona was relentless. Maybe the missing bag wasn't an oversight on his part but a carefully calculated plan by the sly woman sitting across the table. "I'm making an effort. I invited Fiona to dinner." Gavin laughed at the simplicity of his reply. Other ideas crossed his mind.

"Did she accept?" Aunt Joan bit into the soggy biscuit.

"Sort of." He shrugged. "I'm not sure she's ready to accept my apology."

"Think about what you're apologizing for. The two of you have to get your priorities straight. Will you be competitors or something more intimate?" She raised her brows and smiled.

"Enough about me. Tell me about Paul." He glanced at the whitewashed clock. The big hand pointed to the twelve, and the little hand pointed to the four. Emily wouldn't be home for another hour.

"It's not a complicated story. In today's world, we would be the artistic relations—back then, we were rebels, misfits, or bad kin."

Gavin had so many questions, but he didn't interrupt.

"Paul and I hired a lawyer to oversee my affairs with SIREaC. The law firm still handles everything by proxy—including my right to vote. When we opened the conservatory, we put the surrounding land into a trust to protect the surviving spouse." She looked into her cup and sighed. "We kept our new life separate from family connections. The conservatory was *our* joint venture from the money we earned giving music lessons. In the seventies, vanishing in a place like this was easy—no GPS, tracking apps, or social media. Locals liked having the conservatory here. They kept our secret safe, even though the family persisted in searching for me. Thanks to the people in this town, when a detective hired by my father traced us here, he hit a dead end."

"If there's anything this town is good at, it's keeping secrets." Gavin laughed.

"I'm not surprised. After all, the town has a strong Scottish heritage." She coughed and sipped from her cup. "How's your Gaelic?"

"I've still got an ear for it." His parents' insistence that he and his siblings attend Gaelic classes paid off many times over. He tolerated the classes but was more interested in sports and girls.

"Do you remember what your grannie would say when *bairn* spread idle gossip?" She winked. "*Is ná clois a geloisir. Is ma fusfraitear. Abair ná.*"

"Don't hear what you hear. And if asked, say you

don't know." Gavin admired her perfect Gaelic. He heard Grannie's voice. She would like Highland Falls and the people. He'd like her to visit and meet Fiona.

"Well done." She smiled.

"Tell me about your musical careers." He glanced sideways at his crafty aunt.

"Paul and I stayed under the radar regarding our music and family connections. His family wasn't exactly the type of people McIvers associated with. We'll have plenty of time to hear about my past." With a wave of her hand, she ended the conversation. "What did the article say that upset Fiona?"

She had an uncanny obsession with Fiona. Was he wrong to send her to the inn? "A reporter from a financial paper spotted me at the Scottish games. The article mentioned me by name and title and insinuated SIREaC chose this town for another big project." Gavin ran his hand over his face.

"Poor Fiona." Joan shook her head. "Discovering something like that, whether true or not, through a third party can complicate a relationship." She reached across the table and patted his hand. "You can't go back and take away what you did. Look to your future. You want a future with her, don't you?"

"More than anything." He smiled. Aunt Joan's presence could be the link he needed to mend things with Fiona.

Chapter 16

Gavin started the SUV, adjusted the phone holder on the dash, and connected the infotainment screen. He then sang along to a rock and roll song from the sixties.

The music was interrupted by a local weather alert.

"Strong winds from the west with thirty-five to fifty mile per hour gusts will make driving hazardous. Gusts up to sixty miles per hour can be expected at higher elevations."

Wind-tossed branches and leaves covered the dark road out of town.

Turning back was not an option. He promised Joan he would retrieve her tote.

A loud crash of thunder preceded a sudden downpour.

The day he met Fiona was a stormy day, too. Was it a warning of a forthcoming relationship? *Och.* He was thinking like Grannie. He pulled around the driveway as close to the side door as possible. Before stepping out, he checked for flying branches. Off to his right, the old barn creaked and groaned against the wind. He slipped his hands into his pockets and took the steps two at a time. At the top of the stoop, he reached for the handle on the storm door and tugged against the wind's resistance. He stepped into the small mudroom and almost collided with Fiona.

She stepped back. "I heard a car drive up. I

couldn't imagine who would be out and about in this weather." She waved with a potato in one hand and a peeler in the other. "All my guests are in for the night. Only mad dogs and crazy Scots go out in this kind of weather." She laughed.

"No argument there." He ran a hand through his hair. Outside, the wind howled, reminiscent of Highland weather. Inside, her gentle laugh rippled through the air, creating a warm, enchanting space.

"Why are you here?" She raised her brows.

"Joan left a bag behind." He hung his jacket on a hook and followed her into the kitchen.

"Couldn't it wait until morning? No one should be out on a night like this." She walked toward the table and tossed the potato into a bowl. Water splashed on her shirt.

Gavin gazed at her T-shirt. "I'm afraid not. She needs her meds." The worn shirt didn't leave much to his imagination. This wouldn't be the first time he had a perfect view of her soft curves. Some mornings, she went about her chores in form-fitting exercise clothes. On other days, an apron covered those curves. She was a contrast of sexy, sweet surprises. *Focus on why I'm here*. He looked away. Damn. He missed those mornings.

"Check the alcove in the hallway." She grabbed a towel and dried the water on the table.

"I'll look on my way out." He wasn't in a hurry to leave. Her welcoming smile and the scent of a freshly brewed pot of mint tea encouraged him to stay awhile. Aunt Joan and Emily could use the alone time to get better acquainted.

"Can I pour you a cup?" She didn't wait for his

answer, reached for a mug, and poured an earthy green brew.

"Are you making Tottie scones?" He pointed to equally disturbed piles of sliced potatoes on the table.

"Potato scones do sound good. Maybe I'll whip up a batch this weekend, but scones are not on tomorrow's breakfast menu." She pointed toward the whiteboard on the wall behind him. "Sophia's assistant, Alana, is working on a cookbook. She asked me to test a potato pie recipe. It's quite good." She slid her tongue over her lips. "If you've been to The Doric Pub, you might have ordered the pie."

"Aye, more nights than I can recall." He watched her move around the kitchen, and potato pie was the last thing on his mind.

"The recipe's been in Alana's family for over a hundred years. Her cookbook is inspired by local dishes and authentic pub food." Fiona reached for a measuring cup and filled it to the four-cup line with thin slices of crisp white potatoes. "I offered to do a taste test on my guests."

"That's a lot of pies. If it's like the one on the Doric's menu, your guests will be back for seconds."

"Now that you're here, I'll make some extra for you to take home for breakfast." She glanced sideways. Damp, loosely braided hair slipped across her shoulder. "Unless you have other plans?"

Fiona had a generous heart, but was it unselfish enough to forgive? "Honestly, I haven't given much attention to tomorrow's breakfast. I'm sure Aunt Joan and Em would prefer one of your pies to toast and jam." He glanced at the kitchen gadgets on the table. "How can I help?"

"If you're not in a hurry, start scraping." She handed him a potato peeler.

He looked at the peeler, shrugged, and pushed up his sleeves. How hard could this be? He was good with tools and should have no trouble whittling away at a spud.

"How was your dinner?" Fiona reached for a heavy sack of potatoes sitting on the floor.

"I've got it." He rested a hand on her fingertips. Her skin was soft and inviting. For a minute, he forgot what she asked. "Dinner was okay. We tried the Mexican fusion restaurant near the museum. Emily settled for a mushroom taco. Aunt Joan ordered tortilla soup and a beet salad. The Doric Pub would have been a better choice."

"I imagine you're more of a haggis and mash family." She slipped her hand out. "Have you heard about the pub's monthly tribute to Robert Burns—complete with haggis, whisky, and poetry reading?"

"Whisky and Burns sounds like home. Aunt Joan might like to go." He lifted the bag and placed it on the table. "Do you remember any of Burns' poems?"

She looked him straight in the eye. " 'O my Love's like a red, red rose newly sprung in June: O my Love's like the melody sweetly played in tune.' "

"Well done, lass." He applauded a perfect recitation of the first verse of "A Red, Red Rose."

"What about you? Did you pay attention in school, or were you too busy breaking hearts?" She tapped him playfully on the chest with a peeler.

"I'm afraid you have the wrong impression." He placed a hand over his heart and forced a hurt expression. "I wanted to be the next Burns. I memorized many of his poems. 'As fair art thou, my bonnie lass, so deep in love am I...' " With a soft glance and gentle bend from the waist, he swept into a grand finish. " 'And I will love thee still, my dear, till all the seas go dry.' "

She watched his lips move. A blush colored her cheeks.

The poetry charged the narrow space between them with suggestive tension.

"You're impressed. I can tell." He made light of the verse's awkwardness. Maybe he should have considered the words' implications before dazzling her with his poetic proficiency. The poet had conveyed his feelings to a *T*—if she'd only give him a chance.

"I might have misjudged you." She stepped a fraction of an inch closer. "If you're a Burns purist, do you think celebrating Robert Burns before his birthday celebration in January is sacrilegious?"

"Do you?" He inhaled her just-washed hair, and the scent drew him closer. Which homemade shampoo did she use—lavender, lemon, or verbena?

"Not at all. I'm considering having a man in a kilt recite poetry at afternoon tea." She leaned against the table.

"Have anyone in mind?" He half smiled and wiggled his brows.

"I was thinking of my brother. But he's too busy working at the dig site and museum." She clasped a peeler in her hands. "You interested?"

"*Verra* interested." He took the gadget from her and placed it on the table behind her. "You've seen me in a kilt and heard my poetic prowess. Do I have the necessary qualifications?"

****

Gavin stood toe-to-toe in front of her. She couldn't move. "You're more than qualified." She cleared her throat. "Will you be around in the spring?"

"I'm working on it. I like Highland Falls a lot." He brushed a palm along her cheek.

His hand, warm and gentle, left a tingling sensation. Her heart beat faster. Gavin, despite her rash judgment, was a magnetic force she couldn't resist. The thought of him leaving was unbearable. Was the strong physical attraction enough to make her forgive and forget? Before she could overthink further, a soft tap on the kitchen door hurled her back to earth.

The door creaked open. The slow movement added to the tension in the room.

Gavin stepped back toward the counter.

"Sorry. I thought Fiona was alone." The man with the craggy face held out an empty mug. "Is it too late for a cup of hot coffee? The pot on the buffet is empty."

"I apologize. A lot of guests were drinking coffee this evening." Fiona reached for a carafe and filled it with a fresh brew. "There's a pot on the burner. Help yourself. I'll be right back." She glanced from the guest to Gavin and smiled, a bittersweet reminder of the choice she had to make. Business before pleasure was never a choice until Gavin came into the picture.

****

Fiona disappeared, leaving Gavin alone with her guest. He watched the kitchen door close and sighed. "I'm sorry. Did you say something?" He turned toward the man.

"No problem." Craggy Face nodded at the door. "Can I pour you a cup?"

"No thanks." Gavin leaned against the counter and picked up a mug of cold tea. He toyed with the handle before sipping.

"Lovely young woman. You and those adorable little redheads made quite a picture this afternoon. I thought they belonged to you and Fiona, but she quickly corrected me."

Gavin hesitated. He didn't know how much information Fiona shared with her guests regarding her relation to Simon and Sara. "No, we're not family." He shook his head. Their relationship, however, was one he hoped would change. Was Fiona on the same page? "I've got an adorable redhead, too." He pulled a wallet from his back pocket and showed the man Emily's picture.

"Oh." The man raised a brow. "Does your wife have red hair?"

"No, my *ex*-wife was a blonde." He quickly corrected any implication the man might be suggesting. Craggy Face couldn't have been more wrong if he believed Fiona let the coffeepot go dry while she amused herself with a married man.

"Your accent suggests you're not from around here. Did you and Fiona know each other back in Scotland?" Craggy Face added cream to his coffee.

"We met through a local business associate." Much like today, the memory of that day was etched in Gavin's mind.

"You on KP, young man?" The man looked at the bowl of peeled potatoes and smiled. "What'd you do to deserve the job?"

"It's a long story." Gavin walked toward the table and opened the bag.

"I'll leave you to your chores." Craggy Face raised his coffee cup and left.

****

Fiona passed her guest leaving the kitchen.

"Delicious coffee." He smiled. "Had an interesting chat with your young man."

She returned the smile, entered the kitchen, and placed an empty carafe into the sink. "What was that all about?"

Gavin stood by the side of the sink. "Your guest was concerned about your virtue. He believed you were cavorting with a married man." He wiggled his brows.

"What did you tell him? I wouldn't call assembling a potato pie cavorting." She laughed at the amused shift in his voice. "My guests worry over me like a beloved granddaughter. They want me to meet a nice man and have kids." She glanced at Gavin and hid a smile.

"No worries. I corrected any misconceptions." He glanced at the potatoes. "Let's get these pies done before I leave."

Half an hour later, all the pies were assembled and placed in the fridge. Fiona glanced around the kitchen. Emptiness settled in the pit of her stomach. She didn't want him to leave. "I'll wrap up your breakfast pies while you look for Joan's bag. In the morning, pop them in a 350 degree oven for forty-five minutes." The evening was pleasant, with no mention of the conservatory or SIREaC. She listened for sounds on the other side of the kitchen door. The room was silent. She released a slow sigh and looked around the kitchen. Except for Gavin's pies, the kitchen was calm and clean.

Out of nowhere, a wind howled, and thunder

rumbled over the roof and across the yard. Outside, tree debris blew by the window.

Gavin rushed in with Joan's tote bag.

Fiona looked toward the stairs leading from the kitchen to the upstairs apartment. She hesitated at the bottom of the staircase and listened for footsteps. Everything was quiet.

"Do you want to go upstairs and check on the twins?" Gavin placed the tote on a chair.

"I don't want to disturb them. Sara and Simon are sound sleepers." She listened again.

A crack and a *crash* ripped the air.

She dashed toward the mudroom door. "The barn?" She glanced at Gavin, stepped into mud boots, and grabbed her jacket.

Gavin pulled a flashlight from a shelf over the coat rack. With the light in his right hand and his left on her arm, he guided her around debris on the path toward the barn.

Although she hoped otherwise, she wasn't surprised the old barn couldn't withstand the strong wind. She turned the corner from the house. *"Uggg."* The damage lay at their feet. A section of rotting wood had torn off the east wall, taking a piece of the tin roof. She pulled away, stepped over the mess, and ran toward a gaping hole the size of a barn door.

The wind howled between the remaining sideboards. Old planks fell short of the inner shed.

Fiona glanced at a tangled mess of dried leaves and rotten wood. Until now, the aging barn had fought a good battle against the elements. "We should go inside and gather any salvable herbs before the wind rips them to shreds." She ignored the wild strands of her braid whipping across her face.

"I'll go in first. Follow my steps and be mindful of the debris." Gavin glanced at the roof. He stepped through the opening and passed the light over the support beams.

"How's it look in there?" She trusted his expert judgment.

"The majority of the metal looks secure. A small section of the roof and some rotted boards are the only casualty." He kicked the wood at his feet. "I'm confident the outer structure won't cave around us."

She stepped inside. The remains of the old barn rattled but held in place. She worked by Gavin's side. Without considering the potential danger, she pulled swaying branches of lavender and mint from the rafters and placed them in a small bucket. She rescued all she could and followed him out the hole in the wall.

"Nothing more we can do tonight." Gavin glanced over his shoulder. "Things will look different in the morning." He opened the door to the mudroom and let her pass.

"Thanks for your help. What would I have done if you weren't here?" Fiona placed the bucket of herbs on a shelf over the clothes dryer. She'd deal with them in the morning.

"You'd handle it like you always did." Gavin stepped inside and wiped damp stands off of her face.

"I'll call Jack and his dad tomorrow." She shook her head and sighed. "I can't leave such an eyesore on the property." A lump stuck in her throat, and she fought back tears. She wouldn't break down now—not in front of Gavin. She blinked and swallowed. "Do you think they can salvage some of the sideboards?"

"We'll have a better view of the damage in daylight. Let me make the arrangements. I'll bring the Drummonds and a crew out here first thing in the morning." His palm rested on her cheek.

She never had someone step in and take charge. During the last few years, the house, the property, and the repair decisions were hers alone. But Gavin had responsibilities, too. "What about your aunt?"

"She won't mind the change of plans. She's dying to check out the town." He slipped into his jacket and kissed her forehead. "Don't worry. Everything will work out. Not all the planks were destroyed."

"Wait." She rushed into the kitchen and retrieved the tote bag and potato pies. "You forgot this. You'd have to drive back again."

"Hmm." He raised his brows and smiled. "I wouldn't mind at all."

She stood at the storm door until his vehicle's taillights disappeared into the dreary night. When they were no more than a dim fog, she sighed, hugged her arms around her waist, and walked upstairs. Despite a long, tiring day, she'd like it very much if he found another reason to return.

Chapter 17

The following morning was frosty but bright and sunny.

As promised, Gavin showed up with Jack and his dad. They wore heavy work boots and carried tool belts over their shoulders.

"How about some breakfast before you check out the barn?" Fiona put away the last breakfast dish as they entered the kitchen. Glancing at the just-cleaned counters, she didn't mind messing them up.

The men tossed their tool belts over the back of a chair and accepted her offer of warm coffee and the last slices of potato pie.

"This must be the potato you peeled." Jack laughed and held up a fork, which held a steamy slice of potato in a curvy shape.

"Eat your pie and shut up." Gavin pierced a potato with his fork.

"Gavin's surprisingly talented with a potato peeler." Fiona made a silly face behind his back.

"You're not the only one impressed with my skill. Emily and Joan were surprised I helped make the pies. I heated the pie according to your instructions but left before it was out of the oven." He glanced over his shoulder and gazed at her eyes. "Everything that comes out of this kitchen is delicious."

"It's Alana's recipe, not mine." Fiona reminded

him. Guests complimented her on the delicious food she served, but no one looked at her as Gavin did. Mindful of not touching him, she hurried between the chairs and turned her attention toward Jack. "What's your plan? Do you think the barn will come down today?"

"Give us about an hour or two to access the wood," Jack devoured the last piece of pie. "We should have a good idea of what's salvageable."

"I hope the weather doesn't get much colder. The weather lady predicted a three-layer day."

After her morning chores, Fiona planned to serve hot beverages and snacks to the crew.

Outside, the sun was shining without a cloud in the sky.

"The colder, the better," Gavin said. "Even a little snow wouldn't bother me."

"Less chance of finding snakes in the floorboards." Jack launched into a running list of all the critters he had saved during previous demolition jobs. "Rabbits don't hibernate, so they dig holes in warm spaces. Then there are field mice..."

Fiona cringed. Cute little rabbits were one thing, but mice were not her favorite breakfast conversation.

"This might be a long shot, but would you happen to have blueprints for the barn?" Gavin interrupted.

Jack said no more about the mice.

"When Ian initiated a historical search on the property, he found construction plans for the house and barn. I have a cyanotype document dated 1880." Fiona glanced at the cluttered desk in the corner. "Anything can go wrong in an old house. I keep the documents handy."

"Are you interested in architectural documents?" Gavin smiled.

"Only when I need them." She handed him a copy printed on greenish-blue paper with white lines. "Ian looks for a historical explanation for everything." She read the note taped to the document.

Sir John Herschel created the very first cyanotype similar to this one using paper coated with a solution of iron salts, sun, and water.

"That's impressive." Gavin teased her with a crooked smile and unrolled the document. "When the cyanotype process was discovered, builders mass-produced prints like this. Architects no longer relied on draftsmen to copy their drawings for distribution. What else do you know about the process?"

"That's it." Fiona had years of experience tuning off her brother when he went off on tangents.

The men finished eating and put their plates in the sink. Jack grabbed his tools and joined Mr. Drummond.

"Do you want me to put these in the dishwasher?" Gavin turned on the faucet, and warm water washed away the scraps on his plate.

The cool air and heated water hit the plates like a steamy waterfall.

"Leave the plates. I'll stack the dishwasher later." She placed the dirty mugs onto the counter. "Simon and Sara were looking forward to hiking today." Their sad expressions were still vivid when she explained the barn situation. "They've been through so much. I hate letting them down." Their disappointment quickly resolved when she allowed them to hang out upstairs and watch cartoons. An addiction to American TV allowed her to breeze through breakfast and talk to Jack and Gavin without interruptions.

"I wish I hadn't mentioned hiking to Em last night." Gavin rolled the blueprint. "I don't see why we can't go tomorrow." He reached for his tool belt and fastened the buckle low on his hips.

Fiona watched him reposition the pouches over his right hip. In slow motion, he adjusted the position of a hammer, a putty knife, and pliers. "Did you bring these tools from Scotland?" The tools were well-maintained but lacked the luster of newly bought gadgets.

"I inherited them from Granddad." He winked, hung his jacket over his shoulder, and joined Jack and his dad outside.

So, even grumpy Granddad McIver had started at the bottom. She smiled and watched Gavin walk away. The tool belt swayed against his hip. A warm sensation rushed to her toes. Who would ever imagine tools could look so sexy on a man? The door banged shut, and she returned to cleaning the table.

"Why aren't you outside with the boys?" Cora entered with a bucket of cleaning supplies.

"Jack is assessing the damage. I'd be in the way." Fiona didn't need to see the hole in the wall in daylight. "I'll leave the work to the professionals."

"Why don't you go upstairs and help Mabel? Making beds and emptying trash won't take long." Cora glanced around the kitchen. "I'll finish in here."

"Sounds like a plan," Fiona said without argument. She joined Mable in the front room at the top of the stairs.

Mabel hummed along to a tune on her earbuds.

Fiona welcomed the lack of conversation. She smoothed the quilt and moved to the windowsill. The window had a good view of the barn and Gavin. She dusted the ledge.

"What a mess." Mabel joined her at the window. "Are you still planning to reconstruct the barn into a party venue?"

"Now more than ever. I can't have an eyesore on my property." Fiona caught a glimpse of Gavin and Jack. "The barn *was* a charming part of the landscape." She shook her head. "The wind blew an ugly hole in a side wall last night."

"Don't worry." Mabel touched her shoulder. "Everyone knows the Drummonds are the best in the state for restoring old buildings. My dad surprised my mom with a shed built with wood from an old spring house."

"I remember that. Your mom told me how the spring ran down the mountain for centuries. When ski lifts were built, the spring changed course." Fiona used the edge of her apron to wipe a smudge off the window. Gavin and Jack were out of sight. "It always amazes me how resourceful people like your great-grandparents were. Imagine building a shed over a portion of a spring to protect the water from leaves and dirt." Was the old barn constructed to protect the herb shed?

"After that, my grandparents used the shed to keep metal milk cans cold." Mabel tossed the dirty linen into a basket. "I can't imagine working so hard for clean water and cold milk."

"I agree." Fiona laughed. "I don't envy the lifestyle like my brother."

"Hunky Mr. McIver knows his stuff, too." Mabel followed her glance.

"Yes, he does." Fiona smiled. "This is the only

vacant room. I hope the guests arriving today don't mind the noise." The room facing the barn was always popular. Guests enjoyed an evening drink and watched the sunset from the window. "The old barn resting against the hills offers the best view on the property."

"I wouldn't worry," Mabel said. "The work will be done during the day when guests are out. I'll update your list of things to do in the area. Guests will be eager to start early and hardly notice what's happening." She straightened a pamphlet on the bedside table and left the room.

After a quick once-over the vacant room, Fiona checked the bathroom toiletries with the new B and B logo. The imprint of a willowy thistle stem on the labels was another of Mabel's beautiful ideas. The logo offered the Scottish feel the tourists enjoyed. Fiona considered adding soaps to the herbs and teas she sold at her roadside stand in the summer. Unfortunately, with the loss of her shed, the project would have to wait. She placed a fresh soap bar on the dish and glanced out the window over the tub.

Gavin and Jack walked along the damaged side of the barn.

Jack pointed upward.

Gavin grimaced and held a phone up to the busted wood.

No use standing around speculating. She picked up the overflowing laundry basket and carried it to the upstairs washer. *Whites go in the washer, and colors stay in the basket.* Sorting was a mindless task, leaving her thoughts free of Gavin or the barn for a few minutes.

Swoosh and thump. The washer started its first

spin.

Fiona removed her apron and took the back stairs to the kitchen. "Is it tea time already?" She crossed the room toward the counter. Cora had placed a mug, a Brown Betty, and a sugar bowl next to the kettle.

Gavin leaned against the sink with his thumbs hooked in his tool belt.

Cora and Mabel sat at the table, sipping tea and listening to Gavin.

Mindful of the steam from the kettle's spout, she reached around the kettle's handle. "Would you like a cup of tea?" she asked Gavin.

"Let me help." Gavin spooned loose leaves into the teapot. "I was discussing the possibility of Mabel doing her internship at a new SIREaC property on the east end of Long Island."

"Sounds like a great opportunity." Fiona poured water from the kettle.

"I appreciate the offer." Mabel glanced from her mom to Gavin. "I planned to ask Fiona if I could intern here."

"I'm honored. But you should consider Gavin's offer." Fiona took the seat across from Mabel. She didn't want her to miss out on the valuable experience SIREaC offered. "Having an internship with an organization like SIREaC would be impressive on your resume." She glanced at Cora. What did she think of her daughter working for SIREaC? Would she be troubled if she moved far away?

"It's her decision." Cora pressed her lips together.

"Highland Falls has changed so much since I started college." Mabel shifted in her seat. "Except for ski season, it was an out-of-the-way town tourists found on their way to someplace else." She straightened her shoulders. "So much is happening here—like Sophia and Ian's discovery at the Logans' farm. The museum is expanding, and State University of New York offers satellite classes." She glanced at Gavin. "And don't forget the old conservatory."

"What about the conservatory?" Fiona turned toward Gavin with wide-eyed concern. "Is something happening there?" Since he contacted his great-aunt, he hadn't mentioned anything about the building on Joan's property. Was it wishful thinking, believing his plan to build an eco-resort had changed? The future of their relationship was at the heart of this matter.

"Joan told me she has plans for the old place." He lifted a shoulder.

The simplicity of his answer surprised her. Gavin didn't give up easily. McIver's business was just that— McIver's business. She stood and carried her cup to the sink, stopping inches away from Gavin. "And *your* plans for the property?" She placed a hand on his forearm, muscles flexed under her fingers.

"They've changed." He placed a hand over hers.

Cora cleared her throat. "Mabel, go check on Sara and Simon. When we get them ready, we'll take them into town." She nudged Mabel toward the stairs. "We'll keep them busy while Fi deals with the mess outside."

"Sure, no problem." Mabel winked at Fiona. "Yeah, I definitely want an internship here."

"Thanks, ladies." She laughed when Mabel and Cora disappeared at the top of the stairs. "You and I are on Mabel's list of Highland Falls' happenings. Last year, Sophia and Ian were the hot topics." She studied Gavin's expression. Was he up to the challenge?

Gossip, although harmless, was annoying at times.

"The town's live reality show." He chuckled. "Should we give them something to talk about?" He put an arm around her waist and pulled her close.

A buckle of his tool belt pressed against her. "Ouch." She wiggled free. The handle of the hammer pressed into her hip. "Tell me, what *are* your new plans?"

"Talk about the conservatory can wait. A barn out there needs rebuilding." He adjusted his belt and rubbed a hand through his hair. "Let's do a walk-through, lass. You'll get a better idea of what Jack and I discussed. Make sure you dress warm. The clear skies are deceiving."

Fiona slipped into mud boots. She grabbed a jacket and wool beanie and followed Gavin. She wanted to know all about his plan for the barn. The conservatory plans would have to wait for another time. Gasping, she stopped and stared at the hole in the barn wall. "Wow." A sudden coldness ran through her body. "During the day, the barn looks just as bad." She had avoided checking the barn once the sun was up. "Is it safe to go inside?" She slipped her hands into her pockets and approached with trepidation. "It's strange how this was the only area damaged. What caused this section to collapse?"

"All the rain over past few months damaged the old wood. Water and wood never mix well." Gavin pointed toward the hole in the roof. "The roof was compromised. Water pooled and rolled off, hitting the rocks and gravel." He kicked at small loose rocks along the sidewall. During heavy rainfall, water bouncing off these rocks splashes up and hits the old sideboards."

A jagged hole in the metal roof let in enough light, making navigating inside easy.

Mindful of the splintered wood and protruding nails, she slipped past the broken boards. A sweet, spicy scent of dried herbs still lingered. Overhead, a few lone sprigs dangled from a beam. The sight stabbed at her heart.

"Sorry about your herb shed, lass." Gavin followed her glance.

"I appreciate everything you did." She ran a hand down the sleeve of his jacket. What choice did she have? The shed was useless, and the barn walls needed repair. She sighed. Unforeseen circumstances dictated that she proceed with her plan.

"I have some good news." He took her hand and led her toward the back of the barn. "The rear wall is in perfect condition. Jack and I think this section was replaced not too long ago. We'll see the difference when we compare the wall to the original blueprints." He released her and pointed toward the top of the window. "See this tie log? The structure around the log is sturdy and firmly sets the window." He tapped the window trim. "Once we secure the side walls, we won't have much to repair on this wall."

Fiona nodded and glanced toward the view of the foothills. The view had sold her on the property. When plans were drawn, she'd suggest a larger window.

"Are you listening, lass?"

"Yes." She stretched an arm and placed a hand on the wall. "You said it's sturdy, but it's only one wall. What about the other three?"

"Let's walk the outside perimeter," he suggested. "Remember the initial assessment I did? A lot of boards are still salvageable." He guided her out with a hand on her back and took the lead.

How could she forget the rainy day he stepped into her leaky old barn—a handsome stranger who knew everything about barn wood? Focusing on his broad shoulders and confident stride, she took long steps to keep up.

He led the way past the window toward the far side of the barn. Around the corner, he removed a tape from his tool belt and measured the planks. He ran a callused finger along the boards. "These pieces of barn wood are in good condition." He pointed toward the logs he marked weeks ago. "Depending on the dimensions of your new barn, we can easily cut and repurpose them."

Why was he using the word *we*? Was he referring to his company? She took a determined step forward. "Just to clarify, I want you to understand I hire local. The Drummonds will get the restoration work—not SIREaC. I'd make the same decision regardless of how I felt about the other party."

Gavin turned and reached for her arm. "No worries. I got the message loud and clear the first day we met." He rubbed his free hand across the back of his neck. "I should have been as straightforward as you from the beginning."

"It would have prevented…" She let out a slow breath. No need to keep hashing over the article. "I hated being blindsided."

"Yeah, I get it. No more secrets. I promise." He gave her arm a gentle squeeze. "So, you should be the first to know. I'm going into business with the Drummonds."

"You're what?" Overwhelmed by the implications

of the surprise announcement, she shook loose from his grasp and stepped back. "What about SIREaC? Why would you want to do this?"

"One question at a time." He waved an open palm. "To answer your last question—I want to stay in Highland Falls. Emily's happy. I'm happy." He gazed at her eyes. "And Aunt Joan is considering buying the house I rent."

"Will you all live in the little house?" She couldn't image coming home to such a confined space.

"I'm looking for another house—something more suitable for a family." He wiggled his brows. "I have plans for a future here."

He had family here. Emily and Joan were family. Perhaps his future plans included marrying again. However, she couldn't ignore the consequences of an international development company at the town's back door. "Does your plan include opening a SIREaC office nearby?"

"I don't plan on working out of an office." He waved a hand in the air. "This will be my office."

"You're leaving the family business?" She couldn't believe what she was hearing. "Will *you* retain your company shares?"

"I'm not leaving the company. I'm just changing my operating method. I'll be more hands-on." Gavin touched her shoulder and guided her closer to the wall. "Great-Granddad ensured no McIver would ever lose their place in the company. Aunt Joan brought that to my attention. She's been voting via proxy and collecting her share of revenue for years."

A cold breeze blew down from the hills.

"What about the Drummonds? Do Jack and his dad

understand the ramifications of a deal with SIREaC?" She pulled her beanie farther down and adjusted her collar. "I'm assuming you'll place the Drummonds on the board." Without a say, they could lose control of their company. "What kind of deal are you proposing?"

He stepped closer and blocked the wind.

"Jack understands fully the type of acquisition I'm proposing. Remember we were at uni together in Glasgow. Our lawyers will see that the Drummonds retain control and decision-making over their company."

"Sounds like a decent deal." She nodded. The Drummonds' company was no match for SIREaC financially, but their local company brought a lot to the table—reputation, additional facilities, and an expanding regional market. "An acquisition's not so bad if it provides them with more money, new technology, and a solid structure to improve on what they already do." She glanced at his face. "A successful acquisition will help increase your market shares, too."

"An acquisition is a good move for everyone." He placed a hand on the barn wall. "Too bad I didn't know you when you were a hotshot CFO." He smiled. "I like a smart, sexy lady in high heels."

"You might not have liked me. I was ambitious and career-driven." She raised her head and met his gaze. "Those days are long gone."

"The only thing that's changed is your motivation." He stepped back and pointed at her mud-caked boots. "And the way you dress."

She laughed and tapped her heels against the barn wall. Caked-on mud fell off her boots. "Back then, I was all about big gains and minimal losses. I was responsible for other people's money. They understood the risks. My responsibilities are less forgiving now. My schedule revolves around Sara and Simon." She touched the splintery wood. "This old barn and a house full of guests keep me busier than ever." She wouldn't change her new life for anything. She gazed at Gavin. She'd gladly add him to the list, if he planned to stay.

"Do you ever take a break? And I don't mean a morning visit to Sophia's where you help when the shop is busy." He leaned a shoulder against the barn wall and crossed his arms.

"I have a secret place," she whispered, pointing over his shoulder toward the foothills. "Maybe I'll take you someday." Her fingers brushed along his jaw.

"Hmm...a secret hideaway? I can't wait." He moaned, placed a hand behind her neck, and lowered his lips.

Gavin tasted like coffee and smelled like a crisp autumn day. In a profound and unforeseen way, her smothered feelings and uncertainty faded with the kiss. Breathless, she pulled away. Cool hands cupped her heated cheeks. Eager for another kiss, she placed her hands on his and stepped closer.

The crunch of heavy boots on the gravel path forced them apart.

Along with her responsibilities came a lack of privacy.

"Aye, right." Jack cleared his throat. "I was looking for you two." A momentary look of amusement tilted his lips in a one-sided smile. "Sorry to bust in on this little business meeting. We've got work to do and a crew waiting."

"How long have you been standing there?" Gavin

snorted and slid a protective arm around Fiona's waist.

"Long enough." Jack returned the greeting with an approving grunt. "Good on you, lass. My friend here can be a little slow on matters of the heart."

Gavin glanced at Jack with narrowed eyes.

Fiona bit her lip and held back a laugh. She didn't need Jack or a TV psychologist telling her a relationship was two-sided.

"I have a crew on standby all morning." Jack rubbed a hand through his hair and glanced at Gavin. "Will we need them today?"

"We haven't gotten to that part yet." Gavin shifted his weight and let his hand slip from her waist.

"Understandable, mate." Jack nodded and chuckled.

"I think I've seen enough to give the go-ahead." Fiona glanced from Jack to Gavin. "Gavin explained the first step is securing the back wall. Can you do that today?"

"We're ready to go." Jack clasped his hands together.

"I guess it's now or never for the old barn." Fiona sighed. "Let's go inside and check the blueprints." Glancing over her shoulder at the weathered walls as she led the way to the house, she regretted that, once again, business came before pleasure.

The blueprints were where she had left them—on top of the old desk. She handed them to Gavin.

"This will save a lot of time." He walked across the kitchen and unrolled them on the table.

"There's fresh coffee in the pot." Fiona was uninterested in the technical details. "I'll be upstairs if you need me."

The rest of the day was noisy and dusty. The construction crew hammered and sawed until dusk, completing more than expected. By the end of the day, the back wall was secured, and most of the damaged wood lay in a large trash receptacle.

"How long will that eyesore be here?" She stood between Gavin and Jack and stared at the useless weather-beaten wood sticking out of the container.

"All trash will be gone by the end of the week." Gavin placed a hand on her arm. "Tomorrow, Jack will bring in heavy equipment and remove the larger debris."

As she led the way to the house, she glanced over her shoulder, a pang of nostalgia washing over. She couldn't help remembering the first batch of herbs she successfully dried in the shed. She was saddened by the loss of the barn, but she chose to see the bright side. The years of weathering had created some beautiful wood. *It's time to move on.*

The sun had set when the crew entered their vehicles and drove away.

Inside, she and the twins enjoyed a simple mac and cheese casserole for dinner. Despite the eyesore outside, everything was calm. As she tucked Sara and Simon into bed, she listened to their animated excitement about the upcoming hike. Finally, alone in a quiet kitchen, she sat at the table and rolled dough for tomorrow's breakfast scones. She placed a tray in the refrigerator and turned off the light. Her day was over. "Good night," she whispered to the silent house.

Upstairs, a light glowed under the door of the twins' room.

She opened the door.

They were wide-awake and sitting on Sara's bed.

A glowing moon-shaped night lamp cast a soft shadow on their silhouettes along the back wall.

"It's past midnight. Why are you two up at this hour?" This wasn't the first time she heard them whispering in the middle of the night. Usually, they shared something they missed back home or a memory of their parents. Tonight, she sensed the tone was different.

"I don't like Emily anymore." Simon flapped his hands.

"Did something happen? Fiona glanced from Simon to Sara. The comment was typical of a six-year-old boy who didn't want to hang out with girls—his sister being the exception.

"Emily and her auntie, who lived with the *Trows*, were at Auntie Sophia's bakery." Sara took over when her brother was silent.

"Sara." Simon wrinkled a brow and covered his head with a pillow.

"Are you worried about the *Trows*?" Fiona wished Walter had never told the old tale. When she was Sara's age, stories about *Trows* were just as scary. "Joan never lived with *Trows*. It's only a silly story."

"I'm not scared of *Trows*." Simon peeked out from under the pillow.

His false bravado didn't hide the fact something was wrong. Fiona joined them on the bed. She sat cross-legged, facing them. They looked worried, not frightened. "Do you want to tell me what happened?"

"Emily said she'll live in Highland Falls all the time." Simon tossed the pillow onto the floor.

"Is she unhappy about moving here?" Fiona was

unsure where the conversation was going.

"I don't think so." Sara rolled her shoulders and glanced at her brother.

"She likes living here," Simon said.

"Why don't you like her anymore?" Fiona couldn't imagine Emily being cruel.

"Tell her." Simon elbowed his sister.

Sara grabbed her pillow. "She said you're going to marry her *da* and live in a big new house together."

"Really?" Fiona kept her expression neutral. "Maybe Emily misunderstood." Would Gavin discuss a marriage proposal with his aunt, or was it a romantic embellishment of a clever little girl?

"If you marry him, will you send us back to Scotland?" Simon sniffled again.

"Never." Fiona pulled them into her arms. "Emily didn't say that? Did she?" She didn't have much experience with kids but understood they didn't have the best filter system. Their thoughts translated freely into words without careful consideration of the consequences.

"No," Sara said between sobs. "But…but Simon knows a boy who lives with his mother one week and his *da* the next."

"We don't have a *ma* or *da* anymore." Simon's eyes filled with tears.

"No one is sending you away. This is your home—with me." She tightened the hug.

"If you marry Gavin, would he be our *da*?" Simon wiped his nose with the sleeve of his superheroes pajamas.

Fiona handed him a tissue. "No one's asked me to marry them." When the twins first arrived, she and Ian faced more challenging questions. They quickly learned children wanted honest, straightforward answers. "If I get married someday, it would be like having a bonus dad."

"What's a bonus *da*?" Sara sniffled.

"It's someone who's not your real father but would love you very much." Fiona wiped a tear off Simon's cheek with her thumb.

"Okay, but when you marry someone, I hope Gavin is our bonus dad." Simon's lips came together in a serious smile

"We'll see about that." Marriage wasn't something she considered. Could it work with someone like Gavin—combined families, separate businesses? With a shake of her head, she dismissed the silly romantic notion.

Simon yawned and crawled under Sara's unicorn blanket.

When the twins arrived, they often slept in the same bed. She and her brothers had found the same security when times were tough. Her niece and nephew, however, had a different devotion—the kind twins shared. Their closeness helped them through a terrible time. "Let's get to sleep. If we're hiking in the morning, we need a good rest." She softly kissed Simon's forehead.

Sara, the hugger, threw her arms around Fiona's neck.

Tonight, the hug was tighter and longer.

Once their heads hit the pillow, they quickly fell into a deep sleep.

Fiona cuddled under Simon's superhero comforter and studied the warm amber glow of the nightlight. She closed her eyes, but she couldn't sleep. Her mind entered a worrisome spiral as she reconsidered Sara and Simon's heart-to-heart. Broaching the subject with Emily or Joan was out of the question. How would Gavin react if she asked about a conversation his daughter overheard? *Is it true? Will he ask me to marry him? The bigger question is; am I ready to take the step?*

Chapter 18

Fiona rolled to the edge of the bed and glanced at a hippo alarm clock on the bedside table. Next to her, Sara and Simon were in a deep sleep. Even a heavy metal band couldn't disturb them. She shut off the alarm, set to go off in five minutes at five a.m. The hike could wait another day. In her previous life, she, too, had the luxury of sleeping late on weekends. She smiled and tiptoed out. She dressed quickly in jeans and a sweatshirt and went downstairs. In the kitchen, she glanced at the recently purchased coffee brewer. Today was not the day for wrestling a new appliance. A kettle and coffee press provided a more than adequate cup of coffee with less effort.

Outside the window, the sun rose above the hills.

She sighed. The day was perfect for hiking.

Pwwwwwpphht. The kettle whistled.

She heated the glass beaker with the boiling water, then emptied the beaker and scooped a heaping tablespoonful of a dark brew. She poured enough water for two cups of coffee. A four-minute steep allowed enough time to text Gavin and tell him about the plan change.

—*Good morning. Sleep well?*—

Was he looking forward to today, too?

—*Just going to text.*—

Her heart skipped a beat. Had something

happened? Was *he* canceling?

—*Everything ok?*—

—*Em and Joan practiced violin last night. Em's out cold. Hate to wake her.*—

She breathed a sigh of relief and chuckled.

—*Same here. The twins talked until midnight. They're still asleep. We can schedule for another time? Kids will be disappointed.*—

She sent a thinking emoji. Referring to *the kids* as a family unit sounded lovely in a weird way.

—*Joan offered to take the kids to the museum and lunch. You can show me your secret hideaway.*—

He sent a silly face with a finger covering closed lips.

How could she resist such an offer?

—*K. I'll check with Cora. She'll be here soon.*—

—*See you soon. Can I bring anything?*—

No need for Gavin to rush over. Cora would say *yes* without any encouragement.

—*I brewed a pot of coffee. Save you a cup?*—

Spending the morning with Gavin replaced the caffeine rush she needed earlier. *Beep, beep*—the timer went off. Did four minutes pass already? She pressed the plunger, filled a mug halfway, and listened for sounds from upstairs and outside the kitchen door. Everything was quiet. Without traffic, Gavin would be here soon. She grabbed the mug and took the stairs two at a time. When she returned to the kitchen, she saw Cora slicing bread.

"Good morning. You look nice." Cora glanced over her shoulder. "Are the twins dressed?"

"Simon and Sara were up late last night." Fiona nodded toward the top of the stairs. "I decided to let them sleep."

"You already spoke to Gavin?" Cora glanced at her watch.

"I let him know the plan changed." She was having second thoughts about not spending the day with the twins.

"You look like you're ready for a hike." Cora glanced at her pants and hiking boots.

"He suggested we go on our own. Joan offered to take the twins and Emily to the museum and lunch. I don't know how long Sara and Simon will sleep. Would you mind getting them ready?"

"No problem. You deserve a morning alone—well, not exactly alone." Cora winked. "The guest list is light." She glanced at the whiteboard. "Scones and French toast special for four. I've got it." She grabbed an apron.

"Thanks." She could always rely on Cora. Any second thoughts disappeared. She tossed a few protein bars in a backpack and filled two takeaway cups with freshly brewed coffee.

"You'll need more coffee and a hearty breakfast if you're hiking. Maybe you should fill an insulated tumbler with coffee." Cora handed her sliced bread. "You toast the bread. I'll scramble the eggs."

"Two cups are enough. Don't fuss—jam and cheese will do." Fiona removed slices of Swiss cheese and a jar of peach preserves from the refrigerator.

"Hmm. These look good." Cora layered cheese between slices of toast, smeared the bread with jam, and took a bite. "We should add this to our tea sandwich menu."

Fiona placed coffee cups next to a backpack on a

mudroom bench. She sat and laced her hiking boots.

Outside, the sound of tires crunching on the gravel driveway announced Gavin's arrival. He parked the white SUV by the door.

"Gavin's here." Fiona slipped on a jacket and grabbed her backpack and the coffee cups.

"Morning, lass." Gavin opened the door and stepped inside.

A warm tingle surged to her toes despite a gust of cold air.

"Don't forget breakfast." Cora rushed in and handed Gavin the bag of sandwiches. "You two have fun. And don't worry. Joan and I can handle the kids."

"Thanks for the sandwiches." Gavin peeked inside and gave Cora a thumbs-up. "Is everything about food with Cora?" He followed Fiona to the vehicle and opened the passenger door.

"She firmly believes everyone should start their day with a hearty breakfast." Fiona welcomed the heated seat inside the vehicle. "Joan's offer was kind. Do you think she can handle three active kids?"

"Don't worry. Joan will be fine." He backed up to avoid a pothole and turned onto the road. "She's looking forward to visiting the museum."

"Turn left here and then right at the intersection." Fiona adjusted her seatbelt. "I'm sure a lot has changed since Joan lived here."

At the intersection, a sign pointed east toward the town and west toward the mountains.

"Last chance to change your mind." Gavin slowed down and laughed.

"Are you reconsidering being alone with me on a trail?"

"Oh, you have no idea how I'm looking forward to no interruptions." He turned onto the road going west.

Soon, the foothills were visible from both sides. This was as good a time as any to ask about Joan. "We never discussed the plans for the conservatory yesterday. Did your aunt mention the property?"

"Aye, lass, she did. You and I had more exciting things to do." He wiggled his brows.

The short kisses behind the barn were thrilling, but she needed to know if *he* still planned to develop Joan's property.

"She plans to turn the conservatory into a community center offering music programs and concerts. I told her about my meeting with Professor Cappella." He adjusted the rearview mirror. "She's eager to contact the professor and discuss a satellite program similar to Ian's with university students developing music programs."

"What a great opportunity." She breathed a sigh of relief. The town no longer needed to worry about a fancy resort.

"Aye." Gavin shifted gears as the car approached an incline. "Building costs are astronomical. Between Jack and SIREaC local subsidiaries, we'll have enough surplus building supplies to start construction at a minimal cost." He picked up speed as the road flattened.

She was wrong to let her perception of his money cloud her judgment. He would do the right thing for his aunt. "I like Joan's plan. Are all McIvers born with a successful business gene?"

"Some of us more than others. I'll check with Ian to determine whether it's dominant or recessive." Gavin laughed and placed both hands on the steering wheel. "How'd you find this trail?"

"I didn't. While searching for artifacts left behind by early settlers, Ian and his students found the path." She liked hiking's solitude and the quiet language of the hills. Guests appreciated her firsthand knowledge of the trails. She kept this one a secret—until today. "Make a right after you pass the next crossroad."

A stone wall hid the parking lot.

"I can see why this place is a secret." He shut off the engine and rushed to open the passenger door.

"Looks like someone beat us to the trails." Fiona stepped out of the SUV and glanced at the vehicle parked alongside. To avoid weekend hikers, she purposely planned an early hike. "Can't beat them all. This starting point, although remote, is popular with experienced hikers." She placed the paper bag and coffee cups on the car's hood. "Sorry, the coffee isn't hot." The cups were lukewarm. The unexpected change of plans set her off a bit.

"No worries. I'm so hungry, I'd eat anything." Gavin reached for a sandwich and coffee.

"Tell me more about Joan's plans." She nibbled on a sandwich. The sharp cheese and sweet jam were addictive. She took another bite.

"You already know she's interested in buying the rental." He took a bite of his sandwich and washed it down with coffee. "The mayor's secretary mentioned the owners would stay in Florida permanently." He tossed the empty cup into the paper bag.

"And you? Did you find a house?" She crossed her fingers behind her back and waited for an answer. He had the means to live anywhere he wanted.

"I've been talking to Walter's family about the farmhouse and land. I noticed the house the day you took me to the barn. The day was a good one for everyone involved." He smiled. "Renovating an old house is more exciting than building a massive resort."

She sensed his excitement. "You plan on becoming a farmer." She finished the last drop of lukewarm coffee and added the cup to the bag. "The property hasn't produced anything in decades."

"I like working with my hands, but farming, *ach*, it's never been my thing." He held up a callused hand.

"Would your bid include the barn? I heard there were several offers for the wood." Planks of Prescott's barn wood would add character to her new barn.

"My lawyers have drawn up a contract that includes all structures on the property. Barring any unforeseen problems, the Prescotts will sign within days. In a few months, Em and I will have a solid place to call home."

She refrained from doing a happy dance. "Isn't a house that size a lot for you and Emily?" What a silly thing to say to a man used to estate properties and luxury apartments.

"We should get going." Gavin gathered the trash and looked for a trashcan.

Any more conversation about the house would have to wait. "You have to carry out whatever you bring in." Fiona pulled her backpack from the backseat and handed him an empty bag.

Gavin placed the garbage bag in the trunk and retrieved a backpack.

"The main trailhead starts over there." She pointed toward a signpost covered with morning frost. The path started with a steady incline and leveled off at a fork.

"Which way?" Gavin stopped under a tall pine tree.

"We'll go left at the bend." She gazed at a white pine behind him. "Let's take a water break and chat some more." She hung her backpack on a low-lying tree branch.

"Anything in particular you want to talk about?" He took a swig from a water bottle. His Adam's apple moved with each swallow.

She inhaled and stepped back against the tree. "Tell me about the house. I've never been inside."

"Adrian loves the bones of the old place." He shoved the water bottle into the side pocket of his backpack and placed a hand on the tree over her shoulder. "She agrees with my plans for four or five bedrooms on the second level."

"So many rooms—you could open a B and B." She relaxed against the tree.

"No worries, lass. I don't have a guesthouse in mind. I'll fill the place with lots of kids." He stepped closer. "But, first, I need a wife."

"Anyone special?" Her heart beat fast. Was this the conversation Emily overheard?

"I considered the lady who works at the post office. She's always tempting me with her apple pies."

"If you like older women, she's a good choice." She slipped under his arm, grabbed her pack, and jogged past. "And she's already married." Fiona pushed through scrub and low-lying branches.

"Hey, is this even a trail?" Gavin grabbed his pack and followed.

"A secret one." She smiled over her shoulder. "The path gets more challenging up ahead. The rock scramble can be difficult, but it's worth the effort. On the ledge, it opens to an amazing valley view." The trail was narrow, with low-lying branches on both sides. A bare branch brushed her shoulder, catching the end of her braid. She tried to pull away.

"Hold still or you'll make it worse." Gavin rushed toward her. "When Ian found this trail, was he specifically looking for artifacts?" He snapped off the branch and pulled her braid loose.

"They were just a starting point. The association of American Mountain Men holds its annual event in Highland Falls. Ian experiences history firsthand. He's known for going off the beaten path." She adjusted her cap and tucked her braid under her collar.

"Life must have been tough for those early settlers." He brushed stray pine needles off her jacket. "Lead the way."

"This overgrown path is nothing compared to half the holes he's crawled into." She pointed to a canopy of spindly hemlocks along rocky terrain. "Feels like the temperature is dropping. I hope it doesn't snow." Snow flurries weren't unusual at this altitude, and a light dusting made the scramble slippery.

"Let's keep moving." Gavin tested his footing and proceeded.

The first rock was always the most challenging. Maintaining three-point contact, she took a deep breath and looked up. *Just do it.* She focused on the bright yellow lines on his hiking boots. He had all the qualities of a mountain man—strength, confidence, and determination. Living in the past Ian loved might be tolerable with someone like Gavin. She leaned into the rock and started her climb. "I'm right behind you." The last set of rocks leveled off to a plateau, giving her incentive.

Gavin had reached the secret place. "Amazing." He stood dangerously close to the edge.

She stepped gingerly toward him, but not all the way. "A park ranger once told me you couldn't assume a million-year-old rock, with no support from below, won't break loose." She grabbed his forearm. Unlike the rock, his firm arm provided an unquestionable sense of safety and security.

"Warning taken, lass." He glanced over the protruding edge and stepped back.

"You can admire the view just as well from here." She gestured toward the valley. "On a clear day, you can see ten miles in any direction. The town is way down there." The scene reminded her of a still life painting waiting for an animation artist to create movement.

Slowly, the valley came alive. Black dots moved along Main Street.

"Looks like the early risers are up and about. Next time, we'll bring binoculars. Never know who we might find coming out of the wrong house." He slipped his arm protectively around her waist.

"I never took you for a gossipmonger." She laughed.

Overhead, a loud flapping drew their attention. A flock of winter geese soared in a V-formation. Their black wing tips were barely visible from the ground, and at this altitude, they were a stunning contrast against the blue sky.

"If you follow the birds' flight, you'll see my inn." The old barn didn't look so bad from up here. She glanced sideways at Gavin.

He stared out at the valley.

She waited a few seconds. "Remind you of home?"

"It's obvious why so many Scots settled around these hills." He sighed.

A cold gust of wind brushed her cheek.

Nature's paintbrush scattered swirls of burnt orange leaves over the valley.

They stepped back under a low, overhanging rock for protection.

"This is a tidy spot. I can see why you like it." He turned toward her and circled her waist with both arms.

"When I see the town from up here"—she glanced toward the edge—"We're so insignificant in the big scheme."

"No detail about you is ever insignificant." He tightened his hold. "You found the perfect hideaway in a town where everyone knows your business. Thanks for sharing."

"I'm glad I brought you here." She gazed over his shoulder at the blue sky. The intimacy of her secret place always provided refuge from everyday ups and downs. Now, sharing it with Gavin made it even more special.

He placed a rough palm on her cheek. "Can you forgive me for not telling you the extent of the family business? I believed I was living the life I aspired to. Spending time with you, the twins, and the Drummonds showed me how I had built a life on other people's expectations." He released her and held up his palms. "I'll work with my hands and build our future together."

"I was wrong to let the article cloud my

perception." She slipped her hands into her jacket pockets. Her attraction was solidified the day he participated in the games—rich or poor, it didn't matter. He was honorable, skilled at whatever he touched, and a good dad.

"I meant what I said about filling the house with kids."

"Don't you need a wife first?" She inhaled a cold breath and held it.

"If the right one said yes. I'd marry her tomorrow." His smile was full of anticipation. "Are you interested?"

"Tomorrow's so soon." She giggled with palpable excitement. A puff of condensation settled between them. "Could you wait a week or two?" The invitation was a passionate proposal. She couldn't resist. She wanted him back at the breakfast table as soon as possible.

"You're right. Tomorrow is too soon. We'll need at least a week." He rushed his words and smiled. "No, two weeks."

"Yes." She removed her hands from her pockets and nodded. "Two weeks is better."

"So, is that a yes?" He circled her waist and pulled her close. "Granddad will be here in two weeks. Jack and I need time to gather a construction crew. With a good crew, the barn walls will be up by the end of this week." He gazed at her with a wide grin and waited.

"A simple proposal will do." Overwhelmed by his plan to be married as soon as possible…and in *her* barn, she gazed at him and managed a nod. She couldn't imagine building the next chapter of her life with anyone else.

"You can invite the whole town if you want. I know it's last minute, but your family can fly over on Granddad's jet." He held her at arm's length. "I've made many errors in judgment in the past...and recently, too. I don't want letting you go to be another mistake. I don't want to pass you in town or at school. Will you marry me and help me fill the Prescott house with lots of *bairn*?" His breath stilled. "I love you, Fiona Campbell. Marry me."

"You underestimate your power of persuasion." Her insides felt like she was soaring with the geese. Her answer was a rapid thud of her pulse. She waited a split second until her heartbeat was normal again. "How can a girl say no to such a proposal?"

"I'll take that as a yes." He kissed her forehead. "Let's get back and share the good news."

She nodded. "Simon's already told me if I considered getting married, you'd better be my choice."

"Smart lad—but where did that come from?" His brows furrowed. "What about Sara? Will she be okay with her auntie getting married?"

"She misses you." A knot rose in her throat. "I miss you, too," she whispered. Asking about Simon and Sara touched her heart in a big way. "Emily overheard you and Joan talking. Apparently, she told the twins you wanted to marry me."

"Did she now?" He threw back his head and laughed. "And what did you think?"

"Hmm..." She placed her hands on his chest. "I was delighted."

"Simon and I will be outnumbered." He touched her face. "If we plan to even out the ratio of boys to girls, we'll have our work cut out."

His eyes blazed with a raw, sexy tenderness. "We won't have much say in how that turns out."

"Then we'll keep trying until we get it right." His mouth covered hers hungrily.

The touch of his lips was a delicious sensation. She melted against his body. "A quick wedding sounds perfect," she whispered. "We won't have to worry about town gossip if you and Em move into the inn while you renovate the farmhouse. And I can kiss you whenever I want."

"We'll always agree on that." He kissed her again.

"Do you know the old legend about throwing the shot?" Her heart pounded hard in anticipation.

"Aye, I do, lass. The distance a guest of a Scottish landlord threw the stone of strength determined the sleeping accommodations he could expect. I have no regrets that I didn't win the Highland competition." He grinned. "I still won the *best bed* at the inn." He tilted her chin. "That's a title I won't give up easily."

Thank you for purchasing
this publication of The Wild Rose Press, Inc.

For questions or more information
contact us at
info@thewildrosepress.com.

The Wild Rose Press, Inc.
www.thewildrosepress.com